THE MERGE

Love Yourself to Freedom

Morgan B. Holland

MULLEN PRESS

www.mullenpress.com

Morgan B. Holland/Mullen Press
4600 Powder Mill Road
Beltsville, MD 20705
www.mullenpress.com
contact.us@mullenpress.com

Publisher's Note: This is a work of fiction. Names, characters, places, and incidents are a product of the author's imagination. Locales and public names are sometimes used for atmospheric purposes. Any resemblance to actual people, living or dead, or to businesses, companies, events, institutions, or locales is completely coincidental.

Cover Artist: Armend Meha www.armejndi.com

The Merge:Love Yourself to Freedom/ Morgan B. Holland. -- 1st ed.
ISBN: 978-1-7323458-0-5 (paperback)
ISBN: 978-1-7323458-1-2 (e-book)

This one's for you, Cuz

Nicholas Andrew Battle, 1991 - 2012

"The function of freedom is to free someone else."

— TONI MORRISON

CONTENTS

Acknowledgments

I am grateful for the Divine's love and the abundance she readily provides. I am grateful to everyone I met along this journey of bringing this story out of my head and into a book. I would like to thank the following people for providing sound criticism throughout the writing process: Kalya Holland, Shanna Morgan, Crystal Robertson, Tiffany Spriggs, Patresa Day, Sheree Brown, and Nichole Davis. Thank you for listening to me and pushing me to write this story and to get this message out. I am grateful for my mother, Helen Holland, for her constant support and encouragement. I am grateful for my father, Julius Pittman, for always being available to listen to his daughter dream out loud. Most importantly, I thank the Divine in advance for the conspiring of the Universe to work in my favor to make all of my dreams come true. Amen.

THE MERGE

CHAPTER ONE

FOUR INCH HEELS

"Mye!" yelled Truman startling her. She jumped slightly while closing her laptop.

"I hate when you do that," Mye said.

"I know," smiled Truman while typing on his cell phone. "Now can you please get out so Alex can close the door?"

Alex stood 6 foot 1, 200 pounds in a perfectly tailored black suit waiting patiently with a smile for Mye to exit the car. It was a cold March day in Washington, DC. Mye held her coat closed tight as Alex helped her out of the car.

"I'm going to tell him today Truman. I'm confronting all of my fears and desires. From this day forward, I will be stepping into my truths," said Mye.

"Good," said Truman, "perhaps then you can promise never to bring the topic of "Him" up again once he royally disappoints you. He is not going to take it well," he added.

"Shut up Truman. You're the brother I'm glad I never had," said Mye as Alex closed the door.

Truman replied, "Aww, that's the nicest thing she's ever said to me. Let's go, Alex. I have a meeting in 30 minutes."

***

"Must you make me a witness to this murder?! Nobody told me it was Slay Day!" said Kara as Mye walked into the office. Mye blushed and gave a slight smirk at her assistant's dramatics. She recently celebrated her 38th birthday but appeared to have found the fountain of youth. She was a vegetarian and a yoga enthusiast before it was cool. Her style is a blend of sophistication with a sexy flare, and her shoe collection is unmatched. She has her own private practice, amongst other businesses. She's an author, wife, and mother to a beautiful son and daughter.

"Happy Anniversary!" said Kara as she handed Mye an envelope with a gift certificate for a full body massage at Taime Out Studios.

"Thank you, Kara," said Mye as she hugged her, "you really didn't have to do this," added Mye.

"Please Doc, after all you've done for my family and me, this is the least I can do. Plus, this is your 20-year wedding anniversary!" said Kara clapping her hands ecstatically. "Wait, didn't you just turn 38 like 3 days ago? So ya'll literally got married as soon as you turned 18. He was pressed!" Mye laughed and started walking to her office.

"Oh Dr. Hart, your 9 o'clock, Congressman Harrison, will be about 20 minutes late, and you have a walk-in in the small conference room. She seems a little off," said Kara.

"Thank you, Kara. Can you send the walk-in to my office in about 10 minutes? And you can call me Mye," she replied.

"That's gonna be a no for me Doc. You spent too many years in school to be a Mye. You are Dr. Mye Hart. The go-to psychologist for the rich and disturbed," said Kara.

Mye laughed at Kara's response and shook her head as she walked into her office and closed the door behind her. She put her things down on her desk and began to get lost in her thoughts. Today is her 20-year wedding anniversary, and all she could think about was Emerson Avery Birch. They met nearly 25 years ago in high school under a sycamore tree. Mye daydreamed about how different her life would have been if he had just stayed that night after the school dance. A cold chill ran through her back as she thought about that awful night.

However, now with spouses, kids, careers, reputations, and so much more on the line. Mye knew she could not risk it. She couldn't risk shaking up everyone's life around her for her desires, but she couldn't help but feel that she's so caught up in keeping others happy that she's not even living. Busy making grand plans for a life she's not even a part of. She felt stuck, and her growth was stunted trying to keep from overshadowing her husband.While she was both eternally grateful for all she has accomplished, she was still deeply unfulfilled. She wasn't willing to risk it all for Emerson because that would be foolish. To risk it all for a feeling that might not be mutual, or worse, not sustainable. That's a chance no one should take. However, Mye was willing to risk it all for herself. Win lose or draw. She was willing to face whatever consequences she had to face on her path to speaking her truths and becoming her authentic self. The knock on the door snapped Mye out of her trance.

"Come in," she said as she stood up and straightened her black Cleo knit pencil skirt that accentuated her broad hips and fell to a high-low flare at the hem. Her Cushnie Et Ochs crisp white blouse fitted her perfectly as if it was designed for the 12-inch difference between her bust and waist. Her Iman Red lipstick popped on her perfect white teeth. She smiled as she walked over to greet her guest reaching out to shake her hand with perfectly almond shaped nude nails. The sun shined through her office aiding in the natural glow of her flawless deep mahogany skin. At 5'8", 150 lbs, her hourglass physique was exceptionally toned, and her body gave off a natural seductive scent. She embodied what it means to be a successful black woman, and she represented the culture well.

"Have a seat," Mye said to her guest as she pushed her long straight black hair behind her ears. With legs crossed Mye said, "Hello, my name is Dr. Hart, and it's a pleasure to meet you. Unfortunately, I don't have much time, and I don't usually take walk-ins, however, how can I help you?"

The lady looked at Mye with squint piercing eyes and through clenched teeth took a deep breath in her mouth and slowly let it out through her nose. Mye took notice of the woman's behavior but remained calm and relaxed.

She leaned back in her chair and asked again, "How can I help you Ms.-"

"Jager," replied the woman. "Lo-Ruhamah Jager," said the woman. Mye was slightly puzzled trying to figure out why that name sounded oddly familiar. Lo-Ruhamah crossed her eyes and said, "It's not a random ghetto name."

"Its Hebrew?" asked Mye. "I'm just trying to remember where I've heard it before."

The woman looked surprised by Mye's response. "I've never met another person with my name, and I'm probably the first black person of Jewish descent you've met," said Lo-Ruhamah.

"No, actually I know a guy," said Mye and she grinned as she thought about Emerson.

Annoyed by the happiness on Mye's face Lo-Ruhamah reached into her purse and pulled out a big bag of pills and handed them to Mye. Mye began to read through the pills becoming a little more concerned with each bottle she read.

Lo-Ruhamah then said, "I need you to wean me off of these pills."

"I am a psychologist," said Mye.

"You've weaned others off of pills," snapped Lo-Ruhamah, "you've helped others get off pills. Why can't you help me?" Lo-Ruhamah said as she leaned in towards Mye.

"I've helped people get off of 1 or 2 different types of pills that were used for lower degrees of various disorders, and I did this in conjunction with their psychiatrist," explained Mye in a calm manner.

Lo-Ruhamah stood up and slammed her hands on Mye's desk and yelled, "You are a psychiatrist! You know what each one of those pills is for and you know the side effects!"

"I also have a pretty good idea of the reason you are on them," said Mye as she stood up and slowly backed away from the woman. "And for the record, I am not an acting psychiatrist. Yes, I have a MD. However, I chose the field of psychology over psychiatry. I am a licensed psychologist."

"You chose psychology because you believe people are over medicated and the pharmaceutical industry is a big scam working in conjunction with the doctors," said Lo-Ruhamah.

Mye clasped her hands together and said, "While I do have my thoughts on the pharmaceutical industry, and practices of certain pharmaceutical sales representatives, it's not that simple. I believe that we must consider the mind, body, and spirit of a person and not just consider one area at a time. The Human experience is multi-faceted. Sometimes mental disorders are a result of something that's unresolved from the past or currently ongoing. Certain traumas cause chemical imbalances, some deficiencies are attributed to genetics, and some people's everyday faculties and behaviors are just at a certain point on the spectrum that the norm is not comfortable with accepting."

Lo-Ruhamah sat back down on the loveseat seemingly pleased with Mye's response.

Mye said, "I know why I'm here and why I chose to do this work. Why are you here? What do you want from me?" asked Mye.

Lo-Ruhamah replied, "I need you to recommend my doctor to take me off of those meds."

Mye watched as the woman's face changed expressions rapidly. She could tell that Lo-Ruhamah was trying her best to remain in control, but this was ultimately a losing battle.

Lo-Ruhamah said, "If you can get me off the meds then my Mom won't think I'm crazy and I can get what's left of my family back," said the woman as she began to slightly twitch walking slowly towards Mye. Suddenly, 2 police officers barged in, grabbed Lo-Ruhamah, and detained her.

"You called the police!" yelled the woman. Mye stood up and let out a long sigh. Kara walked in and hugged her.

"Are you alright?" Kara asked.

"I'm fine, thanks," replied Mye.

"You owe me!" yelled Lo-Ruhamah. "You ruined my life! I came here to give you a chance to make things right! Now you will pay! I will ruin your family like you ruined mine!" yelled Lo-Ruhamah.

The police yanked the woman out of the office, "Let's go ma'am!" yelled one of the officers as he pulled her out of Mye's office.

Mye grabbed the woman's bag of pills and gave them to the other officer.

"These are her meds; she is severely mentally disturbed. She's an outpatient at this mental hospital," Mye said as she wrote the name down on a sticky note. "I think she may be having an episode, but you can find her doctor's info on her medication. Thank you, officer," said Mye.

"Anytime ma'am, I'm here to serve. I hope your day goes up from here," said the officer as he smiled and walked out of Mye's office.

"Even in the midst of turmoil, you can still pull em!" said Kara as she watched the police officer turn the corner down the hall. "He's cute, young but cute. That silent alarm came in handy," said Kara.

"My son is probably 2 or 3 years younger than that officer," chuckled Mye.

"I'm glad you were here," said Mye.

"I saw that red light and sprung right into action!" said Kara. "That's because I went to that Beyonce concert last week. Now I know how to hop in formation!" said Kara.

Mye laughed, bending over holding her stomach, as Kara acted out how she saw the light and called the police with extensive animation.

"I needed that Kara. Thank you," said Mye.

"No, thank you," said Kara, "there's no way I was gonna let a crazy take you out on my watch," she chuckled.

"Oh yea, the congresswoman had to reschedule, should I reschedule the rest of your clients for the day?" asked Kara.

Mye thought for a moment and said, "Sure, thanks Kara. And you can leave too. It's Friday, go ahead and start your weekend early."

"It's ok, I can finish archiving some files. I mean we only work 4-hour days. I feel like I get off early every day," chuckled Kara as she walked out of Mye's office closing the door looking back at Mye with a smile. Mye put the phone on speaker and pressed 3. She waited as it rang.

"Hey Mye," said a smooth, rich, deep voice. "Are we still on for lunch today?" he asked.

"Well, I would like to know if we can move it up to brunch? If you're free," said Mye.

"Actually my next surgery was just rescheduled to later today, so I'm free. I can leave the hospital in about 20 minutes. Are we meeting at our spot?" he asked.

"Yes," she replied.

"Ok cool. See you soon."

***

Mye arrived at their spot early. Her driver opened the door for her and helped her out of the car.

"Thank you, Alex," said Mye as she exited the car. He replied with a smile. With her journal in hand, Mye walked to the picnic table under a gazebo. It was a quaint space. Quiet, except for the sound of birds and a small stream nearby. She began to write as she waited for him.

Emerson arrived a few minutes after Mye started writing. Emerson parked his car and waved at Alex as he watched him drive off. Alex never left Mye alone; he always waited until Emerson arrived. Emerson lived for these days. Usually, the 4th Friday of the month he and Mye would meet for lunch at the park. Emerson chuckled to himself thinking about the cold DC winters when they would eat lunch together in their cars. Thankfully it warmed up a lot since early this morning. That's DC weather for you. You can get Winter and Spring on the same day. This place was special not because it was the most beautiful park but because of that sycamore tree. This sycamore tree stood tall beside the gazebo and reminded the two of when they were kids, where they first met. Emerson admired Mye's beauty both inside and out. He loved to watch her write. He could listen to Mye read and talk for hours. He simply enjoyed being in her presence. They met when he was 17, and she was 14. Occasionally he would allow himself the opportunity to dream about what could have been, but then he would quickly snap back to reality. He had his chance and let her slip away. He never forgave himself for that.

Mye could feel Emerson looking at her. She always arrived before him because sometimes her knees would get weak when she saw him, and she could not risk the embarrassment of him being able to tell he had an effect on her. The wind brought his cologne to Mye before Emerson arrived and even though her eyes never left her page, she knew he was close.

Mye looked up and saw Emerson standing over top of her as she sat at the picnic table. She said, "Em you smell amazing."

Emerson let out a slight chuckle. He loved when she called him Em. He never had a nickname, and she was the only one who gave him one that stuck. 24 years and counting and he's still Em. Emerson said, "You say that every time." She smiled.

"You look radiant as usual," said Emerson.

Mye closed her journal and replied, "You say that every time."

Emerson placed his foot on the picnic bench to tie his cognac Mezlen cap toe oxford shoe. Mye admired Emerson in his entirety. At 6'1" 215 pounds, he was a work of art. A solid muscular build with broad shoulders and smooth dark chocolate skin. His low haircut perfectly sculpted his face along with his thick eyebrows and chiseled chin. His smile was bright and white surrounded by full luscious lips. He has a classic, sophisticated style. Although his hands were huge, they were always gentle to the touch. He even made tying a shoe sexy. Emerson caught Mye staring and asked, "What? Am I doing it wrong?"

"Shut up," replied Mye. Trying to play it off. *Let me check myself,* Mye thought to herself. *We will never be more than what we are or could we? There is something about a man like Emerson,* she thought.

Their lunch arrived just in time before things got too awkward. The two began to eat. "Em does the name Lo-Ruhamah mean anything to you?"

Emerson thought for a second as he finished chewing his food. "Lo-Ruhamah is the daughter of Gomer, Gomer is the wife of the prophet Hosea," said Emerson as he took another bite of his sandwich. "Why do you ask?"

"I met a woman today by that name," said Mye. Emerson looked puzzled, "Why would someone name their daughter Lo-Ruhamah? Lo-Ruhamah basically means 'no mercy' or 'no compassion for you,'" said Emerson as he took another bite.

"Dang. She walked in today and had a bizarre episode. Kara had to call the cops," said Mye as she paused from eating her pasta.

"What! Are you okay? Do you want security detail? I think that would be best," said Emerson in a firm tone.

"No, no Em, it's not that serious. She was just an outpatient who appeared to be off of her medication," said Mye.

Mye replayed in her head repeatedly the incident that happened today and couldn't understand why she felt a need to make sense of it. She'd witnessed patients having episodes before, but there was something different about this one. This woman knew Mye was a psychiatrist, but how, she didn't advertise that. And the lady was convinced that Mye was somehow at the root of all her problems. However, Mye couldn't figure out why.

"Stop it Mye," said Emerson as he took the last bite of his sandwich.

"Stop what?" Mye asked sheepishly.

"Somethings can't be made sense of, and that's alright," he smiled.

The two laughed and joked around for about 30 more minutes. Mye's and Emerson's phone vibrated simultaneously.

"I have to head back to the hospital," said Emerson.

Mye started cleaning up and said, "No worries Alex will be here any second." Alex pulled up in the black Mercedes S class with mirror windows.

Emerson said, "Let me walk you to your car." As Mye approached the car, Alex stepped out of the car to get the door, but Emerson waved him to get back in the car.

Emerson opened the passenger side back door and saw Truman.

"Hey Truman," said Emerson. "Preparing for court?"

"I don't have to prepare because I stay ready," said Truman while checking an email on his phone.

"Why did you even ask him?" giggled Mye.

Emerson shrugged his shoulders and shook his head, "I don't even know," he said through a slight chuckle.

"Bye Em, love you," said Mye as she hugged Emerson then kissed his cheek.

Emerson thought to himself how he wished he could hold on to her forever.

"Ditto," replied Emerson smiling at Mye. She smiled back.

He helped Mye into the car and closed the door. He watched as she rode away and stared at the car until it was out of site.

"Soooo," said Truman, "did you tell him?"

"Who?" replied Mye.

"Now you're an owl," said Truman.

Mye ignored Truman and looked out of the window. Truman sat legs crossed in a Reiss modern-fit air-force blue suit with a textured black silk tie and wingtip Ferragamo's to match. Completely unfazed by Mye ignoring him. Truman is the best lawyer in a 5 state radius, and that's not debatable.

"Review these," said Truman as he handed Mye some papers.

"Why do you care if I told him or not?" asked Mye.

"I don't care," said Truman. "I just want you to tell him so that he can do absolutely nothing with the information, and then you can move on with your life," said Truman.

"How can you say that?" asked Mye.

"Say what?" replied Truman. "The truth?" he added.

"You... talking about the truth?" chuckled Mye.

Truman replied, "I always tell the truth. Depending on the setting, determines the version, but it's always the truth. And like everything else in this world, it is subject to interpretation, and I cannot be held responsible for how someone interprets my truth."

Mye rolled her eyes. Truman continued, "I get it. You like him. You have history. He looks good on paper but come on Mye. It will never work," said Truman as he began to pack up his briefcase.

"You sound so confident Truman, but how can you be so sure?" asked Mye.

"Mye, I've known you since you were 17-18, I know you. You need ambition-"

"He is ambitious," said Mye cutting Truman off mid-sentence. "He is an accomplished neurosurgeon; he's a philanthropist, he's spiritual, he's-"

"Basic!" said Truman. Mye laughed.

"Shut up Truman," she chuckled.

"Yeah, he's a neurosurgeon, but he doesn't take on any cases that don't have at least a 70% chance of success. He's not on the cutting edge of any new surgical methods, he gives to the same charities we give to, and he's Jewish. You're not even Jewish. You're some spiritual, non-religious, give thanks to my ancestors person."

"Shut up Truman," laughed Mye.

Truman continued, "Emerson likes to be the big fish in a small pond, that's why he looks so accomplished. He does what comes easy for him. Yes, he's better than the average man, but the standards are so low that the title "above average" means nothing. If you must have a man, he needs to be an ambitious man."

"Like you?" asked Mye.

"Oh no no. You cannot handle a man like me," said Truman. Mye chuckled.

"You need someone around half the man of me. Then you'll be fulfilled. You need someone who cares. And you know me. I don't care. Trust me Mye, I'm a lawyer who doesn't lose. If life was a game of chess, I play 10 moves out. Don't waste your time thinking about this guy," said Truman.

"You were born for this," said Mye as the car came to a stop in front of the courthouse. Alex opened Truman's door and grabbed Truman's briefcase from him. Truman got out standing about 6 feet even at about 190 pounds. His dark red hair was neatly in place, and his brown eyes were steady and intense. His skin was extremely fair during this time of year making his freckles more noticeable. Truman was the best of the best, like a young Bruce Cutler. He was not to be messed with. Truman leaned into the car to help Mye get out.

"Look Mye. I need you to focus. We have voir dire today. Now let's go select this jury so I can do what I do best," said Truman as he grabbed his briefcase from Alex and proceeded to walk into the courthouse. Alex closed the door behind Mye.

"Thank you, Alex. I'll text you when I'm ready."

***

Truman sat in his counsel seat. The plaintiff frowned, *I didn't know he was his counsel,* thought attorney Henry Green.

He has heard about Truman. Truman's client sat in a cheap too big black suit with a white shirt and a black tie. He was fidgeting his fingers and repeatedly looking back to the entrance of the courtroom.

How can this clown even afford Truman? thought Mr. Green as he walked over and held out his hand to Truman.

"I know you know who I am and that I don't do handshakes," said Truman without looking up from his file.

Mr. Green turned red slightly and tugged at his suit jacket trying to regain his composure. Everyone knows Truman didn't touch people or liked to be touched by people.

Germ freak, Mr. Green thought. With his hands in his pocket he asked, "So Truman, I've heard you've been spending more time in civil court. I can't imagine you've somehow run out of drug kingpins, murders, and pimps to represent."

Truman closed his file and turned his chair towards Mr. Green. He leaned back in it, crossed his legs and said, "To be frank, I got bored. The States Attorneys' don't put up a good enough fight anymore. I mean let's be honest, the real attorneys are in the private sector. Corporations hire the best legal counsel. Look at you guys," with his hand extended toward the plaintiff's team. "You guys are some of the best! Probably top of your class. Now you guys are a better opponent than any State's Attorney hands down. Although you probably can't tell, but inside I get very excited when I come into a courtroom and see such a stellar team across from me. This is my idea of fun."

Truman's client was fidgeting uncontrollably and staring back at the entrance to the courtroom. Truman went back to reviewing his files. Mr. Green stood tight-lipped in utter confusion by what he heard.

Is this guy serious? he thought to himself. Mr. Green turned to walk away when Truman called out to him.

"Hey! I just have one request of you. Can you try to hold out on settling until after we pick the jury? That's one of my favorite parts," asked Truman with a "Cheshire Cat" grin.

This arrogant asshole, thought Mr. Green. "We have no intentions of settling," he replied.

"You never do," said Truman. "Can I just have your word that you'll wait until after jury selection?" asked Truman.

"That much you can guarantee," replied Mr. Green. Mr. Green spoke to his team. As of lately, Truman often settled out of court. The plaintiff and his team believed he's a little rusty and not prepared to go to trial. They've built a strong case and were eager to build a name for themselves. Mr. Green was ready to go round for round against Truman in court. Abruptly attorney Jones walked in the courtroom and headed straight to Truman.

"What are you doing here?" he asked through a forced smile.

"Surprise," said Truman with a big smile on his face.

"Are you doing pro bono work now because it's no way he can afford you?" asked attorney Jones while looking at his client. "Are you trying to redeem yourself helping people like him get over on companies like us? If your client is innocent, then he has nothing to worry about," said Mr. Jones.

"Your company has a legal team of 4, and you now make 5. My client makes slightly too much to get a public defender but not enough to hire a lawyer. My last case ended early, and my next case isn't for another hour. I see a man representing himself in a jury trial against a fortune 500 company and I ask him if I can be a part of the fun. Now here we are," smiled Truman.

"Besides, let's be clear, no one can afford me. Even when I get paid 7 figures, I still consider it charity. So, let the fun begin!" said Truman.

Mr. Jones frowned and walked to the first chair motioning for Mr. Green to move. All the attorneys moved down one chair.

Truman said to Mr. Green, "Even though you are now second chair, you still have to keep your promise."

Mr. Green frowned and clenched his hands tight. "You might as well ask to reschedule your next case because there is no way you are getting out of here in an hour," said Mr. Jones. Then he leaned into Mr. Green and asked, "What is he talking about?"

Bailiff announced, "All rise. The Court is now in session, the Honorable Judge Hillman presiding." Everyone remained standing until the judge entered and was seated.

"You may be seated," instructed the Judge. In walked Mye.

"Hi, Mye! It's good to see you!" said the judge. Truman's client had a sigh of relief and a big smile on his face when he saw Mye. Jones' chest instantly caved in as he hung his shoulders low.

"Damn it," whispered Mr. Jones.

"Excuse me?" asked Judge Hillman.

"My apologies your honor," he replied.

"Hi, Judge Hillman. The feeling is mutual," replied Mye.

Mye leaned over the divider to shake Truman's client's hands.

The client leaned into Mye and said, "This is all new to me, but I trust you. Thank you for everything."

"You're welcome and don't worry. Everything will be fine," said Mye.

The client sat down completely relaxed by her words.

"May we approach the bench?" asked Mr. Jones.

"Yes," replied the judge. Truman sucked his teeth and slowly approached the judge.

"What is it counsel?" asked the judge looking at Mr. Jones.

"We would like to settle out of court."

The judge looked at Truman, "Any objections?" asked the judge.

"No," said Truman, "but I'd like to go on record saying that counsel's second chair promised to not give up until after jury selection."

"Stop wasting the court's time Truman," said the judge. "Now settle this out of my courtroom," said the judge as she hit her gavel.

Both attorneys walked back to their seats. Truman handed Jones a file.

"Those are our terms. It's triple my client's initial request," said Truman. "Sorry but you think too small," Truman said to his client. "You have to think bigger." Truman looked at Mr. Jones, "I expect this document to be signed and delivered to my office first thing Monday morning or we will start negotiations at double this amount," said Truman as he walked out of the courtroom.

The client watched Truman walk out of the courtroom and frantically made eye contact with Mye, "What does this all mean?" he asked.

"It means you won," whispered Mye. The gentleman leaned across the barrier and gave Mye a big hug.

"Thank you so much!" said the client. "You don't know what this means to my family and me. You saved my life. I could never afford a lawyer like him," pointing towards the door where Truman exited. "Now I can pay you back," he said.

"No, that's not necessary," replied Mye, "just promise me one thing," asked Mye.

"Anything," said the client.

"Promise me that you'll live the life you've always wanted to live. Become the person you've always wanted to be. Can you handle that?" asked Mye with her hand extended. The client shook her hand and said, "You gotta deal!"

In the hallway outside of the courtroom, Mr. Jones said, "You should have called me when you found out Truman was his legal counsel Henry."

"I can handle him," said Mr. Green.

"You were put on a case when the accuser was representing himself, and you were still given a team of 3 to assist you. You cannot handle Truman. You've heard stories about him, but I've seen him in action. It would do you well to know when you see him; you see a team of 10. Never underestimate him," said Mr. Jones as he watched Truman in the distance checking his phone.

Out walks Mye and the client. They walked over to Truman. The client hugged Mye one last time and stuck his hand out to shake Truman's hand.

"Truman won't even shake his own client's hand," said Mr. Green.

Mr. Jones replied, "He doesn't touch anyone, and he doesn't allow himself to be touched. He's had 4 people charged with felony assault just for bumping into him by accident. There was a rumor that he has a mental condition disorder or something. I don't know. I do know that the last thing you need is a mentally ill, grade A lawyer, with a 97% success rate on your ass," said Mr. Jones.

Mye grabbed the client's hand and smiled at him. Then she looked at Truman with a tight lip. Truman gave the client a fake overly enthusiastic smile while holding his phone tight with both hands. Truman sarcastically said, "It was a pleasure to be of service."

The client walked towards the courthouse exit and looked back one last time and mouthed, "Thank you," to Mye.

Mye interlocked her arm in Truman's and started walking towards the exit.

"You're always trying to low-key ruin my reputation," said Truman still looking at his phone.

"What!" said Mye.

"What's next? You gonna start leaving your earrings at my house?" asked Truman as he chuckled to himself.

"Whatever," said Mye as she pushed Truman slightly knocking him off balance.

"Alex is here. I'm about to go to the center and then to the clinic. Are you going to pick up your suit for tonight or do you want Bhavani to drop it off?" said Mye.

"I don't pick up stuff," said Truman.

"Of course you don't. I'll have Bhavani and Jia drop it off with your doorman. Alex will be back here to pick you up after he drops me off at the clinic," said Mye as she walked down the courthouse steps.

"I hope the results are negative!" yelled Truman.

Mye looked at Truman with a straight face and said, "That's.... That's not funny," as she chuckled to herself and walked to her car.

Mr. Jones watched Truman as he walked down the hall into another courtroom. "Henry did you see that woman with Truman?" asked Mr. Jones.

"Yes," said Mr. Green.

"Well, if Truman was Superman, which he isn't, she would be the sun. She doesn't hang out at the courthouse often, but when she does, he's always on his A game. She assists him with jury selection, and he has never lost with her in the room. She's very selective with the cases she works on with him, yet won't work for anyone else," said Jones.

"Is that why you chose to settle today instead of going to trial?" asked Mr. Green.

"Hell no, I'm not afraid of Truman. I can't wait to redeem myself against him. We settled today because someone high in the company said to settle if Dr. Mye Hart gets involved," said Jones. "Truman may have the power but Mye Hart, she got the juice."

***

Alex opened the car door for Mye. She asked him to take her to the Child Development Center. Mye was reviewing some emails when her daughter Bhavani Face-Timed her.

"Hey, Bhavani how are you doing?" Mye asked.

"Ma I'm doing fine. Jia and I are going to be on our way soon to get your dress. The tailor said they had a few more things to do to it and then she'll be ready in about 2 hours, so I'll see you later on this evening. I'm also getting a second back up dress just in case," said Bhavani.

"I don't need two dresses, one dress is fine; no one needs two dresses for one night," said Mye.

"Mom you can never have enough options. Jia agrees," said Bhavani. Mye could see Jia in the background shaking her head in agreement.

"Oh yea Truman asked if you could pick up his tux and drop it off with his doorman," said Mye.

Bhavani and Jia laughed together. "Ma we know goodness well that Uncle T didn't ask for anything," chuckled Bhavani.

"Yea G-Ma, he just expected it to be done," added Jia.

"Well, can you do it?" asked Mye.

"It's already done," said Bhavani.

"Thank you, ladies," said Mye.

"My line is beeping. It's your brother, hold on one second," said Mye.

"No Ma you can't," said Bhavani as Mye was accepting her son's FaceTime call.

"Hi Tem!" said Mye. Tem was laughing uncontrollably, and you could hear Bhavani in the background yelling.

"What's going on Tem? You guys are all together? Of course, you guys are, you are always together," added Mye.

"No no," said Bhavani, "I'm always with Jia, yes-"

Her mother cut her off and asked, "And Tem is always with Jia?" asked Mye.

"Yes!" said Bhavani.

"So you are always with Tem?" asked Mye.

"No!" said Bhavani.

"But you guys are all together now?" asked Mye.

"Yes!" said Bhavani. "But, I'm with Jia, and Tem stalks Jia, and that's why we seem like we are always together. But we're not. I don't like my brother Ma. I don't like being around him. You couldn't just stop with me. You had to have him."

"I was born first stupid," said Tem. "How does what you said make any sense?"

"I see you didn't deny the stalking Jia part," said Bhavani.

"I peeped that too," said Jia through a slight smirk.

"I'm breaking records as a sophomore quarterback at a D1 school. I'm heading straight to the NFL. I'm not stalking anyone. I get stalked," replied Tem.

"By losers," said Bhavani.

"Ok, but why did you call me Tem?" asked Mye.

Bhavani snatched the phone from Tem. "Ma he didn't want anything. He just saw Jia and I talking to you on FaceTime and knew if he called you, you would click over and that would end our FaceTime call because you always forget that when you click over on FaceTime, it hangs up on people," said Bhavani.

Tem was laughing uncontrollably in the background.

"Ma, you birth a jerk!" said Bhavani.

Mye laughed, "Look, I have some more work to get done today. You guys be ready for tonight and Tem can you follow up with your dad and make sure he shows up on time?" asked Mye.

"He would be the type to be late to this event," said Tem sarcastically.

"What did you say, Tem? The phone was breaking up," asked Mye.

"Nothing Ma, I got you," said Tem.

Mye replied, "Thank you, baby, I'll talk to you guys later I'm pulling up to the Child Development Center now.

***

Mye arrived at the Child Development Center as some of the children were getting picked up by their parents. As she made her way into the building, children were waving frantically and giving her hugs. Parents gave head nods and a quick wave as they did their best to gather up their kids. Mye founded this center when her children were toddlers because she couldn't find a center that met her needs. Both of her children had needs that required unique attention. Tem had a form of arthrogryposis, and he couldn't stand, move or walk properly. Bhavani had a bad seizure that nearly put her in a vegetative state and drastically affected her motor skills. Mye couldn't find a child care center that fit all of her needs, so she started her own. She opened DEON (Day, Evening, & Overnight) Child Development Center nearly 15 years ago and gave priority to children with unique needs and children whose parents had unique needs.

The director of the center Ms. Hawkins was a stern but lovely woman. She adored the children and had great patience for them. However, she had little patience for their parents. The DEON Child Development Center has an extensive waitlist. Children who didn't do well in other schools excelled here. Children who were labeled with mental or physical special needs excelled at this center. Children learned in huge classrooms with half walls, a minimum of 4 teachers with 50 plus students in each class. Previously labeled special needs children learned alongside the other children. The director Ms. Hawkins ran a tight ship as far as the parents go and the teachers were the law in their classrooms. Mye came to the center at least 3 - 4 times per week to help out in any way she could. When Mye walked into the building, Ms. Hawkins immediately made eye contact with her and motioned her to come over.

"I'm so glad to see you. How's your day coming along?" said Ms. Hawkins quickly.

"All is well," said Mye sensing Ms. Hawkins urgency. "What's going on? How can I help?" asked Mye.

"There is this parent, or I should say, guardian, that has been bringing her grandson to school, later and later every day. Today she showed up about 15 minutes before you walked in the door," said Ms. Hawkins.

With her head slightly tilted through squint eyes, Mye stated, "It's nearly 4 o'clock? What would be the point in bringing him now? Is he also one of our overnight children?" asked Mye.

"No," said Ms. Hawkins. "She usually picks him up at 5 pm," she added.

"So she dropped him off and will pick him up at 5?" asked Mye.

"No," replied Ms. Hawkins.

"What? So she's here?" asked Mye.

"Yes!" said Ms. Hawkins. "The grandma, I'm sorry her name is Mrs. Robinson. Mrs. Robinson, the grandma, said she would wait here since she has to pick her grandson up at 5 anyway. Look Mye, if this were another parent, I would be really concerned, but besides the tardiness, I don't see any other red flags. The kid looks happy and healthy. He's very affectionate towards his grandma and teachers. He has lots of friends, and he's very well behaved. I'm concerned that maybe, I don't know, I have no reason to speculate there is a problem in the home. However, I have to address this matter with Mrs. Robinson. Her grandson is in kindergarten, and he has to come to school on time. I don't want to report her but if she keeps this up my hands will be legally tied, and I will have to inform the authorities," said Ms. Hawkins with deep regret in her eyes.

"I understand," replied Mye. I will talk to Mrs. Robinson. Where is she?"

"In the infant room," said Ms. Hawkins. "She volunteers there when she comes late to drop off Kiam and leaves when it's time to pick Kiam up. The teachers in there call her the baby whisperer, and she's great with helping new moms with breastfeeding and getting their babies to sleep at night. She's great Mye, it's just rules are rules," added Ms. Hawkins.

"I understand," said Mye.

Mye walked down to the infant room and stopped just outside the door. She listened as Mrs. Robinson comforted Tiffany, a new mom having anxiety about dropping her 3 month old infant off as she headed out to go to work.

"I feel like a bad mom," said Tiffany. My daughter is barely 3 months old, and I'm already leaving her with a sitter."

"Oh hush there child," replied Mrs. Robinson, "you're doing the best you can, and you have your child at the best overnight child care facility in the area. You can see your baby on the lil webcam thingies, and everyone here is top notch. You know that founder Dr. Hart?" asked Mrs. Robinson as she leaned towards Tiffany as she was holding the baby. "She's like a top-notch psychologist, lawyer, author, doctor, mom. And she has 2 kids of her own who had severe physical disabilities, and she nursed them out of it," added Mrs. Robinson.

"What? What do you mean?" said Tiffany.

"You see how all kids learn together. She sees the goodness in everyone and strengthens that part of them. She sees past the present into what could be. You're leaving your child with a company that sees the beautiful essence of your child," said Mrs. Robinson.

Tiffany smiled as she began to feel more relaxed about leaving her daughter. "Don't you work over at that fancy alternative therapy healing touch clinic?" asked Mrs. Robinson as she made funny faces to Tiffany's baby.

"Yes," said Tiffany in a confusing manner. *How did she know that?* thought Tiffany to herself.

"Well, it just so happens that Dr. Hart is part owner over there too! Tara Jones is the main face of the clinic though. I know you love working there," said Mrs. Robinson. Mrs. Robinson caringly motioned for Tiffany to place her baby in her arms and Tiffany watched as Mrs. Robinson rocked her baby to sleep.

Tiffany said, "I love my new job. I knew it was affiliated with this daycare, but I didn't know it had the same owner. They treat their people really good over there, and they have extremely low turnover."

Mrs. Robinson gave the sleeping baby back to Tiffany. Tiffany looked down with tears in her eyes and said, "What if she doesn't remember me? What if she doesn't remember my face? I work 12-hour shifts," said Tiffany through sniffles.

Mrs. Robinson replied, "To be honest with you sweetie, your baby has pretty crappy vision right now. She probably can't recognize anyone by sight."

Tiffany bust out laughing startling her daughter out of her sleep.

"I mean faces are pretty much a blur to your baby, and she can only see a few colors," chuckled Mrs. Robinson. "Besides, you work the night shift. Your baby will be sleeping most of the time," said Mrs. Robinson as she wiped a tear from Tiffany's face.

"Thank you, Mrs. Robinson," said Tiffany, "I needed that."

Mye smiled to herself as she smoothed out her skirt before walking into the infant room.

"Excuse me, Mrs. Robinson. May I have a word with you?" asked Mye.

Mrs. Robinson beamed with excitement as she clasped her hands together. "Of course! I've been waiting for you!" said Mrs. Robinson.

Mye looked puzzled.

"Is she here? Is she here?" asked Kiam as he went running in the Infant room bumping into Mye. He tripped and fell into his grandma's arms.

"She is," his grandmother whispered in his ear looking at Mye.

"What's wrong with her hair and eyes?" Kiam said in an extremely loud whisper. Mye traced her hands over her eyebrows and smoothed out her hair.

"It's a part of her disguise," said Mrs. Robinson.

"I don't know grandma. I have a hard time reading her. I must be sure," said Kiam as he got up and walked to Mye.

"Can I see your back?" asked Kiam.

"Oh no no," said his grandmother, "that won't be necessary," she added. Curious about where all this was going Mye obliged.

"It's okay Mrs. Robinson. We encourage curiosity here," she smiled.

Kiam smiled, "Can you lift your shirt in the back please?" asked Kiam. Mye untucked her shirt and lifted the left back side of it.

"No the other side," said Kiam. Mye slowly lifted the back right side of her shirt exposing the right part of her lower back. Kiam gasped and fell back into the diaper station.

"It's okay Kiam. It doesn't hurt," said Mye as she quickly began to tuck her blouse back into her skirt. Mye had a bad scar on her back that looked like a tree's roots. Kiam got up and started to jump up and down speaking in a loud whisper, "I knew it! I knew!" as he ran to his grandma nearly knocking her over.

"Ha ha ha!" laughed Mrs. Robinson. "So now do you believe me?" Mrs. Robinson asked her grandson. "Now do you believe me when I say everything will be alright?" she added.

"Yes I do!" said Kiam as he hugged his grandma tight. "I love you, grandma. You're the best grandma a kid could ever ask for," said Kiam.

Mye cleared her throat and asked, "Can I speak to you for a minute Mrs. Robinson?"

"Oh, yes yes. Oh before I forget. Can I sign Kiam up to be picked up and dropped off from school? I'm getting kinda old, and I get my times mixed up sometimes," said Mrs. Robinson.

Mye smiled a huge smile of relief, "Of course you can Mrs. Robinson, Ms. Hawkins can take care of that for you at the front. Mrs. Robinson and Kiam started to walk out of the infant room when Mrs. Robinson turned around and asked, "Oh yea baby. Was there something you needed to talk to me about?"

"No ma'am," replied Mye. "Have a great weekend!" Mye added.

"See you on Monday!" said Kiam, "I'll be ready with my bag," he added while tapping his book bag. Mye chuckled to herself as she began to make the rest of her rounds through the center. A little five-year old girl named Bliss came running down the hall with some papers in her hand.

"Hey, Mrs. Hart!" she said as she hugged Mye's legs tight. Mye kneeled down and gave her a big hug.

"Hey, Bliss. How have you been?" she asked. "I can't wait until my dad gets home," she said.

Bliss looked around then leaned into Mye's ear and whispered, "I don't like my mom's new friend. He tastes salty."

"What do you mean taste?" said Mye looking Bliss in the eye.

"I meant smell," smiled Bliss nervously. Mye stared at Bliss for a couple of seconds then forced a smile. Bliss smiled back. She then gave Mye the papers she was holding.

"It's a book for my dad. I made it for him. Can you give it to him when you go see him? My mom said she's not taking me to see him anymore because I talk too much."

"I'll be sure to give it to him the next time I see him," said Mye.

"Katie!" yelled Bliss as she ran to her best friend who was standing next to her mom.

"Joyce, can I speak to you for a minute?" asked Mye.

Katie's mom Joyce walked over and said, "Hey Mye what's up? Is everything okay?"

"I know this is quite forward and I'm likely about to cross the line here, but do you mind asking Bliss's mom if she can stay with you this weekend? I have a weird feeling about her mom's boyfriend."

"Say no more. I don't know what's going on, but I get a bad vibe from him too. When he comes to pick her up, she looks scared and is reluctant to leave with him," said Joyce.

"Oh my goodness, I didn't know. I'll have something figured out by Monday, and the girls can come to the center over the weekend for the overnight shift so you can get a break," said Mye.

"Oh we can do this every weekend!" added Joyce.

Mye laughed, "Joyce you have to figure out a way to convince Bliss' mom to let you keep her this weekend."

"That's not a problem Mye. That woman will pass that poor girl off to nearly anyone. I just finished my foster care classes; following in your footsteps. If anything pops off and you need me just let me know. I'm available," said Joyce.

Mye was appreciative of Joyce's willingness and understanding. She watched as Joyce stopped Bliss' mom and chatted with her for a bit. Next thing you know, Bliss was jumping up and down waving bye to her mom as she skipped out of the door with Katie and her. While this wasn't a permanent fix, Mye was happy knowing Bliss would be safe for now.

***

By the time Mye reached the clinic, it was quarter past 5 pm. Alex picked up Truman since he got out of court early and took her past the clinic to sign some documents. She had to be quick because Truman hates waiting. Mye rushed into the office she and Tara shared to find John pinning Tara in a corner.

"Come on guys. Seriously?" asked Mye, "we've been through this," said Mye as she went to her desk and turned on her computer. While typing she added, "John you've got to be the freakiest conservative that I've ever met."

John dressed very conservatively and presidential. In a navy blue suit with a red tie. He stood 5 feet 10 inches in his polished wing-tipped Allen Edmonds. His blond hair was neatly trimmed, and his blue eyes sparkled through his transitional lenses. John was from old money, and he dressed like it.

"Can I just buy her out?" John asked Tara. Tara smiled as she fixed her perfect bone straight bob cut and her lab coat.

"No babes," chuckled Tara, "she's my partner. We started this together." Tara stood about 5'5", petite, and was impeccably dressed. She has flawless light honey skin and her Tibetan roots shined brightly through her epicanthic folds, dark brown eyes and naturally blushed cheeks. She wore designer apparel before it hit the runway and fashion was her guilty pleasure. She is a style icon. Under her lab coat, she wore a Chanel knit sleeveless dress that is black and white with a scoop neck, pleated hem and woven trim around the waist, and neck. The metal cap toe on her black Chanel flats perfectly matched her Rolex. While John looked like he was always wearing the same suit, Tara always looked dressed for a magazine cover.

John pulled Tara close, "I love how you bronze in the sun," he whispered into his wife's ear. Tara giggled.

"That's her skin, John. It's called mel-an-in. You wouldn't know about that. As a matter of fact, it looks like you burned a little, right there, on your forehead," Mye added while pointing at John's forehead. John put his hand over his head and looked at his wife.

"Am I sunburned?" he mouthed.

"No," whispered Tara while chuckling.

"Let me buy her out," said John.

John was from old money. His net worth was about 250 million shy of a billion. With all the money in the world the only thing that mattered to him was his wife, Tara. He met this beautiful Tibetan medicine woman nearly 20 years ago while touring in China. And at 39 he hasn't lost his passion and love for her over all these years.

"Babes," said Tara to John. "Who was there for me in the beginning?" asked Tara.

"Oh not this again," said John.

"Seriously babes. She's like my sister," said Tara.

"I'm your husband," said John as he pulled her close.

"She's the mother of your Goddaughter," added Tara.

"I'd like to go on record saying I asked you," said Mye pointing to Tara, "to be my daughter's Godmother, he became a Godfather by default," Mye added as she was signing some papers.

With his hand over his heart, John replied, "I'm the best Godfather there ever was. Bhavani loves me."

"You spoil her," said Mye.

"I do not," chuckled John.

"You bought her 4 cars for her 16th birthday," said Mye.

"She deserved it," said John.

"No one deserves 4 cars, no one needs 4 cars," said Mye.

"Well, my Goddaughter does," replied John with crossed arms.

"And 3303 Walters Street? A corner penthouse with a view of the water? Don't you think that's a bit much for a 17-year-old?" asked Mye.

"Almost 18-year-old this November. And no, I don't think it's too much. She graduated high school and college the same year, and she'll be done her masters in Economics by the end of the summer. Bhavani deserves all I give her and so much more. Her time here is borrowed, and I'm just trying to make it as amazing as I can for her," said John with sincerity.

"I understand, and I appreciate it. I just think that sometimes you don't think your gifts through," said Mye.

John replied, "Name one gift I gave that wasn't-"

"I can name a gift," said Mye cutting John off.

He replied, "No, not that, you always bring that one-"

Mye cut John off and said, "Who buys a kid a 10,000 piece Princess lego set?" said Mye loudly. "Who's putting that together?"

"I sent a lego team to put it together," replied John.

"Who's letting a group of strange adults put lego pieces together with their daughter? I couldn't walk barefoot in my house for 2 years after that," said Mye.

John whispered to Tara as she laughed at the 2 of them, "That was like 10 years ago; I really wish she would let it go."

Mye's desk phone rang, she noticed it was Truman and answered. "Hey Truman, you are on speaker, and I'm with Tara and John."

Truman replied, "I don't care. Hurry up!" Then he hung up the phone. Mye laughed and rolled her eyes.

"I have to go," said Mye as she began to gather some documents and put them in her briefcase.

John whispered to Tara, "So is this a bad time to tell her I bought the adjacent unit for Bhavani's birthday?"

"Yea, not a good time babes," whispered Tara.

Mye hugged Tara, "I love you girl. Don't be late tonight and bring John only if you must."

"Bye Mye!" said Tara. "See you tonight."

CHAPTER TWO

OH WHAT A NIGHT

Alex pulled into the three-car wide semi-circle driveway in front of a 6 bedroom white colonial house. Parallel 2 story pillars lined aside 6' x 8' mahogany double doors.

"Truman, please behave tonight," said Mye as she reached for her briefcase.

"I make no promises," he replied. Mye paused and looked at Truman as Alex opened her door, "Truman," she pleaded.

"Get out, get out, get out," said Truman as he shooed her out of the car. "The makeup artist needs at least 2 hours for your face, and it's already 6," he said. Mye knocked his phone out of his hand, "Tonight behave," said Mye as she got out of the car.

"Yes master," said Truman as Alex closed the door. Mye thanked Alex and went inside her house. She was walking to the table in the foyer when she noticed William was in his office. She smiled slightly as she put her items down and walked over to him. She admired his midnight skin and smooth bald head. He's only about 5'10," but is impeccably built. He works out religiously, and it shows. His white shirt was tailored to fit his broad shoulders. He wore a grey-black button sweater, with a thin black tie, black dress pants, and Pelle Tessuta triple stitch slip-on sneakers. Ermenegildo Zegna from head to toe.

"Well, this is a pleasant surprise," said Mye as she grabbed his hand to admire his new watch. "It's a Bvlgari Diagono Chronograph," said William.

"It's nice," said Mye.

"It's an anniversary gift from a very special lady," said William flashing his million dollar smile.

Mye smiled back. "What kind of anniversary are you celebrating?" she asked.

"Wedding. It's my wedding anniversary. In fact, it is today," he added.

"Oh congratulations," said Mye, "how many years?"

"20. 20 beautiful years and she looks the same as the day I met her. She gave me 2 beautiful kids. A son and daughter who make me proud to be their father and she makes me proud to be her husband," he added.

Mye looked down at the ground trying to hold back her tears. He gently lifted her chin and added, "Who would have thought that a couple of kids could stay married this long?" Then he kissed her gently on the lips. Mye looked him in the eye and let a single tear fall.

"I thought I left some papers here, but I must have left them at the precinct. Since I'm going back to Baltimore, I'll just get dressed at my apartment there and meet you at the Peabody Library. Tonight is going to be amazing. A night to remember," said William. He kissed his wife's forehead as he grabbed his briefcase and walked to the front door.

"Happy Anniversary baby," said William as he closed the door behind him.

Mye locked the door and leaned on it as she shook uncontrollably. She took deep breaths trying to calm herself and regain her composure. She walked over to the foyer table and opened her briefcase. She pulled out an 18k white gold case. She opened it and admired the way the light reflected off of the Rolex GMT Master II watch. She cried as she began to finally admit to herself that her life with her husband was a huge lie and she was beginning to buckle under the weight of it all.

She's known this truth for years, but she chose not to face it. She chose to ignore his infidelities as long as they didn't cross over into her world. But now her husband is so dumb that he unknowingly pranced around in a 16,000 watch gifted to him by another woman, but bought on Mye's American Express card. Mye thought about how her husband was getting sloppy and reckless. How he so easily lied to her face. She has been keeping up with appearances for years and has grown accustomed to it. She's always trying to reduce her light so that her husband could shine brighter. And now he has whores spending her money. Mye let out a lone tear earlier when she was with her husband because she was gathering all her strength not to slap him.

She used to wonder how leaving her husband would affect her children and his image. However, she never wondered how staying with her husband would affect her. Until today.

"It's Mye time," she said with deep conviction instantly feeling lighter. She relished in the joy of deciding, considering herself more than anyone else and discontinuing to settle for the sake of comfort and normalization. She flipped her hair off her shoulders and with her head held high, walked to her bedroom to prepare for tonight. While everyone thought they were going to a 20-year wedding anniversary celebration, Mye was preparing for her coming out party.

***

Emerson walked into the house and admired his beautiful wife as she talked on the phone in the sitting room. Delilah was radiant. Her fair skin was slightly tawny and flawless. She was a slender, toned woman with big brown eyes and high cheekbones. She dyed and permed her long hair blonde, and over the years her once thick hair began to thin out, but it was always styled to perfection. She exercised daily and only wore the latest designers. Emerson watched her as she laughed on the phone and took in her beauty. While her beauty was undeniable, he always had a void. She never fully satisfied him intellectually. Delilah's a pharmacist, so she's no idiot, but she was always about appearances. Inside his heart occasionally, Emerson yearned for Mye but he missed that train, so he focused everything on making his marriage work. Emerson's parents had been married for over 43 years now, and divorce wasn't an option for Birch men.

Emerson snuck up behind Delilah and grabbed her. "Dave-ry," she said when she turned around then pulled away from Emerson. Emerson had a puzzled look thinking to himself, *Who the hell is Dave?* Seemingly reading his mind, Delilah said, "I was trying to say, don't and Avery at the same time. You know, your middle name," giving Emerson a weak smile.

"But you never call me Avery," he added.

"So Mye is the only one who can pass out nicknames," Delilah hissed.

Emerson rolled his eyes. Whenever Delilah got caught in the wrong, she always managed to drag Mye into the conversation. When she overspent on the Amex for the 100th time, she dragged Mye in it. When she bought the Porsche without talking to him, she somehow brought Mye in it. Whenever she does not get her way or messes up somehow, she always manages to bring Mye into it.

This was all too familiar and starting to get old to Emerson. Instead of responding, he went into the kitchen to get something to drink. Delilah followed him hot on his heels upset about him dismissing her.

"So you guys had your little date today?" she asked.

Emerson didn't respond. He didn't keep any secrets from his wife. She knows about Mye and his lunch dates. They weren't a secret. Often their kids joined them. He and Mye were just friends, and Delilah knew that when they met.

"I'm not going to argue with you. Instead, I'm going to go upstairs and get some rest before the party tonight," said Emerson.

He walked out of the kitchen and left Delilah standing there heated. She knew he and Mye didn't have anything going on. He was too much of a square to actually do something like that. However, she also knew if he had the chance to do it all over, he would pick Mye over her. Delilah felt that she deserved a man to love her how Emerson loved Mye. Her phone was vibrating in her hands, and she saw the name David on her screen. She smiled as she answered it, walked into the sitting room, and closed the door.

***

"Good Evening Mr. Hart!" greeted the doorman of the 24-story luxury condominium. The building was in the Baltimore Harbor with 360-degree views of the city skyline. William nodded at him with a slight smirk. He pressed the up elevator button and admired his watch as he waited for the elevator to arrive.

"I got a good one," he whispered to himself as his smirk turned into disappointment. The elevator arrived, and he pressed the button for the 19th floor. "I didn't even get her anything," he said. *I honestly thought the party was our present to ourselves. I'll order her something nice on the way to the party,* he thought.

He walked off the elevator and pulled out his keys. Before he could put the key in the lock, the door opened.

"Hola bebé," said Emely, "no esperaba verte hoy."

William stared as he admired the way her brown skin glistened in her deep V red lace lingerie romper. He was mesmerized.

"In English baby," he replied in a sexy tone as he walked in the condo. Emely closed the door behind him and added all of the locks. William began to get excited as he watched her from behind. Emely favored Jill Scott and often got asked for her autograph. It wasn't until they heard her accent that strangers knew she wasn't Jill.

"You look amazing," said William.

She looked back at him and smiled. She slowly walked over to him and said in a thick Dominican accent. "I did not expect to see you today. Today is you know... that dreadful day," she said as she rolled her eyes.

"It's a formality baby," said William as he pulled her close.

She smiled as she inhaled his cologne.

"Las pendejadas," said Emely through a smirk. William was laughing when his phone started to ring. He looked at his phone and put up his hand, "One second, it's my son," he said.

Emely rolled her eyes and sat on the bar height chair beside him.

"Hey son!" said William.

"Dad, please. I'm just calling to make sure you have your tux and to remind you that the party starts promptly at 9 pm. Don't embarrass Ma and be late," said Tem in a matter of fact tone.

"Who do you think you are talking to?" said William.

"Dad I don't have time today. You can play Ma and Bhavani like a fiddle, but game recognizes game. You getting sloppy and none of them broads can hold a candle to Ma. Just do something for Ma for once in your life.

Don't be late and don't show up smelling like cheap perfume," said Tem.

Emely could hear some of what Tem said, and she slipped and spoke out loud saying, "No juegues conmigo."

William covered his phone and snarled at Emely.

"What you get? A knockoff version of Ma?" said Tem.

"Your mom's perfect huh?" said William through clenched teeth.

"No, not perfect dad; just better than you. Don't be late," said Tem before he hung up the phone.

"Look I'm out!" yelled William as he grabbed his coat.

Emely begged him to stay, and William ate it up as he watched her apologize over and over again offering to do anything to make it up to him. William fed off of women needing him and wanting him. He loved when a woman knew her place, which was to serve her man's every need. Mye served William but she was also way more successful than him, and he envied her for that. Mye was good at everything, and William only wants her to be good at being only one thing... his wife.

"I'm out. Maybe next time you'll watch your mouth," snarled William as he slammed the door behind him.

William left Emely mad but regained his composure as he walked to the elevator. He pressed the up button and went up to the penthouse. He walked to the end of the hallway and pulled out his keys. He slowly opened the door to find Leah, a beautiful caramel skinned woman with almond-shaped brown eyes standing in the nude dripping wet. He watched her intensely as she slowly sucked her fingers and traced her breast until she entered her valley doing figure 8's, moaning in almost a whisper. She laid back on the couch so he could get a better view and pleased herself as if she was putting on a performance, rotating her hips and grabbing her breast. William froze in excitement wanting to watch and join at the same time. By now he was naked and at full attention. He started kissing her knees and slowly made his way up to her inner thigh. He devoured her and took over without missing a beat. The caramel beauty slipped from underneath him and sat on his face. William palmed her assets while she rode him to ecstasy. She could barely control herself as she drifted into euphoria. She climaxed, reached over the couch, grabbed William's tux, and threw it at him.

"It's already 8:45 and you don't want to be late," she said.

He was mesmerized by her beauty, he knew he had to get dressed and get to his anniversary party, but he wanted Leah. He wanted her now. Leah could read William like a book. She knew he was one of those misogynistic types who need a woman with mass sex appeal and little brains. But Leah had a whole lot of brains, and she knew how to get what she wanted.

"So tell me, William, do you want to be in here?" Leah asked while holding up his tux. "Or here?" she asked while fingering herself.

He snatched the tux from her hand and picked her up. She wrapped her legs around him, and he said, "I want to be here."

"Then divorce her," Leah whispered in his ear. She squeezed her valley tight in a rhythmic manner. William could barely contain himself. As good as she felt, he knew he couldn't divorce Mye. William burned through his trust fund years ago and was living the fabulous life because of Mye. He made good money but spent frivolously. Mye was the brains behind their portfolio. He has political ambitions, but Mye has the connects. Divorce was out of the question.

William's knees began to weaken, so he sat on the couch as Leah continued working her magic. She whispered, "You are self-made baby, and half of what you and your wife acquired is yours. Divorce her and just take what's rightfully yours baby. You earned it. I have some ideas on how we can build our own empire."

William thought about what Leah was saying and knew it was a lie. Most of all of what he had was because of Mye. But his ego was loving what Leah was feeding him.

"Tell me more," he said as he flipped her over his shoulder and carried her into the bedroom.

***

The party was in full swing, and people were laughing and having a blast. The venue was amazing. The space had high 5 story ceilings with books all around. Gold lights draped high across the opening. The roundtables were covered in black linen with gold wooden chairs and gold chargers with plate setting for a 3-course dinner. The tables were covered in white candles of various heights with a tall, elegant gold centerpiece adorned with crystals and a huge arrangement of white flowers. A

Tribe Called Quest was performing live as people danced and feasted on food by Baltimore's top chef Dash Mason. No expense was spared. Dignitaries flooded the space, all of the top influential DC and Marylanders were there amongst a few out of state celebrities. This was a Who's Who affair. Even Commissioner Davis stopped through to congratulate the couple, but his deputy wasn't there.

Tem called his dad for the 15th time and left another voice message. "Look, you're an hour late, and even your boss doesn't know where you are so don't come to her with some I was working late bull." Tem was beyond mad at his dad for pulling this stunt.

Tem watched his mom in the distance dancing and laughing with her friend Tamron Hall. He admired his mom's resilience. She was perfect in his eyes and couldn't understand how his father could treat her this way. Tem was no saint, and he loved the ladies. He was an 18-year-old sophomore in college. He was brilliant and could double up his caseload and graduate in a year, but he's trying to get noticed so that he could make it pro. Naturally, he has a variety of women he beds. However, he was always upfront about what it was, and he never had a relationship because he never had any intentions of being with any woman for too long. He viewed marriage as something sacred but never saw himself as the married type. He briefly caught Jia looking at him and instantly became aroused. He loved her deeply but knew he didn't deserve her. He was too young, and then there was his condition. Tem and his sister Bhavani are medical miracles on borrowed time. Tem knew sooner or later he may start to regress and would hate to become a burden to anyone. So marriage was out of the question and so was Jia.

Tem watched his mom enjoy her anniversary party even though her husband of 20 years was missing. What Tem didn't know was Mye danced hard and enjoyed herself because in her mind this party was just for her. She called the event planner an hour before the party and asked her to remove the vow renewal set-up. It was no need for it tonight. After tonight, she would embark on a soul-searching adventure with no formative plan. She would just let the divine be her daily guide as she broke free from any attachments that kept her from evolving into the woman she yearned to become. Mye was finally free, and this was her big hooray.

William was rushing into the building quarter pass 10 when his phone rang again. It was Tem. Again. But this time he left a message. William shook his head because he knew he messed up. He found his way to the entrance of the hall and noticed Tem standing there with a look of disgust on his face. Tem was built like his dad with broad shoulders and defined muscles. While his dad was bald, Tem had a low cut Caesar with deep waves. He stood about 3 inches taller than his dad at 6'1" with smooth deep cocoa brown skin with a strong muscular jawline and high cheekbones. He has his mom's thin slanted eyes, full lips, and million dollar smile. However, he wasn't smiling now. He stood tensely in his William Malcolm tux with his 44th Legacy cufflinks. William walked up to his son and stood beside him in silence.

"It's nice of you to join us," Tem said through clenched teeth as he looked at everyone enjoying themselves.

"Who's the father and who's the son?" asked William.

"I don't know. You tell me," said Tem looking at his father for the first time. "Nice watch," Tem added.

"It was an anniversary gift from your mother," William said.

"No it wasn't," said Tem slightly annoyed by his father's blatant lying.

Bhavani walked up behind her dad and gave him a big hug. "Are you feeling better?" she asked. William looked puzzled as he looked at Tem to throw him a bone.

"Yeah, G-Ma said you had a mild case of food poisoning, so you'll be a little late. Feeling better?" Jia asked.

"I'm feeling a lot better. Thank you for asking," William replied.

"Nice watch," said Bhavani.

"It was an anniversary gift from your mother," William replied.

"Please, you ain't gotta lie to kick it. That's the same watch Ma got Tem for his 18th birthday. Surely she wouldn't gift you both the same watch. Plus that one is flashy like for a rapper or a stunter like Tem," said Bhavani as she pushed her brother.

Tem raised his arm to show he was wearing the same watch. "Guilty as charged," he added.

"We'll go find Ma so you two can make a grand entrance," said Bhavani as she grabbed Jia's hand and made her way through the crowd.

William stood there looking puzzled.

"You honestly thought Ma bought you that watch didn't you," said Tem with a quizzical look on his face. "But you don't even screw women who can even afford to buy you a watch like that. So your whore probably bought you that watch with your own money!" Tem laughed at his father. "You better take that watch off before Ma see you and for God's sake put on your wedding ring. Here comes Ma."

***

Delilah watched Jia and Tem sneak glances at each other throughout the night. Her daughter was stunning in a gold well-fitted gown with glossy embellishments all-over it. She stood about 5'7" with a slender frame. She favored her mother greatly except she had long, thick brownish sun-kiss blonde hair that she currently had pulled into a high ponytail with a long braid that went down her back. Jia had thick perfectly arched eyebrows with long full lashes and small pouty lips. Her big brown eyes and dimples are what Tem found to be her most irresistible features. Jia was a triple threat. On any given day you could find her in a tutu with combat boots and a lab coat. She was a 1st-year resident, a ballerina, and an activist for social change. She, Tem, and Bhavani were homeschooled by the best teachers starting at age 7 because back then DEON Child Development Center only went up to the 1st grade. Jia and Bhavani earned their first degree by age 13. Jia knows everything about Bhavani and Tem's condition and understands why Tem keeps his distance, but it doesn't make it hurt any less.

Delilah walked over to her daughter and handed her a glass of white wine. "I'm 17 mom I can't drink. Besides, there are cops here," said Jia sarcastically. Being that William was the Deputy Commissioner in Baltimore, there were a lot of officers there.

"Fine, more for me," said Delilah as she downed her daughter's glass of wine. "I see you looking at Tem," said Delilah.

Jia blushed. She truly loved Tem, but he was so aloof. She knew he was young and had girls throwing themselves at him, so she always played it cool.

Jia's mom added, "He's a good catch. He's likely going to go pro. You gotta get him now while he's young. He's handsome and rich. Your children will be trust fund babies. Be smart Jia. For every million girls like you, there is only 1 guy like Tem. Be smart. This is a chance of a lifetime. Act now, or you'll regret it," said Delilah as she grabbed a glass of champagne from the server's tray who was passing her. "Straighten your hair a little. A matter of fact, get a perm and lighten it up. Go platinum blonde. You're light as me; you can pull it off. I've seen the girls Tem dates. Go light and bright, and you'll be alright. Listen to ya momma."

Jia shook her head in pity at her mom and walked off gracefully.

"Ignore her," said Bhavani. As she made Jia start dancing in circles around Truman laughing as he got annoyed. Mye laughed at them in the distance as Truman tried to get John and Tara to make the girls stop. Tem eventually pulled Jia away and then Truman and Bhavani proceeded to roast everyone who walked past them. It was a party to remember and the night was just getting started.

***

Alex dropped Mye and William home around 2 am. William was exhausted and wanted to take a shower and go to sleep. When he came out of the shower, Mye was standing there with a bag packed.

"Where are you going?" asked William.

"Nowhere," replied Mye.

"So who's the bag for?" he asked.

Mye looked around and said, "You."

"What's this about baby?" asked William.

"Don't William," replied Mye as she stopped him from trying to hug her. She stepped back and fidgeted with her wedding band as her marriage flashed before her eyes. The memories caused her to grimace in pain.

"No more pretending William," she whispered as she slid her ring off and laid it on her vanity. She looked him directly in the eye and with all sincerity confidently said, "I want a divorce."

A million and one thoughts ran through William's head. He didn't initially comprehend what Mye said. He heard her, but he didn't understand. Why now and why tonight of all nights. He began to panic wondering if she knew about his affairs and how much she knew exactly. While William's mind was racing, Mye threw a small but heavy box at him. He caught it knocking himself out of his trance.

"That's your anniversary gift," said Mye as she turned to her vanity mirror and began to take her gold earrings off. William opened the box and couldn't believe his eyes. As soon as he saw the 18k white gold case, he knew what it was. It was the watch of his dreams. He opened the case and gawked at the Rolex GMT Master II. He eagerly took the watch out of the box and went to put it on when he realized that he was wearing the other watch that he thought was a gift from his wife. He instantly got mad at himself because his son told him at the party to take the watch off, but he didn't listen. Mye had her back to William, but she could see everything playing out through her vanity mirror.

"What's the matter William?" asked Mye as she turned to face him. "You can always put the watch on your other wrist," she added.

William stood dumbfounded quickly thinking of a way to talk himself out of this hole, however, he wasn't having much luck.

"I bought this watch as a gift to myself," he said. "As a way to bond with Tem. You see, we have the same watch," added William.

Mye clasped her hands together and rested her chin on them. She could believe that her husband would lie to her face and drag their son in it. That was very believable to her. William was notorious for lying, sneaking around, and dragging their kids in his lies to help persuade her to believe him. What she couldn't believe was that she allowed a man to feel confident enough to lie to her at this degree and to treat her like this. She couldn't believe that a woman as brilliant as her would not consider this treatment to simply be intolerable.

William watched Mye dazed out and thought to himself, "*That was a close call. I gotta find out who got me this watch.*"

Mye glanced up at her husband and became slightly annoyed by the look of relief on his face. The old Mye would let things go, not only to avoid confrontation, but most importantly to avoid the truth. Her husband was community property, and she paid all his expenses. You never ask a man about his extramarital affairs unless you've come to terms with leaving him. Before now, Mye didn't want to leave her marriage because she felt she was partly the blame for her husbands cheating. William was very misogynistic, and Mye's successes made him fill less than. William believed a woman's place was underneath her husband and he envied Mye. She made substantially more money, and she had many connections to people in various high places.

Mye tried to play smaller and downplay her accomplishments to make William feel better. She would turn down jobs or do them in secrecy to keep from bruising her husband's ego.

However, today was different. Today she decided that she's going to live free and authentic to herself. Mye didn't know what that meant exactly, but she was going to say to William exactly what's on her mind and in the process likely surprise herself.

William pulled the covers back to get in the bed. Mye thought to herself, *this negro really thinks he's spending the night here.*

Mye asked, "What card did you use?"

William scrunched his face, "What? What card? What are you talking about?" he asked.

Mye pointed to the watch on the nightstand. "What card did you use to buy the watch? Did you get reward points or air miles? What? What card did you use?"

William jumped up in anger, "Are you questioning me? Questioning me about my money!" he yelled.

"No, it's my money! I'm questioning you about my money!" she yelled banging on her vanity. William was taken back by her yelling.

"It's my money, and apparently I bought you two watches!" said Mye. She got up and began to pace the room.

"I'm tired of pretending we are something we are not William and I be damned if I continue to let you let some broads spend my money! You did not buy that watch William! Some young girl who watches a lot of music videos did, and she did it with my money!" she said.

"Our money!" said William.

Mye took a deep breath, "Go find a lawyer and have them write up something fair," said Mye in a calm manner.

"Why can't Truman do it? You tell him everything anyway," huffed William.

"Truman will take you to the cleaners and leave you with nothing. I'm doing you a favor," said Mye.

William knew Mye was right, Truman never liked him from day one, and he's a ruthless attorney. William tried to plead with Mye.

"Let's do counseling. We can work through this," he pleaded.

"To be blunt William. I don't want to work through this. I don't want to be with you. You have a problem with my success, and I'm tired of making myself small for you. I want to do more and accomplish more, and I can't do that with you," said Mye.

William was heated. Never has a woman made him feel so small and inadequate.

"That's why I screw other women. You don't appreciate me! You don't know how to take care of your man!" yelled William. "You work 4 hours a day! You don't have a real job. You live the sweet life. A life I built for you. This image of having it all together is because of me. If you lose me, then you lose the image and then what would you have? I'll tell you what. You'd have nothing and be just another broke down black woman who can't keep a man. That's what's wrong with y'all new generation woman. Y'all don't know how to shut up and play your role. My mother knew that, and her mother knew that. Keep it up Mye. Please know that once you lose me, you will slowly start to lose everything else."

Mye sat down on the bed as the harsh reality of his words began to sink in. She looked up to William with a slight smirk and said, "That's the plan."

She then added, "I don't want you anymore nor do I need any of this. And we new generation women as you call us are different from the older generation. We, A, care more about our mental, physical, and emotional well-being than older generations. That's a luxury most of them didn't have. And B, we don't have men providing and taking care of us as the older generation women did. At least not most of us anyways. Y'all new age men want 50/50. I'm up every day from 5 am to 9 pm working nonstop, and I deal with difficulties every step of the way. This morning, I was nearly attacked by a deranged patient, went to court to assist a client going up against a major corporation and won, had to figure out on the fly how to handle a possible molestation of a 5 year old little girl, signed contracts and reviewed files for the expansion for the clinic and all that was before 6 pm. I've spent the last 20 years creating multiple streams of income, multiple businesses, buying assets, wisely investing, and all you did and still do is spend, spend, spend! You need this image and this life. This is your key to becoming a future Mayor. You need all of this William! Not me! And now you have another woman spending my money too! I worked hard for everything, and you have just been enjoying the ride."

"What do you expect from me Mye? You haven't put out in like two years! Did you honestly think I was celibate too?! Let's not play these games. Look I'm sorry about the watch but let's not pretend I'm the only one at fault here," yelled William.

"Who said I was celibate?" asked Mye as she sat down at her vanity and began to wipe off her make-up. William looked stunned and then began to get tense with anger. Mye looked at William through her vanity mirror.

"You've been unfaithful for more than two years, and I couldn't continue to expose myself to whatever you were doing out there and lose money at the same time." Mye turned around and looked him in the eye.

"Yeah, you had a trust fund, but you blew through that. Then you started blowing through my money." Mye got up and began to walk towards William. "Now you have another woman blowing my money. It's like I'm taking care of you and that cum bag. Hell, she might as well be my side chick!" yelled Mye.

William couldn't believe what he was hearing. Mye never spoke like that. She was like a different person. She stood tall, confident, and secure with herself spitting venom. He knew what she was saying was right, but who was she to address it? William racked his brain trying to flip the argument in his favor.

He replied, "All you keep talking about is money money money. You don't care about losing your husband? You never cared about me, only my money! Only my family's money! You married into a prestigious family. You only have a family because of me! You have children because of me! You were born into dysfunction, so it is second nature to you. Where is your father huh?! You put him up in a fancy home with nurses and servants, but you don't visit him. What kind of person does that make you?! And what about your kids? Are you going to leave them too like your mom left you?" spat William.

William's words sliced to Mye's core. Painful memories flood her mind all at once. There was pain in the truth he spoke. She tried her best to maintain her composure. At 6 years old, Mye's mom was abducted right in front of her and has never been found. 32 years later, the incident is still fresh in her memory as if it happened yesterday. Mye began to get angry as she thought about how her mother didn't leave her but instead was taken.

William married Mye with every intention of her being his trophy wife just as his mom was for his dad. He thought he had a malleable naive 18-year-old girl with no friends or family that he could control to his likening. He strategically picked Mye just like his father taught him, and William pursued Mye pulling out all the stops. He never noticed the ambition that hid behind the hurt in her eyes. And as she grew and prospered, he resented her more and more. Despite how perfect their lives looked to others, William didn't believe that Mye knew her place. And so he cheated with many women for years who he believed knew their place. This was William's chance to break Mye all the way down so that she can get with his program. He knew he crossed the line by talking about her parents, especially her mother. However, he wasn't going to lose without a fight. Plus, he couldn't face his father if he and Mye divorced. His father heavily disapproved for years of how active Mye was outside of the house. If William and Mye divorced, then his father would feel that William had lost full control of his wife and was less of a man.

Mye threw the bag at his feet and said, "Get dressed and get out! You can come back Monday to get the rest of your things. I need the weekend to gather my thoughts. When I get out of the shower, I want you gone."

William threw on some clothes and left.

***

It was 3:15 am when William finally got in the bed to get some sleep. He was beyond tired. He snuggled up to Emely gently waking her. She greeted him with a kiss and turned around to go back to sleep. He whispered to her, "I'm still mad about what you did earlier, but you can make it up to me now."

"Anything for you," she replied. Then she proceeded to plant kisses from his neck to his manhood where she proceeded to do what she does best.

The next morning, Emely woke up excited about having the chance to cook her man breakfast and just love him. She turned over to ask him what he wanted to eat and noticed he was already gone. She knew there was no need texting or calling him because he would not reply anytime today. She reached in her nightstand and re-read the job offer she received. It was 50% more money than she was making now in a city with a lower cost of living. She had until Monday night to accept the offer. She had discussed the offer with William briefly, and he said they would think it over. Emely just wished he would hurry up and make up his mind before time ran out. She really loved William, and she would turn down the offer if it meant they could finally start a family here in Baltimore.

***

"What the hell is your problem?" yelled William waking Leah up out of her sleep as he threw his expensive watch at her.

"Would you lower your voice please?" she replied picking up the watch. "This is your anniversary gift," she said confused. "Our anniversary is 3 days before your wedding anniversary. What? You don't like it," she said.

William thought about how sloppy he has been. He made their anniversary the same day as Mye's birthday so he would not forget, but now he was just getting himself confused. When he saw the watch in his bag with the anniversary note, he naturally assumed it was from Mye because Leah couldn't afford a gift that expensive. William started getting upset all over again thinking about it.

"How did you pay for this watch?" he asked.

"With the Amex," she replied.

William was furious. "You remember you have a 5,000 dollar budget! You can't go over 5k in a month," he yelled.

"I didn't. I bought it on a payment plan. I stayed well below my monthly budget, and on the receipts, you can't even tell what I bought exactly," Leah replied.

William felt terrible for yelling at her. She didn't mess up. He did.

"I'm sorry for losing my cool baby. It's just been a lot going on," he said.

"It's okay. You can trust me. You can trust me with any and everything," she said.

William felt like he could really trust Leah. She was younger, 28, and William was 41, but Leah always knew her role and played her position well. He would toss other women to the side after a couple of weeks to a month, but he was slowly starting to see that Leah was something special.

"I'm going to divorce my wife," William said nonchalantly.

Leah was ecstatic. She was jumping up and down kissing him all over. William was eating it up. She made him feel so powerful and in control. He didn't plan on divorcing his wife, but if he had to, he was going to make sure it looked like it was his idea. William slowly pushed her off of him so that he could go to the bathroom.

Leah texted an unsaved number, "He's one foot out the door. He's filing for a divorce."

Then she got a text back that said, "Perfect! Now the ball is rolling, and I can finally get what I want, and you can get what you want."

Leah laid back on the bed in utter bliss as she thought about how perfectly her plan was unfolding. She was one step closer to what she really wanted. Access to all of his money.

CHAPTER THREE

IT HURTS LIKE HELL

Mye was in the kitchen cutting fruits and vegetables to make some smoothies while Emerson was checking emails on his phone. After their weekly Monday jog, Mye makes smoothies for everyone accept Bhavani. Mye has a rule, and if you're not exercising, then she isn't making you a smoothie. Bhavani doesn't jog because she doesn't believe in sweating. Jia and Bhavani came running down the stairs just as Tem came through the kitchen door. Everyone grabbed their smoothie while Bhavani stood there pouting. Mye slid the cutting board with the extra cut up vegetables and fruit on it to Bhavani, and everyone broke out in laughter.

"Same time next Monday?" asked Emerson while walking to the door to head to the hospital.

"Of course, bye Em! Love you!" yelled Mye.

"Ditto," replied Emerson. "See ya later baby girl," said Emerson to Jia. "

Bye, daddy! I'll be at the hospital around noon. My rotation starts at 1 pm," said Jia.

"I'll be in surgery, but I'll find you after I'm finished," he said as he hugged Jia and kissed her forehead.

"Let's go, Jia. I gotta get Mrs. Jones paper for her," said Tem.

"Why do you always have to get that woman's paper?" asked Jia.

"You jealous?" smirked Tem.

"Of what Tem? She's like 80 years old? Who gets excited about an 80-year-old checking them out?" laughed Jia.

"Don't forget your weighted vest!" Mye interrupted. "It's a good way to increase the intensity of your workout," she added.

Walking to the closet, Tem opened the door and grabbed the vest from the floor, "I got it Ma!" he yelled. As he closed the door, he said,"Whatever Jia, I see Mr. Jones checking you out. I see you smile at him," joked Tem while poking Jia.

"Whatever, let's go," Jia said as she smacked Tem's hand away playfully. "Thank God G-Ma got you that vest. I was worried you'd blind somebody running around with no shirt on," said Jia as the door closed behind them.

Mye started to wash the dishes when she noticed Bhavani still standing there with her arms crossed. "Now that everyone's gone, can you please make me a smoothie? You know no one makes them as good as you mom," pleaded Bhavani while pouting.

Bhavani shared her mom's mahogany skin tone and hourglass shape at about 5'7". However, she was about 40 lbs heavier closer to 190 lbs. Her body was firm and tight without a roll in sight. Her light brown slanted eyes sparkled through her thick eyelashes. Her cupid's bow is naturally well-defined, her sultry full lips are tantalizing, and the beauty mark on the right side of her nose adds an extra sass to her perfected resting bitch face. Her hair is pulled up into a messy curling bun, however, she has an unmatched collection of the best wigs money can buy and changes up her looks often.

Mye stopped washing dishes and just put her head down for a good 5 secs.

"What's wrong? What are you doing?" asked Bhavani stepping behind her mother with her hand on her shoulder.

"Nothing's wrong with me. I was just saying a quick prayer for your future husband." They both laughed.

"Stop playing Ma," said Bhavani as she sat down at the island. "Why did you marry daddy?" she asked.

Mye paused for a moment, taken back slightly by Bhavani's question. She'd never asked Mye anything about love or relationships before. Bhavani was very different from her mother. Bhavani relied more on logic and meticulous calculation and very little on her intuition. She was confident and put herself first. Not in a selfish way but in a way that demonstrated to others her standards and required level of treatment. Bhavani succeeded at everything she did. No one, man or woman, could outwork her and she enjoyed the glamorous life. She lived like a movie star with the best of everything. While she was more flamboyant with her lifestyle than Mye, she shared Mye's choice to keep the many ways she made her money discreet. Bhavani didn't date because guys her age didn't seem to meet her on an intellectual level which was important to her. Most guys thought she was superficial and was living off her parent's money which was far from the truth. They were nowhere near prepared to handle Bhavani once she opened her mouth. Young men who attempted to court her seemed to be less intimidated by her but more annoyed by her ambition. They didn't understand Bhavani's big why, and so they had a hard time understanding her.

"Ma!" yelled Bhavani, "why did you marry dad?" she asked.

Mye began to sweat a little and Bhavani could see her mother's hesitation. Mye never lied to her daughter. However, she knew if she opened this door, it could lead to a conversation that Mye doesn't want to have. It will force Mye to speak a truth she didn't want to hear and admit a fear she didn't want to acknowledge.

Mye took a deep breath and answered, "Sweetie, I met your father when I was 16, and I didn't think about life like you do now. Back then, I thought about life as making it to tomorrow, and every day I just tried to make it to tomorrow. It was hard for me back then. I had no family, and your father came in like a knight and shining armor offering love and stability. So I married him. 3 days after my 18th birthday. However, I honestly didn't marry your father. I married what I thought your father could provide for me. That's why I'm in the situation I'm in now. See baby, if you decide to marry one day, choose that person, choose to want to marry who they are currently. Not their potential, not what gaps you think they can fill within you, not the image, choose them. I didn't do that. Your father and I had clear differences in our fundamental values, but since I had been through so much, I figured I could handle it. And I was right. I could handle it. However baby, just because you can tolerate something doesn't mean that you should."

Bhavani gave her mom a tight hug. "Mom I'm so sorry you had to deal with so much. I notice a lot that I don't speak on, and I'm glad you guys are getting a divorce. I mean, don't get me wrong, I love dad it's just his behavior, it's borderline embarrassing."

Mye ran her hands through her daughter's hair wrapping a loose strand around her bun. "Bhavani, your father, has his own issues he's battling, and he loves you very much, it's just-"

"No mom," said Bhavani cutting off her mother. "Dad's wrong, and it's okay for me to think he is wrong and it's okay for me to be disappointed in his behavior. You deserve someone who defends your character even when you are wrong. You deserve all the love you give so freely."

Mye got teary-eyed as she began to dry dishes that were already dry.

Bhavani whispered, "Do you regret marrying him?"

Mye spun around quickly. "Oh, no baby. Of course not. I was a young girl ready to run as far away from my past as possible and ran right into the arms of your father. And despite how we both may feel about him, let's be honest, I could have done way worse," they both laughed. Mye added, "I'm so grateful for meeting your father because he gave me you and Tem."

Bhavani added through tears, "You're mostly grateful for me more than Tem right?"

Mye laughed.

"It's okay Ma. You can be honest," Bhavani added.

Mye grabbed some tissue for the two of them and said, "I have no regrets about anything. I'm honored that you and Tem chose me to be your earthly guide to adulthood."

Bhavani said, "Ma, I want someone to love. You know, like, I'm not saying I want to get married, but someone to love would be nice. Have you ever been in love? Like felt true love?"

Mye thought for a moment, "Well there was this one guy I thought I fell in love with when I was really young like 14 years-"

"Ooo, I know who you met at 14 years old! Do it! Eww not do it, do it, but do you boo!" proclaimed Bhavani.

Mye laughed then yelled, "Get out my kitchen girl!"

***

Between heavy breathing, Jia said, "Pace yourself Tem," as she trailed slightly behind him jogging up the hill.

Tem turned around and began to jog backward and chuckled, "By pace yourself do you mean slow down so you can catch up?"

"No," said Jia between breaths. "You know what I mean. You're running not jogging, with a weighted vest on, up the hill, on a Spring day that feels like Summer," puffed Jia.

"I have to be prepared for the season. It's no way I can play pro ball this size," proclaimed Tem as he turned around and ran faster up the hill leaving Jia behind.

"Stop lying Tem!" yelled Jia. She ran up to Tem and stopped him from running. Bent over breathing heavily she said, "I'm tired of you lying to me, more importantly, aren't you tired of lying to yourself?"

"What?" asked Tem confused.

While catching her breath Jia said, "You don't even like football Tem-"

"What!" interrupted Tem. "I've been playing football my whole life!"

"Stop lying Tem! It's me! I've been here since the beginning," said Jia through eyes of concern. "You have nothing to prove to anyone." Tem stood there quietly looking past Jia. "I see the subtle jerky movements. You're pushing your body too far right now, and you need to rest.

Tem looked Jia in the eye and flashed his million dollar smile. "Jia, I have no idea what you're talking about, but I'm gonna be just fine," Tem began to jog in place, "you see, I'm better than fine," then he turned away and returned to running.

Jia ran up to him, and grabbed him aggressively, "I'm serious Tem," she said through clenched teeth. He yanked his arm away smiling, "I'm 18 years old, and you're what 17? Respect your elder's young lady," joked Tem as he returned to running.

Jia grabbed him again, "I'm 17 and 3 months, but more importantly, I'm a 1st-year resident specializing in spasticity. The last 14 years of your life have been a medical miracle. An anomaly, but I fear you are pushing your body backward with your extreme exercise regimens," Jia leaned in and whispered, "some of your old symptoms are returning, please slow down."

"See Jia, this is why you don't have a man," sneered Tem as he stepped away from her. Jia just stared at him with her head slightly tilted to the side with a genuine look of hurt and confusion.

"Are you serious?" she whispered.

"Hell yeah!" yelled Tem with his chest poked out. "That's why you black women can't get a man, and if you do, you can't keep a man. Y'all always nagging and trying to bring a brother down. That's why I don't deal with y'all."

Insulted and infuriated, Jia rubbed her temples and said, "What?! I'm talking about your health, your life, and you want to make me the representative of all black women and equate my genuine clinical cause for concern as a diss to your ability to perform, and you want to use this reason to justify why you don't date black women? Did I get that right?"

A police cruiser patrolling the neighborhood drove by and rolled down their window. Tem raised his hands with palms up and yelled, "What are you looking at?" The police cruiser just drove off.

Jia slapped his hands down and asked, "What is your problem? Do you have a death wish? Don't let your attitude with me for speaking the truth get you killed."

"That officer has seen me around, he knows I'm the one in the tight ass coupe," said Tem.

"What you drive doesn't matter. You're still a black man and it-"

"My father is the deputy commissioner," he said cutting her off.

"In Baltimore Tem, we live in Spring Valley in Washington, DC," said Jia.

"So what? If I get arrested Uncle T will get me off. He never loses. I'm Teflon," he said with a big smile.

Unamused Jia took a deep breath and stepped closer to him. "Uncle T has never successfully tried a dead man either. You gotta make it to the police station first. And I would hate for you to end up dead because some scared ass police officer felt threatened by the presence of your black skin and kill you without due process. You think you have equal protection under the law? No matter how much money we have, we're still black," said Jia.

"This is precisely why I don't date black women! Black this, black that, and you're barely black. You can pass off as white easily. All you have to do is straighten your hair, it's already naturally blondish." Tem started to walk away then he turned back and said, "You should be like your mother. She's black, but she pretends she's white and uses white privilege. You know in school everyone thought you were mixed because your mom looks white. Be that! Isn't it easier to be that? If you were that I might date you," he winked.

She replied, "There's no such thing as barely healthy or barely racist or barely black. You either are, or you aren't. We create degrees to these topics to make ourselves feel better. My mom has her own cross to bear, and as an adult, she does as she pleases. I am black and proud of it. My beautifulness is from my blackness. Every human feature there is or ever was can be found in a black woman. From blonde hair to blue eyes. No matter how wealthy you become, the macro-system you will forever be a part of will attribute to the social-historical context of your race. You can never not be black. You can date or marry anyone you so choose. That's the beauty of love. It sees no color. But the funny thing is whenever shit hits the fan, you always run back to a black woman. You rely heavily on the black woman to lift you up and to look past your faults," said Jia with hurt in her voice.

"Look I don't need you," said Tem.

Jia smirked, "Funny, I never said you did. The truth of the matter Tem is the black man couldn't be the black man without the black woman," said Jia.

"I can make it just fine without you," he said.

"Then bye," said Jia as she turned to jog away. "Oh yeah, there's no way in hell I would ever marry a man as distracted as you. How can you protect and cherish me when you're so busy fighting yourself?"

She turned around and began to jog, then stopped briefly dropping her head seemingly in defeat, "Tem, please try to rest and get the tremors checked out. In the meantime try to stay away from high voltages or just electrical sockets in general. A shock to your nervous system can possibly progress your regression or completely send you back to the stage you were as a kid. It was painful to watch."

"Even more painful to live," Tem said avoiding eye contact with Jia. With a smirk, Tem replied, "I'll do my best not to get electrocuted." Jia rolled her eyes and jogged off.

Tem watched her jog down the street until she turned the corner and he couldn't see her anymore. Then old Mrs. and Mr. Jones broke his trance with their bickering.

***

The doorbell rang and rang as Ms. Dean the executive house manager stood in front of the door looking at it. Mye couldn't help but laugh because Ms. Dean does this to Truman every Monday without fail. She only comes to the house to annoy Truman. She owned one of the most successful Estate Management businesses in the DMV metropolitan area. She managed the chauffeurs, maids, butlers, gardeners, pool guys, bodyguards, etc. She is the go-to person for the elite homeowners; owners of homes valued at 2 million or more. She worked from a referral system only, and she was picky as hell. She didn't work with just anyone. She treated her employees with the utmost respect and demanded her clients to do the same. If she found out that a client disrespected an employee, she would pull all of her employees from that property and from the property that referred them. Ms. Leena Dean played no games. She grew up in the government yards in Trench Town, in Kingston Jamaica, and quoted Bob Marley like the old saints quote scripture. A solid exceedingly curvy woman who stood about 5'9 at 220 lbs with a walk that commanded attention. Saying she is confident, would be an understatement. She knew her worth and commanded it. With big brown eyes, beautiful mocha skin, they only thing that gave away her age was her pencil size grey dreads.

The doorbell rang. "The door is open Truman," yelled Ms. Dean. The knob turned, but the door was still locked.

"Why don't you just open the door?" Truman replied, "Ms. Dean, why must we do this every Monday?"

Ms. Dean opened the door and smiled at Truman, "Cuz mi like fi si yuh tun red," she whispered in her thick native tongue then she winked at him and hit his butt when he walked past her into the house.

"Good day my love! I'll see you later baby!" yelled Ms. Dean in a clear Washington D.C. accent as she left the house.

"Bye Ms. Dean!" Mye replied.

"That is sexual harassment," said Truman as he locked the door.

"No, that's love," said Mye as she put away the last of the dishes in the cabinet.

"No, I'm a lawyer, and that legally constitutes as sexual harassment," said Truman.

"Not if I say it wasn't," smirked Mye. Truman squinted his eyes in annoyance. Mye continued, "I could be a witness for Ms. Dean, and we all know how the law works. It's not what you know, it's not the truth, it's what you can prove," said Mye as she was finishing her smoothie.

"Listen here you little Jack of all trades," said Truman. Mye laughed nearly spitting her drink out. "I'm the lawyer with the 97% success rate. For the right price, I can make anyone Teflon. I'm the man. And if I ever was on trial, you better be my witness," said Truman.

Mye laughed, "But what if I wasn't there?"

"Especially if you weren't there," chuckled Truman. "You better get on that stand and get your Halle Berry on. Nobody is playing with you," said Truman through a slight smirk.

Mye shook her head and began to walk away. Truman turned on the sink and sprayed Mye with the faucet getting her straight hair wet.

"What the hell Truman?" yelled Mye through a chuckle.

"Say you'll be my witness," demanded Truman. Mye laughed, and Truman sprayed her again.

"You're gonna make my hair curl!" yelled Mye.

"You're about to get it washed anyway," said Truman as he tried to spray her again, but he missed.

"I'll be your witness," said Mye while rolling her eyes.

Truman put the faucet back and said, "I would never put you in a position to have to lie for me, but it's nice to know if I did you would. We lawyers don't trust a lot of people," said Truman.

"We've been friends for nearly 20 years. I got your back always," said Mye. "Besides, you know too many secrets for me to ever turn on you," laughed Mye.

The doorbell rang. "Coming!" yelled Mye. It was Tisha, Walt, and Renee. Their nail technician, hairdresser, and stylist.

"Hi guys!" said Mye.

"Why is your hair wet?" asked Walt. "Did you do it yourself? I love it! I love the curls! Is this your new wash and go look?"

"No," said Mye. "Truman was playing and got my hair wet."

"He plays?" asked Walt with his head slightly tilted.

"In that suit?" asked Renee through clenched teeth as she peeked around a rack full of clothes. "That's hand stitched Truman."

Truman looked down at his watch. "I'm on a tight schedule. Can we get this started?"

Tish, Walt, and Renee started making their way to the salon slash dressing room in the house. Renee was pulling the long rack of clothes shaking her head.

"That's hand stitched," she whispered.

"Is it that time of the year again? I see all of the cars lined up outside?" asked Walt.

"Yep, it's the time again," Mye replied.

Every 3 months George, Mye's mechanic, does a multi-check on her cars. He's really big on making sure brakes and tires are in top shape. He got into a really bad accident as a teen because he had bad brakes.

Mye was acting a little jittery as she was trying to flatten her growing hair. When her hair got wet, it got really big, and big hair makes her feel really uncomfortable. It reminded her of a dark time in her life that she always tried to forget.

"Can I get my hair done first?" Mye asked Truman.

"I always get my hair cut first," said Truman as he fixed his suit jacket.

It wasn't until he looked up and saw the pain in Mye's eyes when he remembered. He knew all too well why Mye didn't like her hair curly, and she had a good reason. It was too painful for her to look at. By this time Mye's hair was drier and had grown bigger and curlier. No one can truly understand how much hurt and pain can collect in a woman's coils. Instead of facing the pain, Mye straightened it away. There is nothing wrong with straight hair. The problem lies in why she straightens it. Mye knew that it was time she faced this issue and her need to keep her hair straight. She knew that facing her past was a part of her journey and necessary to grow but facing her past was scary as hell. Mye's hair held an emotional blockage that she needed to undo to move on, so she could stop being at the mercy of her hair.

FLASHBACK - MARCH 1990

"Champ, I think my dad is going crazy. Can you come over quick? I left the side window open. Hurry!" said Mye right before her dad snatched the phone from the wall.

"Who were you talking to?" demanded Elroy.

"No one dad. No one. It's me your daughter," cried Mye.

"Where have you been? You've been gone for 6 years then you decide to come back on your daughter's 12th birthday? Who were you with this whole time," he asked.

"No one dad. It's me your daughter. I'm not mom. Mom's not here. It's me," she cried.

"I know who you are!" yelled Elroy as he slammed his fist on the table.

He was in a full drunken rage. Mye sat in her green dress that perfectly matched her eyes with her hair out in big curls that fell down her back. It was her birthday, so her babysitter Gale did her hair real nice and got her a birthday cake. Mye was sitting at the dining room table waiting for her dad to come home so she could surprise him. He never was the same after her mom was kidnapped in 1985. She spent most of her days with her grandparents or her babysitter Gale with her nephew Champ. But today was her dad's weekend and her birthday, so she was super excited. But when he walked in, he started acting really strange.

"Where the hell have you been?" he yelled.

"Here," cried Mye, "I've been here."

"Don't you love me anymore?" he pleaded.

"Of course I do dad, but you're scaring me," she cried.

"I'm sorry baby. Let me make it up to you. Let me make you feel better," he said.

Elroy opened his arms, and Mye gave him a hug. Then he picked her up and carried her down the hall. He took her to his room and laid her on the bed. Elroy began to take his pants off.

"I don't know where you've been and I don't care. I'm just glad you're back home baby," he said as he began kissing her.

Mye screamed hysterically, "Dad stop! It's me! I'm not mom! Dad stop!"

Champ ran into the room and swung Elroy to the floor.

"What the hell?" he said in disgust.

"What happened?" said Elroy as he saw the fear in his daughter's eyes. He had snapped back to his senses and realized what he did. Reaching for his pants trying to put them on while also trying to cover his face in shame.

"What were you thinking?" asked Champ with his arms around a crying Mye.

"I don't know. I just walked into the house and saw that hair and green dress; she looks just like her mother, I mean I don't know. Every year she looks more and more like her. I just don't know. I told her don't wear her hair like that! She didn't listen!" yelled Elroy.

Champ shook his head in pity. Something in Mye's dad was permanently broken after he lost Mye's mom.

"This isn't the first time, is it?" asked Champ. Mye just looked at the ground.

"He's right. I should have listened. I shouldn't wear my hair this way, and green was mom's favorite color, but it's my favorite color too!" cried Mye. "I can't help I look like her! I can't change my hair and eyes. This is me! How can I change me?!"

"Go pack up your stuff Mye. You're staying with me and Aunt Gale," said Champ. Even though Champ was only 2 years older than Mye, he always appeared to have everything figured out and no matter what Mye could always count on Champ to have her back.

PRESENT - MARCH 2017

"Of course you can get your hair done first," said Truman, "aren't I a gentleman."

"You a something," smirk Mye. "I'm still trying to figure out what though," she laughed. "But I'm good

Truman. No need to break tradition. You can get your hair done first. It's time I get use to these lovely curls and stop running from them."

Truman didn't say anything, but he could see Mye growing, and he respected her for it. She had good reason to be the way she was, but she was choosing to grow past it. Mye had a hard childhood and came far. And something inside appeared to be pushing her to go even further. It made Truman think there could possibly be some hope for him. That's what happens when people start to grow. They give others around them permission to grow too.

***

"Mrs. Jones, are you giving Mr. Jones a hard time again?" asked Tem. Mr. Jones walked into the house and slammed the door. Mrs. Jones loved to sit on her porch and wait for Tem to jog down the street and offer to grab her newspaper. The paperboy did a pretty poor job of tossing the paper close to the front door, but Mrs. Jones didn't mind. She was pushing 80 years old and looking at Tem's sweaty body was her excitement for the day. Tem had his headphones on when he grabbed the paper and began to jog to Mrs. Jones as she sat on the porch smiling.

"Thank you Tem. You're such a sweet boy. You're going to make a fine husband one day," she said.

Tem smiled and jogged across her lawn to the sidewalk. Mrs. Jones took the newspaper and threw it across the yard. She waved frantically to get Tem's attention then she pointed at the newspaper and smiled. Tem shook his head as he jogged to the other end of the yard to get the newspaper then jogged back to Mrs. Jones.

***

Jia had stopped running to stretch and gather her thoughts. She was so disappointed in Tem, but more importantly, with herself. She undeniably loved Tem even though he was a total jerk. She tried to push him out of her mind, but he would always find a way to creep back in. Jia was lost in her thoughts when she heard a single gunshot and loud screaming. The first person she thought about was Tem.

She ran as fast as she could across people's yards and over fences. She couldn't be sure if she was running in the right direction, but she never stopped running. Then she heard a second shot. She ran as fast as she could in that direction and found Mr. Jones holding a shotgun with Tem and a cop on the ground.

***

"I love your hair curly," said Walt, "please wear it curly outside for me one time."

Mye laughed, "Baby steps," she replied.

Mye's eyes have been getting dry lately, so she took out her brown contacts out for a second to give her emerald green eyes a chance to breathe. Her eyes watered slightly as she blinked a few times while sparkling in the sunlight. She wore a black crop top and green cargo shorts. She wiggled her toes trying to help make her white polish dry quicker.

"When are you going to stop wearing those brown contacts Mye? Your eyes are so beautiful," said Renee.

Mye looked down to avoid eye contact with anyone. "I know, I know. Baby steps," Renee added.

Mye felt she could be herself around them. She caught a glimpse of herself in the mirror and cringed slightly in her chair, then immediately regained her composure. The sight of Mye seeing her natural self brought back painful memories, but she was taking baby steps to face them around the people she trusted.

"I see you wearing that midriff Mye," yelled Tish.

Before Mye could speak, the group said, "I know baby steps," and bust out in laughter.

"How come you never get comfortable Truman?" asked Walt. "I mean who gets their hair cut in a suit?" Walt laughed.

"I like to stay ready," replied Truman.

Loud ringing was happening seemingly all over the house. Mye's cell phone was ringing; the house phone was ringing, Truman's, Walt's, Renee's, and Tish's phone were all ringing. Mye's heart started pounding uncontrollably. Unanimous ringing of everyone's phone meant one of two things: either Bhavani or Tem had only minutes to live.

"It's a cold blue!" yelled Mye as she grabbed her phone.

"See Walt," said Truman calmly while buttoning up his jacket. This is why I stay ready.

***

Jia ran to Tem and checked to see if he had a pulse. And he did. Jia could hear the officer moaning, so she knew he was alive. That's when she noticed the bean bag beside him. Mr. Jones was still holding up the shotgun.

Jia slowly pushed his gun to the ground. Mrs. Jones was crying hysterically.

"I didn't mean to kill him. He shot Tem, and I was scared he would shoot my wife too," said Mr. Jones.

"I understand Mr. Jones. Can you go get the keys to your pickup truck?" asked Jia.

"What happened Mrs. Jones?" asked Jia.

"He just shot em," she said.

Jia notices the bullet didn't go through Tem's vest, but she couldn't understand why he wasn't responsive.

"And then he tased him," said Mrs. Jones.

"Oh my God! Oh my God! Oh my god!" said Jia repeatedly.

Mr. Jones came back with his truck keys. "I gotta get him to the hospital before he starts seizing," yelled Jia. "Go inside and don't open the door for anyone but Warren Truman. Don't talk to the police, don't talk to anyone but Warren Truman. He's your attorney and don't speak without him. Go inside now!" yelled Jia.

She dragged Tem to the truck and sped down the street as she heard sirens coming from the opposite direction. Jia called the emergency line, and Mye picked up before the second ring.

"What happened?" asked Mye. She put Jia on speaker.

"Tem's been shot and tased. He is alive but unresponsive. And an officer is down in front of the Jones's house," said Jia.

"Is the officer alive?" asked Truman.

"Yes, Mr. Jones shot him with a beanbag. I told them to go inside and not to talk to anyone but you, " said Jia.

"You gotta get him to Georgetown Hospital as quick as possible Jia! I'll meet you there," said Mye.

"Already on my way," she said.

Mye ran out of the house barefoot just as George was pulling the Hummer in the driveway.

"I got the emergency ring," said George as he hopped out of the truck. Mye jumped in the Hummer and headed to the hospital. She called Tem's doctor and asked him to meet her there. She was speeding weaving that big truck in and out of DC traffic with ease. She prayed her baby would be fine.

Jia was sitting at the light when Tem started seizing. She turned him to his side and used her fingers to help clear his throat of the vomit. Then she drove over the medium and went through the light.

Truman pulled up to the Jones's house to find it surrounded by police cars and officers banging on their door.

Truman said to the officers, "Perhaps I can be of some assistance."

***

Jia pulled in front of the emergency doors and called for help. She went inside and grabbed a gurney as a nurse followed her. Tem was unresponsive again, and now his heartbeat had a crazy flutter. Jia tried to catch the pattern, but it was all over the place. As they rushed him inside, Jia tried to explain his condition and instructed them not to use an automatic defibrillator by any means. She followed Tem as far as she could before the nurses held her back and locked the doors.

Mye pulled up seconds after they took Tem to the back. She ran inside the hospital and found Jia crying. "I tried to explain, but I don't think they listened. He had a seizure and heart palpitations," cried Jia. Mye hopped over the nurse's station and ran frantically down the hall. Busting into each room looking for her son. She heard a loud commotion and ran in the last room on the left to find her son lying on the table with the defibrillator paddles on him. She heard someone yell, "Stand clear," and she jumped on top of her son.

"Ma'am move, what are you doing?" yelled the doctor on call.

"Saving your ass," said Dr. Johnson, Tem's doctor and the chief physician in the hospital.

"He has a rare condition, and his file explicitly says not to use an automatic defibrillator. Along with that piece of information, you can also find a DNR," stated the doctor.

Mye hugged her son and channeled the life energy around her. Her entire body began to tingle, and a heating sensation generated all over her. She poured all the love she had inside her into him. Calling all the energy surrounding her, summoning it to herself, through her body then into her son's. She prayed to her mother's mom, grandma Nuwa. A beautiful chocolate woman with black straight hair that would not hold a curl and a smile so big that it seemingly caused her brown eyes to disappear in the fold.

Mye whispered softly, "Nǚ wā qǐng bāngmáng. Nǚ wā qǐng bāngmáng. Nǚ wā qǐng bāngmáng," over and over again as she held her son tight.

A resident asked, "What is she saying?"

One of the nurses replied, "My Chinese is a little rusty, but I think she is saying 'Nuwa please help.'"

There was so much Mye never said to her son because it was easier to pretend she didn't see his faults than to call him out on them. Parents do their children an injustice by not chastising them when they need it. She was always a little afraid that her boy wouldn't love her the same if she gave him some tough love. But she realized that day, at that moment, that since she didn't check her son and put him in his place, that life did. As Mye prayed, Tem's heartbeat gradually went back to normal, and Mye let out a deep sigh of relief and said, "Thank you Nuwa. Thank you, everyone."

***

William's phone vibrated non stop as he slept. Leah could see it was Mye calling and kept sending her to his voicemail. She hated Mye. She had been playing second fiddle to Mye for nearly 7 years now, and she was getting tired of hiding in the shadows while William and Mye pranced around like the "It" couple. She was happy that William finally agreed to divorce Mye and make her his new wife. Well, he didn't exactly agree to marry Leah, but in her eyes, that was the logical next step. Leah thought about how desperate Mye had to be to keep calling back to back.

"Get over it old hag. He doesn't want you anymore," whispered Leah as she sent Mye to voicemail again.

***

Mye was waiting at her son's bedside for him to wake-up. She hadn't had the opportunity to be this close and watch him sleep since he was a little kid. She missed these moments. Jia was sleeping in the chair beside him. Mye appreciated Jia so much for what she did for her son today. She loved Jia like her very own and couldn't imagine how different this day could have ended if Jia wasn't there. Truman came into the room and pulled Mye to the side.

"So what's the news?" asked Mye.

"Well, apparently the cop that shot then tased him saw Tem running towards Mrs. Jones and assumed he was going to attack her or something. He is claiming that he was protecting Mrs. Jones," said Truman.

Mye looked confused. "Shooting and then tasing someone for that is extremely excessive," said Mye.

Truman shrugged his shoulders. "So do you want me to bring the department down or nah," asked Truman. "I mean Tem is a Grade A Fuck Boy, but he didn't deserve this. No one does," he added.

Mye thought about what Truman said as she walked towards Tem's bed, then abruptly turned around and punched Truman in the arm.

"Don't call my son a Fuck Boy."

Mye watched her son as he slowly began squirming and waking up. Tem let out a soft moan as he put his hand on his forehead. Jia seemingly woke up on cue as Tem was trying to sit up in the bed. She hopped up and helped pull him up as she added an extra pillow behind his back.

"Thanks," he said looking Jia in the eyes with deep sincerity. "What happened?" he asked looking at Jia. Then he turned to look at his mom admiring her natural beauty and said, "I haven't seen you like this since I was a kid."

She chuckled, "I was just thinking the same thing about you? What's the last thing you remember?" asked Mye.

"Well, I picked up Mrs. Jones's newspaper, and I was jogging over to give it to her when I got shot in the back. I fell on my face, and all I can hear was Mrs. Jones screaming. Then a cop flipped me over and stood over top of me with what I thought was a gun, and then I hear a loud gunshot louder than before, and that's' it. That's all I remember," said Tem.

Mye added, "You got shot once in the back and tased once in your shoulder. That loud shot you heard was from Mr. Jones. He shot the cop with a beanbag shotgun."

"What?! What happened next?" asked Tem.

"Tell him, Jia," said Mye. "You were the first one on the scene."

Jia began to tell Tem the story from beginning to end not leaving out one detail.

***

Mye stepped out into the hallway and called William again. His calls kept going to voicemail and she had an idea why. Emerson came running down the hall and hugged Mye really tight. He pushed her big curls out of the way, grabbed her face with both hands, and just stared into her green eyes. He hasn't seen this Mye since they were teenagers. In fact, the last day he saw her like this was the day he failed her for the first time. Emerson felt a sharp pain of regret and guilt for not being there for her that night. Unbeknownst to Emerson, he was always looking for a way to make it up to Mye, but whenever he had the opportunity, he always messed up.

***

Emely went to get her mail and noticed she had a letter from her landlord. The letter informed her that her condo was up for sale and she had some serious buyers interested in it. Emely was annoyed because if it wasn't one thing, it was another. William was acting crazy, she had to make a decision about her job, and now she might have to find a new place to live. Her cell phone rang, and she didn't recognize the number, but sometimes William called her from different numbers, so she answered it hoping it was him.

"Hello," she said in a sultry voice.

"Hello Emely, this is Dr. Mye Hart, William's wife. I need a favor."

***

"Mayor Woller, we have a situation. Another black kid has been shot and then tased by an officer in Spring Valley," said her assistant.

"Why tased?" Mayor Woller asked.

"I don't know. Then the officer in question was shot with a beanbag by a civilian," said the Mayor's assistant. "The officer is fine, but I do not have an update from the hospital of the condition of the kid."

The mayor flipped through the news stations on TV. "I don't see any news on it. What is the press saying?" she asked.

"It's being suppressed somehow, and I don't know by who," replied the assistant.

"Then what's with the theatrics? It seems things are under control," said the Mayor.

There was a knock at the door. "Excuse me Mayor Woller, but I have messages from 2 state governors, a congressman, and 3 senators. They all sound urgent. It's about the boy that was shot in Spring Valley," said the secretary.

"What the hell is going on here?! Who is this kid?" asked the Mayor.

Her assistant looked through her files. "His name is Tem Amen Hart. His father is William Henry Hart, Jr. Deputy Commissioner of Police in Baltimore, MD, and his mom is Dr. Mye Amor Hart. I don't know what kind of doctor though," replied the assistant.

"Damn it! You should have led with that," said the Mayor as she grabbed her jacket.

"Is all of the attention from higher up because his dad is a police officer?" asked her assistant.

"Hell no. It's because of his mom. She's the go-to shrink shared amongst many dignitaries, top politicians, CEO's, hedge funders and more. She's very professional, private and low key. Call my car for me," said the Mayor.

Her assistant called her car and grabbed her documents.

"If she's such a good quiet and professional therapist, then what's the big deal?" asked her assistant.

"When people know the kind of secrets she knows, then you'll want to keep those kind of people happy. I'm imagining her clients are calling me trying to figure out how I plan on keeping her happy. Get the Commissioner on the phone. Let's head to the hospital to see how much damage control we have to do before she decides to come after the entire department with that damn lawyer friend of hers. People have a way of throwing caution to the wind for their kids."

***

Emely stood there frozen in silence. So many thoughts ran through her head. She knew William was married, and she knew his wife's name, but she never thought his wife even knew about her. To find out she knows about her and knows her phone number had Emely shook.

"Hello, Emely. I need you to focus. I need to speak to my husband it's an emergency," stated Mye calmly.

"He's not here," Emely replied softly. "I honestly don't know where he is?"

"I believe you. I know where he is," said Mye.

A confused Emely thought to herself, "*Well, if she knows where he is, then why is she calling me?*"

Mye added, "He's on the top floor of that condominium with his main side piece. If there was levels to this, you'll be number 3."

Emely cried silently from humiliation. She did everything for that man, and he was just using her.

"¿Cómo podría ser tan estúpido?" said Emely in a low whisper.

"Cuando sepa mejor. Lo haces mejor," replied Mye.

"I didn't know," said Emely feeling even worse.

"Yes. I speak Spanish as well as Chinese. And yes, I identify as black. My mother was Dominican and Chinese. My father is a Black American from Baltimore. My grandparents, parents, and myself all share the same brown skin complexion. I respect my history and culture. I choose not to identify as Dominican, Chinese or mixed. Let's be honest; my physical features would never allow me to be accepted in the Chinese community as a Chinese woman. I could identify as Dominican because I speak Spanish or I could call myself mixed because that's true too. However, America's obsession with all things Black, except the people, has not gone unnoticed by me. It's gotten to the point where Black people are trying to escape being black. The irony is, everyone in the world came through the lineage of someone who looks like us. So yes, I identify as Black, until we agree upon another name, for the indigenous darker complected people of America. I'll identify as black. However, no matter my ethnicity, you should never be ok with playing third fiddle," said Mye.

Emley was in full tears crying and sobbing in Spanish asking Mye to forgive her and how she can make it up to her. Mye seemed like such a nice person, and it made Emely feel even worse.

"Emely you can make it up to me by doing this."

***

When Mye ended her call, she looked up and noticed Emerson walking out of Tem's hospital room. She braced herself for what was about to happen.

"Why didn't you call me?" he huffed between breaths. Emerson was in great physical shape, but his anxiousness had him feeling winded. His hands trembled slightly as he rested them on Mye's shoulders.

"Why didn't you call me Mye?" he asked with sincerity.

"I don't want to do this right now," she replied with her hands lightly patting his chest. "I don't want to do this. Not here," she added in a whisper as she cupped his face and placed her forehead on his. "Let it go," she whispered stepping back giving him a slight smile.

Emerson was in awe of her beauty. She was breathtaking. He reached for her hand and asked again, "Mye, please tell me. Why didn't you call me? This was an opportunity for me to be there for you," Emerson said.

Mye was full of emotions. She couldn't do this right now. She couldn't be responsible for comforting Emerson right now. She's always the one having to comfort people and make plans and figure everything out, but what about Mye? The truth is that Emerson did not want to hear the truth. He wanted to be comforted and made to feel better. He wanted Mye to make him feel better about being left outside of the loop. While Mye was strong and had the energy, she didn't want to. She was done with being good for the sake of being good. Unbeknownst to many, Mye had recently adopted a "Be Genuine" attitude. A little softer than the "I don't care" attitude but with a similar premise. If Emerson kept pressing her, she would tell him how she really felt. She would share the painful truth of one of the many elephants in the room that had been there for over a decade.

***

Emely slowly approached the condo that Mye told her about. This is where William stays with his other mistress. Right on top of her head. Emely felt if she could do this one thing for Mye that this could somehow help redeem herself from her shortcomings. Emely had already called and accepted the job offer down south and gave her landlord a 30-day notice. The last thing she had to do is walk up to this condo, knock on the door and follow Mye's instructions. Then, her soul and conscious would be free to move onto another life in another city. Emely lifted her hands and knocked on the door 3 times.

***

Tara came running down the hall into Mye's arms.

"I'm sorry we're late. We had to charter a helicopter. Traffic was horrible. What happened? No no, forget I asked. Later after things settle and you are in better spirits, we can talk about it then. You look amazing, especially considering everything going on," said Tara.

Mye blushed. She loved Tara and secretly wished more people could be as intuitive as her. "Can we go see him?" asked Tara.

"Thanks, and yes you can go see him," she said pointing to his door. Tara quickly darted into the room. John put his hand on Mye's shoulder and gave her a gentle smile.

"You do look good," he added as he walked into the room.

Emerson walked over to Mye with a slight attitude, "I had to find out through whispers in the nursing station that my godson was in the hospital, but you called Tara?" said Emerson. "I'm an actual doctor," he added.

Slightly annoyed Mye responded, "So is she. So am I. So is John. Truman has a J.D. does that count? Since we are listing our friends' credentials."

"I've known you longer," he added.

"I met you at 14, and I met them at 17. It's barely a difference," she said.

"But I was there first," he said.

"But they are there always," Mye proclaimed.

Emerson paused for a moment and stared at Mye as she stared right back.

"Is that why you didn't call me. Because you didn't think I would be there for you?" he asked.

"No. I didn't call you because I wasn't sure you would be there for me and so since I wasn't sure I didn't include you in the plan," she said.

"What plan?" he asked

Mye shook her head in disappointment for even bringing it up.

"The emergency plan. We have an emergency plan for Tem and Bhavani. Because of their conditions, if something happens, we literally have only minutes before things can turn fatal," she said.

"But I heard Jia came in with Tem. Is she a part of the plan? Does she know the plan?" Emerson asked.

"Yes," replied Mye.

Emerson looked upset as he thought about Jia keeping secrets from him.

"But don't get mad at Jia. She likely never brought it up because she assumed you knew about the plan," Mye said.

"But all the time Tem spent with me what if something happened?" he asked.

"Jia would have been there," she said.

"But Jia is a child. Yes, she's a resident at the hospital, but I'm an experienced doctor!" he said.

"But she's reliable," added Mye. "Whenever I've needed you most, you've always let me down."

Emerson knew there was truth to her words. He slumped down in the hall chair and placed his head in his hands.

"Mye, this would have been the perfect time for me to show you that I got your back through anything. This was the perfect opportunity," he said.

"You don't get to prove yourself on Super Bowl Sunday when you choked in the playoffs," Mye said.

"What?" Emerson asked confused.

FLASHBACK - MAY 2004

"Emerson, please reconsider," begged Mye. She had been pleading with Emerson for 2 weeks now to do the surgery.

"Mye I can't. I'm too close to her. Plus I'm fresh out of my residency. I can't attempt a surgery of this magnitude," he said.

"Well, can you try to convince another doctor to consider it? I've been looking around, and everyone is saying no. Maybe you can talk to someone and make them understand," she pleaded.

"Make them understand what Mye!? That you want them to cut half of your toddler's brain out. Make them understand that! No one wants to do that unless it is an absolute medical necessity. They'll think I'm crazy!" he said.

"That's it! There's the truth. Bhavani has an extreme loss of motor functions on one side of her body. The seizures are on a localized part of her brain. She is one seizure away from a complete vegetable state, and you won't help me," cried Mye.

She broke down and sobbed uncontrollably in Emerson's arms outside of Bhavani's hospital room. Emerson held her tight and let out a single tear. He loved Mye dearly, but he couldn't risk his reputation for a surgery that would be a Hail Mary at best.

"Maybe it's God's will for Bhavani to have this disability," Emerson said.

"My child is not disabled," snarled Mye as she pushed away from Emerson. "God gave her every faculty she needs to gather all of the experiences she was sent here to experience, which includes me her mother, and I will do everything in my power to get her the best care! God doesn't give out desires without the ability of them being seen through. Now I don't know how but I do know she will get the surgery she needs and she will get to live the life of her choosing!"

Truman came down the hall staring into his palm pilot then looked up and saw the tension on Mye's face as she stared at Emerson.

"I have some possible good news. I've found 2 doctors, a couple. One is a neurosurgeon, and the other is a cardiologist. They are willing to operate on both Tem and Bhavani," said Truman.

Mye jumped up and down as Truman just held his arms straight out trying not to touch her.

"My suit Mye! My suit," he said. "Now we are still vetting them, but things are looking good. The downside is that the doctors are in India and you will have to fly out to them," he added.

"That's no problem! See Emerson. Things are already looking up! So go ahead and put in your leave so we can get to India!" said Mye.

Emerson looked down as he scratched the back of his head. "I'm not going to be able to go," he said.

"Why not?" replied Mye in shock.

"I have to put in my time here before I go requesting extensive leave. Post op will be at least 2 weeks to a month minimum," Emerson said.

"Well, just come for the surgery and go back afterward," Mye replied.

Emerson closed his eyes and said, "I don't want to."

"Why? I don't understand," said Mye.

"Besides, won't your husband be there? You don't need me to," he said.

"Damn. When the jump-off brings up the husband, then things must be going really bad," said Truman

"Shut up Truman!" shouted Emerson.

"He's not a jump-off," whispered Mye. "He's just a friend."

"Best friend," Emerson added with a smile.

"No, just a friend who thinks I'm sending my children to India to die. But what's more mind-boggling is that you don't even want to be present to console me in the event they did die," Mye said.

"How many times do I have to tell you about this dude. He ain't about that life Mye," said Truman.

"I'm not playing with you Truman," snarled Emerson.

"This was a perfect opportunity to make it up to me. A perfect time for you to somehow vindicate yourself and you've failed again!" yelled Mye. "Your image was all that mattered then, and the same goes for now. Just like you weren't there when I needed you that night after the dance!"

"That's not fair Mye!" yelled Emerson.

"But it's true," said Mye as she let one tear fall.

"I'll be there Mye," said Truman as he typed in his palm pilot.

"No Truman. You're in the middle of a big case," said Mye.

"No, it's cool. I've been dragging it out because litigation is so much fun. I'll shut it down tomorrow, the jury will deliberate for 2-3 days, and my client will be out by the end of the week. We can leave first thing Monday morning. Shall I get the plane tickets?" asked Truman.

"Yes," replied Mye while looking at Emerson.

"Everyone can't be as emotionless as you," said Emerson to Truman.

"I know. What a pity. Apparently, everyone can't be as loyal either," said Truman as he walked away.

"You can go now, Emerson. I'd like to spend some time alone with my daughter," said Mye as she walked into Bhavani's hospital room leaving Emerson standing in the hall.

PRESENT - MARCH 2017

Truman walked up to Mye and Emerson reliving the past.

"Does anybody else feel a sense of deja vu?" asked Truman. "No, in all seriousness, I feel like we've been here before. I think Tara's spooky stuff is rubbing off on me."

"What's the latest Truman?" asked Mye.

"I've suppressed the press, so nothing is going to be in the news about Tem. However, the video of you driving your Hummer into the emergency room and running down the halls is all over social media, and it's only a matter of time before it makes the news," said Truman.

Mye palmed her forehead in disbelief. "What now?" she asked.

"Oh don't worry about the video. We can easily put a spin on it. At least they got your good side," said Truman.

Mye chuckled, "And what side is that?"

"I don't know. I'm convinced they did some photoshopping," said Truman.

Mye bust out laughing.

"Or maybe it's some type of filter. I don't know," Truman added.

The Chief Doctor walked up to Mye with a notepad in his hands. "I'm glad to see you in good spirits Mye. Shall we?" he asked while motioning for her to go inside of Tem's room.

"Hey playa," said Chief Doctor Johnson.

"Give it to me straight Doc. No need to butter me up," said Tem.

"Would you like me to clear the room?" asked Dr. Johnson.

Tem looked down and began to breathe a little heavier. He saw genuine concern in everyone's eyes. His mom's, Jia, Emerson, Tara, John and even Truman's, although Truman tried to hide it.

"No sir, you're good. They are all family," said Tem. Everyone smiled moved by Tem's admission.

Truman interrupted the moment, "I would like to go on record that I am by no means-"

"Shut up," whispered Mye as she elbowed Truman. "Continue doctor."

"Ok Tem. You sustained two injuries today. The first was a gunshot wound to the chest, close range by a government-issued 9mm. Had you not been wearing that bulletproof vest, I'd be having a whole different conversation with your family right now," said the doctor.

"Hold up? Was I wearing a bulletproof vest? I thought that was an exercise weighted vest?" he said looking at his mom. Mye stared at the doctor waiting for him to continue.

"No Tem. You were wearing a vest in excellent condition clearly rated for weapon use. You got lucky today. Twice. The pain and bruising you feel is from behind-armor blunt trauma, BABT, that's from how close the shot was, however, you'll be fine. The second incident is cause for more concern. Getting tased on your right shoulder is what is going to keep you in the hospital to be monitored for a few more days. These so-called less-lethal weapons are being overused by people, poorly trained on the immediate side effects, to punish people for insubordination instead a threat. That taser caused you to have a seizure and did a complete override of your central nervous system. The taser acted like a partial reset. You will start to experience regression and lack of control in that arm sometimes. I do not know if it will be isolated to that location only or not. There are exercises and therapy you can do, but you can not overwork or stress that arm or your body. But you will live a full long life if you just maintain your therapy sessions."

"What about football?" asked Tem. The doctor looked down at his clipboard and shook his head slowly.

"I'm sorry son, but your football career is over. The demands of that arm with you being the quarterback and the demands on your body. It would accelerate your conditions dramatically," said the doctor.

"Can I have a moment alone," asked Tem.

Everyone left Tem's room and gave him a moment to process it all.

CHAPTER FOUR

IT ALL FALLS DOWN

Emely waited nervously as she heard heels clicking on the hardwood floor inside the condo getting closer and closer to her. There was a pause, and then someone unlocked the door and opened it. There stood Leah beautifully dressed in a red wrapped dress with a high split. Emely masked her emotions through a fake, forced smile trying to hide the range of emotions she was feeling. Leah was wearing the same dress William bought for her.

"Hello? How can I help you?" Leah asked snapping Emely out of her trance.

"Hi Leah," said Emely while looking down at the mail in her hands. "I think the mailman accidentally gave me some of your mail," smiled Emely as she handed Leah her mail.

"Oh, thank you, I'm sorry I didn't get your name," said Leah.

"Who is it babes?" asked William from behind the door.

"It's Emely from 1903," said Emely. Leah opened the door wider so William could see Emely.

"Babes it's Emely from 1903. She accidentally got some of our mail, and she was just bringing it to us. Isn't that sweet?" said Leah as she sifted through the mail. William and Emely eyes locked. William looked terrified. He was frozen in fear.

"Leah, can you tell me the quickest way to Georgetown Hospital? My niece Sky's boyfriend Tem was shot. Apparently, he's some big football star, and so everyone's there for him, so I just wanted to be there for her. I was actually on my way there, but I wanted to drop off your mail in case it was something urgent you needed." William's eyes perked up. Was this a joke? Was she serious? He frantically started to look for his phone.

"Oh gosh! No this is just some junk in here. Let me send you the quickest directions to your phone," said Leah. Leah and Emely exchanged numbers, and Leah sent Emely the directions.

"I hope everything works out for your niece and her boyfriend and thanks for my mail. Maybe after everything quiets down we can go out to lunch or something?" asked Leah.

"That sounds great! But it would have to be sooner rather than later. I recently accepted a new job down south, so I'll be moving within a week or so, but we'll talk about that more at lunch," smiled Emely.

"Of course, yes go meet your niece and congratulations on your new job! It was a pleasure to meet you," said Leah.

"The pleasure was all mine," said Emely.

***

Mye and Truman were reviewing case files in the hall while Tem got some rest. Two detectives approached Tem's room and were about to go inside when Truman stopped them.

"Hello, officers. How can I help you?" asked Truman.

"Hello I'm detective Dan, and this is detective Vincent. We are here to ask Tem Hart a few questions. Is this his room?"

"Yes, but you can't speak to him right now because he's resting. You see, today a police officer shot then tased him for getting an 80-year old's morning paper for her. Crazy right?" said Truman.

"Well, that's your version. We want to hear from Tem exactly what happened because one of ours got shot," said detective Vincent defensively.

"With a bean bag. You left off the bean bag part," said Truman.

"Look we can do this here or we can take him to the precinct. Don't make this harder than it has to be," said detective Vincent.

"Do what you have to do," said Truman with his hands in the air.

Detective Vincent became visibly upset, "We don't take lightly one of ours getting shot.

"There, there," said detective Dan calming his partner down. "Look everyone let's remain calm," said detective Dan as he scanned the hallway. "We're just looking for some answers here. Excuse my partner's passion. We get a little emotional when one of ours gets shot. We are just trying to uphold the law and get some answers," said detective Dan.

"Whose law?" asked Mye from across the hall as she closed the file she was holding.

Truman sneezed, "Blue law."

"I don't understand your question ma'am," said detective Dan, "there's only one law I vowed to uphold," he added.

Mye replied, "That much we can agree on, however, it's still not clear what law that is."

Truman sat down crossing his legs and said, "This is gonna be good," through a slight smirk.

Detective Vincent interjected, "Who are you?"

Mye replied, "I'm the mother, of the young man, one of your officers shot then tased. Is that standard protocol? To shoot then tase a person when they're down on the ground?"

The detectives were quiet for a moment. Mye continued, "So I, a grieving mother, is supposed to have the skillset to remain calm when friends of my son's shooter come to speak to him? I am supposed to understand that even though one of you attacked my son that this doesn't mean that all of you are alike? I'm supposed to be able to remain calm because I am supposed to be able to decipher between good cops and bad ones?"

Mye spoke in a very matter of fact kind of tone.

"We are not all the same," said detective Dan sincerely. Mye reached for his hand and cupped it in hers.

"I know. I honestly believe most of you are amazing. But how long do I have to be understanding of your profession's inability to properly vet its recruitments?

You allow one bad apple to spoil the whole bunch. Instead of pointing out the bad apples and getting rid of them, you try to hide them under good apples."

Mye released his hand and sat down. He thought for a moment about what she said and acknowledged some truth to it.

Detective Vincent spoke up, "What about black-"

"Not now," said detective Dan cutting off his partner. "Let's allow this mother time to process it all. She almost lost her son today," said detective Dan as he pulled his partner back.

Truman interjected, "No please detective Vincent. Share your thoughts. Tell us more about what you think about black people?"

Mye added, "Don't take the bait detective. While I've remained calm, this is indeed a very serious matter. And this here is attorney Warren Truman, and he is completely bored with corporate law and is looking for some excitement. He is looking for a reason for me to give him my blessing on bringing a suit on the whole department. So please gentlemen, can we have some privacy?" pleaded Mye.

Detective Dan's phone rang, he answered it and quickly hung up. "That was Captain. He said to fallback now," Dan whispered. Detective Dan and Vincent walked away without saying anything.

"Don't you wanna take him to the precinct for questioning?" yelled Truman with a big grin.

"Let it go," said detective Dan as he pulled detective Vincent down the hall.

***

Tara came back to the hospital to do Therapeutic Touch on Tem with Mye. This was when Mye and Tara both placed their hands on Tem to help him heal quicker. Their focus was to stimulate Tem's own natural healing ability by balancing his overall body energy. Mye and Tara believed that people are systems of energy composed of many layers that interact with others and the environment. They view illness as an imbalance of energy so if they can help balance a person's energy then they can help heal a person's sickness. This technique is used in conjunction with conventional medicine and was used to bring Bhavani and Tem to their level of present physical abilities. This technique is why the clinic has an 18-month waitlist. For some reason, when Mye and Tara come together, their abilities and energy are amplified, and healing happened quicker. The main issue comes in when trying to help patients maintain the balance of energy when they leave their therapy sessions.

Jia walked into Tem's hospital room with food and to warn them.

"Bhavani is coming, and she is pissed, session over get out while you can."

"You are an idiot!" yelled Bhavani as she barged into Tem's room.

"Well, that's our cue Tara," said Mye as she and Tara gathered their things to leave the room.

"Ma!" yelled Tem.

"No Tem. You know I don't like to get in brother and sister arguments. Ya'll work it out," said Mye as she and Tara left the room leaving Tem with Jia and Bhavani.

"I'm convinced you are adopted because no one this stupid can be related to me," said Bhavani.

"I'm not going to be too many more of your stupids," spat Tem.

"Oh no you are going to be as many stupids as I see fit and you are going to listen to everything I have to say stupid!" said Bhavani as she took off her black fur coat and laid it over the chair.

"It's not even cold enough to be wearing that," said Tem.

"Oh but it's about to be," replied Bhavani. "And I'm never caught unprepared," she added.

Jia's phone rang giving her an excuse to leave the room. Bhavani then pulled up a seat and got really close to Tem's face.

"You ready big bro because I got a few choice words for you." She clapped with each word she spoke. "Are you stupid or are you dumb?" she asked.

Tem rolled his eyes and turned the other way.

Bhavani was wearing a one-piece turtleneck long sleeves fitted jumpsuit with suede thigh-high heeled boots. Her hair was pulled back into a bone straight ponytail that fell to her lower back. She stood up and pulled Tem's shoulder causing him to grimace in pain.

"Turn around when I'm talking to you!" she yelled.

"What is your problem?!" Tem yelled holding his shoulder. "You come in here yelling, acting crazy, dressed in all black-"

Bhavani cut him off mid sentence.

"I'm prepared for your funeral because it's obvious you do not give a fuck about your life," she said as she

stared down at her older brother in utter disappointment. She grabbed the chair and sat back down beside
him.

"You don't have to want to live Tem. It's within your
God-given right to not want to live. I've come to terms
with you not wanting to live and I respect it. I do not
agree with it but I respect your decision because I respect you. My problem comes in when you drag the
whole family down with you. You don't want to live but
you got the whole family mobilizing to save you. Jia told
you about your regression. I know she did because she
told me and I warned her that you were not going to do
anything useful with the information. I prepared her for
you disappointing her, which you did.

Tem you don't even like football. You only do it to
prove to dad that you are better than him because dad
got injured and never made it to the pros. You're trying
to one up a man who is never around. Where is he now
Tem? You treat the women in your life, black women
might I add, like shit. Simply because they call you out
on your shit. You don't have a preference for white
women, you have a preference for women who are in
love with your facade. When you look at Jia, mom, or
myself, you are reminded of all the hardships and strug-
gles you went through physically to get where we are today. Instead of being appreciative of the love and sacri-
fice mom, Tara, Jia, and countless others made to get us
here, you are ashamed that you needed anyone's help at
all! You want to pretend the past didn't happen and live
in a lie. So you take issue with people who know the
truth and anyone who looks like her.

The future scares you so much that you do not want to live, but most importantly, you don't want to love. I know what it feels like to be trapped in a body that I can't control. However, you're mentally and emotionally in need of help bro, and you are far more like dad than you care to realize. Is it your fault that you were born into this situation? No. However, it is your responsibility to seek help and to find internal peace. If you don't want to do this fine, I respect that. If you don't want to deal with black women, fine I respect that. If you don't want to live, then fine, I respect that too. But I be damned if you think I'm going to allow you to drag me down this dark rabbit hole of an existence you're building for yourself. I will not be a witness to this train wreck. Now get your ass some help and start acting like a real big brother!"

***

"Hey Ma," said Jia dryly as she answered her phone. She knew her mother was just trying to be nosey because she never called to check on her.

"How is Tem doing? Your father told me that Tem was in the hospital, but he didn't give me any details. You know how he can be," said Delilah.

"He's doing fine Ma. I'll let him know that you asked about him," said Jia.

"Ok good. I'm glad to hear he's ok. How are you doing?" asked Jia's mom.

Jia was taken back by her mom's concern. Her mom almost sounded like a caring mother.

"I'm doing good Ma. Thanks for asking," smiled Jia. "I have to go Ma, but I'll keep you in the loop."

Delilah replied, "Good, because we need to know if Tem can still play football. If Tem is no longer a top consideration for pro ball, then you need to let him go and focus on a better prospect. You have to be smart about these things Jia. Hook em' young and dumb like Savannah did LeBron. Remember, there are a million of you's out there. Don't wait too late to try to pull a good one," said Delilah.

Jia's heart deflated a little. All that Jia accomplished didn't mattered to her mother. The only thing that mattered was Jia marrying rich. That's it. Jia's mother based a woman's success off the success of her husband.

"I gotta go Ma," said Jia as she hung up the phone.

***

The police station was going crazy with rumors of what happened earlier that day. The case has been contained, and the files are only available to a few people. Most of the gossip is speculation and hearsay. 19-year-old Wayne has been over hearing bits and pieces about what went down. However, all he is truly concerned about is getting out of that holding cell and checking up on his family. He hasn't spoken to his grandmother in 3 days since he's been in jail and knows she's likely worried sick. Wayne doesn't want his grandmother to think what happened to his dad happened to him. Wayne brushed his hands over his low cut hair. He stood about 6'2 with smooth chocolate skin. Athletic build, broad shoulders, around 220 pounds. He wore a black shirt and grey sweatpants that did a poor job of concealing his manhood, which was well endowed and had many of the female officers stopping by multiple times to take a long look. His face was a sight for sore eyes. His thick eyebrows and full lashes was a thing to envy, and his smile was big, white, and perfect. But he didn't smile often and right now he wasn't smiling at all.

"Excuse me," he said in a deep, gentle voice to the female officer passing by his cell for the third time. "Do you know when I can make a phone call? I've been here since Friday, and now it's Monday. I take care of my grandma and little brother, and I'm worried about them," he pleaded.

The female officer licked her lips and said, "Let me see what I can do."

Wayne waited patiently to ask the right officer, and he hoped he chose well. The female officer came back and said, "Today is your lucky day. You're free to go. They'll process you out at the front."

The officer who processed Wayne out and gave him his belongings was an ass, but Wayne was used to dealing with cops like him, so he wasn't fazed by it. When he walked out of the building, he took a deep breath of fresh air and smiled for the first time in days when the officer who arrested him grabbed his arm.

"Look, we are going to catch you. Now do yourself a favor and leave town," said the officer.

"Can I have my arm back?" asked Wayne. The officer let go of his arm and took a step back.

"You ran my plates just because, pulled me over because my license was allegedly suspended, and kept me in jail without a phone call for 3 days. Only to have to let me go because my license is not suspended. You needed any excuse to search my car and what did you find...

nothing. Look I have to go check on my grandmother and little brother. I'm out," said Wayne then he walked off.

***

Mye knocked on Tem's hospital door gently. "Can I come in?" she asked.

"Yes," Tem grumbled. "What's wrong with your daughter? She came in here yelling trying to tell me about me. Talking about how I'm disrespectful to you, her, Jia and black women in general, and how I don't care about my life or how my actions affect the people around me," he said.

"Do you think any of that is true?" asked Mye.

"No!" said Tem. "I mean, I prefer white women, yes but so what? That's just a personal preference. It doesn't mean I don't like black women," said Tem.

"What is it about white women that you like?" asked Mye.

"I like how they are ready to accept control and instruction. They are eager to please and very submissive as soon as I meet them. Unlike black women who are angry and always have attitudes. No wonder nobody wants them. They act like they don't need men and that's why they don't have one," said Tem.

"It sounds like you like docile women. Not all white women are docile just like not all black women are angry. Those are just stereotypes that the weak and feeble minded buy into," said Mye making direct unbreakable eye contact with her son.

"Out of curiosity, where is your white woman now?" asked Mye. Tem rolled his eyes and looked out of the window.

"Call her Tem," said Mye as she handed him his phone. Tem ignored her and didn't take the phone.

"Call her!" Mye yelled as she threw the phone at him. Tem was shocked. His mother never got loud with him. She was always poised and well mannered no matter what. He didn't know what to make of her.

"You can't call her because you don't want her to see you this way. This Tem doesn't match the facade you wear for her and all the other women like her," said Mye. Tem could not argue with the truth she spoke.

Mye added, "For years Tem, I've tried to be a good example of what a good woman is. I wanted you to be able to see and experience love from a woman so you would be able to recognize it when you're looking for a potential wife. However, over the years I've watched you down and belittle black women and eat up the stereotypes you hear as if you've never seen a beautiful black woman before. I've tried to keep quiet and not become that stereotype. I've tried to give you space to figure this all out for yourself. I've tried those methods because I didn't want to scare you away by telling you how I really feel because I didn't want to lose the love from my only son. But today is a new day, and if you no longer want to talk to me because of what I am about to say, then it's your loss.

The woman who breastfed you until you were one is black, who pumped milk for you until you were three is black, nursed you from the wheelchair to the walker is black, from the walker to the track is black, from the track to the football field is black. The woman who kept you from choking on your own vomit while you were having a seizure and driving a pickup truck over the medium during traffic is black!

Your attitude is terrible. How you feel about black women is obvious. People tolerate it because they think you are somebody. But honestly, you haven't done anything miraculous. You are privileged. You have a huge head start over so many that you don't care to acknowledge. Yet as you saw today, you are still black and are subject to a certain treatment that not even money can protect you from. What did the old Kanye say, "Even if you are in a Benz, you are still a nigga in a coupe." Today you got hit with a hot flash of reality. Your black mother and her team came right on in to clean everything up. I always take care of my baby boy, but that all ends today.

Moving forward you will be charged upfront for any Therapeutic Touch sessions, and it's $2,500 each for 30 minutes with Tara and myself. Truman requires a 35,000 retainer fee and charges $900 an hour, however, he has been doing some cases pro bono, so you can try your luck. John is no longer your fiduciary and financial advisor, and you simply don't have a high enough net worth to higher him yourself. Forget the book deal, "From the Wheelchair to the Field" that Penelope offered you on my account. I'm sure you can find another ghost writer to finish your book and a publishing company to pick it up. Ashley is the family accountant, so you have to manage and balance your own books and the black card I gave is dead, so don't try to use it. When you get to the point where I feel you actually have respect for me and women who look like me, then we can talk about me reconciling these relationships. Until then, you figure it out," said Mye.

"Ma you aren't like other black women. You don't act black. You're mixed, Chinese and Dominican. You're like an Afro-Asian-Latina. Don't lower yourself to a regular black women status, you're mixed, so you're above them. Don't be a bitter, petty black woman. It's not a good look," said Tem.

"You think I'm bitter? You think I'm petty? I'll see you tomorrow at my house when you are cleaning out your stuff to go take it to your place," said Mye as she got up to walk out.

"The doctor said I will be here for a couple of days," smirked Tem.

"Not after I cut your insurance off tonight. They'll be sending you home by tomorrow afternoon and have fun getting new insurance with your pre-existing condition," said Mye.

Truman walked in unannounced, "Go head Petty Mayonnaise," said Truman in a sarcastic tone. Mye chuckled. Tem rolled his eyes. "The Mayor is on her way to do damage control. She'll be here any minute," said Truman.

Mye looked at Tem and asked, "How do you want to handle this?"

"I don't know? Why does the Mayor even want to see me," said Tem, "what should I do?" asked Tem talking to Truman.

Truman looked at his phone and said, "I don't see your retainer."

"Ma, please," asked Tem. Mye ignored him.

"Listen Tem, Petty Mayonnaise here got the juice. She knows more famous people's secrets than Judy Smith and no one wants her talking," said Truman.

"Ok so what am I supposed to say when the Mayor comes in?" asked Tem.

"Did you send me the money yet?" asked Truman looking at his phone.

"Ma, please," asked Tem.

"Ok," said Mye reluctantly. "This is what you are going to do."

***

Police filled the house and a white sheet lay over a body. The school called the police to do a welfare check after no one answered the door when the school's bus driver went to pick up Kiam and no one returned their calls. The police went to the house and found the door unlocked with the grandma dead in the living room chair. Kiam was upstairs in his bedroom with the door locked. When the police arrived, they made themselves known to Kiam and asked him to unlock the door.

Kiam said, "It's about time you showed up? Is the Amazon Goddess with you?" he asked through the door.

A police officer asks, "Who?"

Kiam slid his sketchbook under the door with a drawing of a beautiful woman. The police asked who the person is, he replied, "The Amazon Goddess and I'm not coming out until she gets here."

Social worker Ms. Gains showed up, and the police showed her the drawing. Ms. Gains smiled, called Mye, and made a strange request.

***

There was a knock at Tem's door.

Mye said, "Come in."

In walked Mayor Woller and her assistant. Mayor Woller proceeded to shake everyone's hand.

"Good afternoon Dr. Hart and Mr. Truman. It's a pleasure to see you again. I wish it were under better circumstances," said Mayor Woller. She walked over to Tem to shake his hand, "Good evening Tem. I'm deeply sorry that you had to experience this tragedy. Mye, Truman, I hope you can allow me the opportunity to have my best men personally investigate this matter. I want you to know that we do not take this lightly and that this isolated incident doesn't reflect our police department," said the Mayor.

"I don't know," said Mye. The Mayor and her assistant had a slight look of surprise on their faces. "What do you think son?" asked Mye.

Now everyone was staring at Tem waiting to hear what he had to say. Tem looked at his mom and smiled.

"I stand behind the Mayor and her promise," he said. Tem then looked at the Mayor, "I trust your people are of high quality and can settle this matter quickly and quietly. I stand behind you Mayor and your plan to find justice for me."

Mayor Woller gleamed with pride. "Smart man," said the Mayor. "My team is already all over it. Thank you for your trust and your time. We'll leave you to rest. Have a nice day everyone," said the Mayor as she walked out of the room.

Mye's phone has been vibrating non-stop, so she stepped out of the room to answer it.

"You see that Tem," said Truman. "Petty Mayonnaise just gave you a gift."

"What gift?" asked Tem.

Truman responded, "A high-level politician now owes you a favor. Now use it wisely or be like your mother and don't use it at all. That's how she got most of her juice."

CHAPTER FIVE

IT'S GONNA GET EASIER CHILD

Mye left the hospital and drove to a small white house with multiple police cars outside. As soon as Mye parked, her phone rang. It was her husband, William. She answered the phone and before she could say anything he said, "Mye sweetie I'm so sorry. I was busy at work, and my phone died."

"William, your son is in the hospital. He's fine now, but he nearly died earlier. Go see your son please," said Mye then she hung up the phone not even waiting for him to reply. She walked towards the small white house. All of the police officers were staring at Mye as she approached the house. She was prepared to explain why she was there but everyone just kept stepping to the side for her to walk pass. When Ms. Gaines saw her, even she looked at Mye stunned.

Mye asked, "Why are you and everyone else looking at me like that?"

Ms. Gaines asked Mye, "Where are your shoes?" Mye completely forgot she left the house in a rush without them.

"Is that why everyone is looking at me?" asked Mye.

"No. It's because of this," said Ms. Gaines handing Mye the drawing Kiam made. The drawing looked just like Mye at that very moment. Same hair, same clothes, down to the missing shoes.

Mye asked, "How did you know it was me? I've never worn my hair like this before, and my eyes are usually brown. And this woman's hair is too big and curly to get a good look at the face and her eyes are green?"

Ms. Gaines replied, "When you were in class to become a foster parent, I noticed your eyes were green when you were putting drops in your eye, and I remembered thinking to myself. Why on earth would someone cover up green eyes? Then there was the root. In the picture, one of your feet is like a root of the tree, and it goes up your leg to your back. I've seen that scar on your back during the CPR training for your foster care certification. I know that's a stretch but just call it a hunch. Look the little boy won't leave the room, and I don't want the police to go barging in there like he's a wanted fugitive. His grandmother was found dead in the chair downstairs for at least 12 hours," said Ms. Gaines. Mye placed her hand over her mouth in shock. "Yes, but it looks like she died from natural causes," said Ms. Gaines. "So I really do not want to make today any more traumatizing than it already is for him. So can you go to the room and try to convince him to come out?" she asked.

"I'll do my best," said Mye. "So what is his name?"

"Kiam. Kiam Robinson," she replied.

Mye went to Kiam's room and lifted her hand to knock on the door. Kiam opened the door with his backpack with a big smile.

He said, "Amazon Goddess!" Then he gave Mye a big hug. "I mean, Mrs. Hart," he said nudging her with his elbow and winking frantically. "I'm ready," he added.

"Ready for what?" asked Mye in a confused manner as she kneeled down to his eye level.

"Ready to go to your house. My new home," he said through a big grin.

Mye stood up and asked Ms. Gaines, "Can I take him home?"

Ms. Gaines thought about it for a moment.

"I guess so. You are a certified foster parent and currently listed as an emergency care provider, so I don't see a problem with you taking him home. You know what, he kind of looks like you," said Ms. Gaines.

Kiam gave a big smile. "Cool. Now let's go!" said Kiam in excitement.

Mye stopped Kiam and put both hands on his shoulders.

"Kiam. There's something you have to know about your grandma," said Mye barely through a whisper.

"I know," said Kiam in a loud whisper. He pulled Mye to the side, "She left me a note to give you. It's in my bag. Now can we get out of here?" whispered Kiam.

Mye smiled, even though she was a little confused and they walked hand in hand. Kiam grabbed his booster seat that sat beside the front door.

"Safety first!" he smiled.

They hopped into the hummer. Kiam rolled his window down and waved bye to the little white house.

***

Emerson was walking to Tem's room to check up on him in between doing his rounds when he ran into Dr. Johnson.

"Hey, Emerson. You know it's truly a miracle that Tem is still alive. If Jia wasn't there, he could have died or worst regressed back to where he started. He needs to marry that girl if he knows what's good for him," chuckled Dr. Johnson as he patted Emerson on the shoulder and walked away.

Emerson knocked on Tem's door before walking in. "Hey, buddy. Are you feeling a little better?" asked Emerson.

"Yeah, but Ma and Bhavani are giving me a headache," said Tem. Emerson chuckled. "Naw it's not funny Uncle E. They are going all black girl magic on me at a time like this. I don't want to hear that," Tem added.

Emerson said, "Well, I think when something like this happens, it makes people do deep reflection and think about all of the things they've wanted to say but for whatever reason never did. They love you and just want the best for you."

Tem thought about what Emerson said for a moment. "To be honest Unc, Jia already warned me about regressing if I continued to push myself hard with my exercise regimens. I was a jerk to her right before I got shot. That's why she ran ahead in front of me. I'm lucky she came back and knew exactly what to do," said Tem in a somber voice. "Now that I'm thinking, I haven't even thanked Jia yet. Unc, how can I be such an ass? The first thing out of my mouth wasn't thank you. Jia literally saved my life, and I haven't even thanked her yet," said Tem as he sat there trying to figure out how thanking Jia slipped his mind.

"Let me tell you a quick story while you sit there and try to figure out why you are a jerk," said Emerson.

"Whatever Unc, but go ahead," chuckled Tem.

"I'm allergic to bees. Mye found out and casually asked me if I told my football coach. I told her no because that would make me sound weak. I was the quarterback, and I have to be strong for my team. She said something like, if I get stung they might not have the medicine I need, and it could be bad. I basically told her to mind her business. 2 weeks later; we were at an away game, your mom was one of the defensive coordinators-"

"Wait! What! How come nobody ever told me this? She was in high school and one of your team's defensive coordinators?" asked Tem.

"Yep. She was only 14 too. She could read the o-line better than anyone. She got offers to assist college coaches. She's good at reading people and even better at communicating with them in a way they are receptive to her. The team and coaches had great respect for her because she never looked for credit. She would study other teams' o-line and go back and tell the coaches what she learned. She was 14, she blended right into the crowd," said Emerson.

"That's tight!" said Tem.

"But let me finish. Ok so 2 weeks later at an away game, when I was about to throw the ball, I got stung by a bee and started to go into anaphylactic shock. Your mother beat the emergency crew to me and gave me an epinephrine injection. She told them my medical history, and they got me to the hospital quickly. If it weren't for her, I wouldn't have made it past the age of 17. So I know what it's like to be a jerk to someone and have them to turn around and save your life. But at least I said thank you," chuckled Emerson.

"Don't do that Unc," laughed Tem. "I'm going to say thank you to Jia," he added. "Ma never told me that story before."

"You know she's not a bragger, but if you ask her about it she'll tell you," said Emerson.

"Ma really let me have it today," said Tem as he stared off into the distance. "I was mad at her at first, but now she's got me thinking. I'm lucky to have her and Jia around me. Remember when Bhavani and Jia used to put on skits and shows for me when I couldn't walk. Bhavani was the more "normal" kid, but she wouldn't go anywhere or do anything without me. I don't know Unc. I don't know what's up with me," said Tem.

Emerson said, "Sometimes, it can be hard to truly appreciate something you've always had. But still, try. You don't want to realize you had something good because that means you've already lost it. You don't want to see your dream in the hands of someone else living a life with someone else all because you realized what you had too late."

"You might be right Unc, but I'm 18. I have time," said Tem.

Emerson grabbed his clipboard and got up to go finish his rounds and said, "That's the problem Tem. You think you have time."

***

William was rushing down the hall and saw Emerson leaving the room walking down the hall in the opposite direction. William hates Emerson. Their rivalry goes back to undergrad where they were always in competition with each other and Emerson was always one step ahead. However, William got the last laugh because he got the girl. William knew Emerson had a deep, genuine love for Mye and that's how Mye caught William's eye. Emerson still had love for Mye, but his goodie two shoe image would never let him act on it. William knew Emerson wasn't a threat because he believed Emerson was too weak to ever go for what he truly wanted. He was a low hanging fruit type of guy. Either way, every time William saw Emerson, he would get irritated by his presence and today was no different.

William walked into his son's room unannounced. "Hey, son. How are you feeling?" asked William.

Tem hated when his father called him son. He really didn't feel his dad was much of a father. His dad was always away, and when Tem was young, he thought it was because of work. At least that's what his mother would tell him. The first time he caught his dad cheating, he found out the truth. He was 15 years old when he got a fake I.D. and snuck into a strip club with his older college friends. That's where he saw his dad following a stripper into a back room. He paid a stripper to get to the back room where he found his dad having sex with a stripper. Tem lost all respect for his dad that day. Tem felt that all those nights he wasn't home and all those games he missed was because he was out with other women. It's one thing to cheat on your wife, but it's another thing to cheat on your kids, and Tem felt his dad cheated him out of part of his childhood. Tem knew he had the perfect mom anyone could ask for, but every boy needs his dad to be present in his life.

Tem stared at his father thinking about how much he wished he never came to the hospital. He felt like his dad was just going through the motions with him just like he was doing with his mom. Tem knew if his dad had his way, he would rather be laid up with a woman instead of checking on his son. William stood at the edge of Tem's bed, and the two just stared at each other.

Jia knocked on the door then came in almost dropping her laptop while trying to balance the food on it.

"I got it, I got it," she said regaining the balance. "I brought you some footage from the last game. Maybe you can help from the sideline. Like be a coordinator or something," said Jia finally looking up seeing William.

"Oh hey, Mr. Hart. I didn't see you there. I'll wait outside," she said turning around to walk out.

"No, it's ok Jia. He was just leaving," said Tem in a cold manner.

William paused for a moment, "That's right. You can stay Jia. It was good seeing you," William added.

Tem was a little disappointed in his father for not having a rebuttal. For not trying to make a connection or effort to be a better dad. But it was something he grew to expect. William walked out of the door without giving Tem a second look.

"Is everything ok?" asked Jia.

"Yea, everything's good. You brought me some real food this time I can smell it. Instead of that rabbit food?" asked Tem.

"Shut up," chuckled Jia. "I brought you a burger and fries," she added.

Tem grabbed the food and took a huge bite out of the burger. "Come on son. This is a veggie burger," he said in disappointment. "You're the vegetarian not me," he added as he continued chewing the burger.

"I see you're eating it. It must taste good," she chuckled.

"It's alright. Where is Bhavani?" he asked.

"She left to keep from punching you in the face," said Jia as she ate her burger.

"What about everyone else?" he asked.

Jia said, "They probably left for the same reason."

Tem asked, "Well, why haven't you left? You don't want to punch me in the face too?"

Jia replied, "Of course I do. I've just mastered the art of restraining to do so. Nearly 2 decades of dealing with you taught me some serious patience and self-control." They laughed and enjoyed their dinner until Tem went to sleep.

***

Wayne left the police station and went to go pick up his car from the police compound. His car was old and beat up. Wayne wasn't a flashy guy for a very good reason. He didn't enjoy the comforts of his labor because he wasn't trying to draw attention to himself. But one way or another, he ended up on the police's radar. It was important than ever for him to hurry up and complete his exit plan while he still had time. When he got to his car, it was completely trashed, and they took his pocket change from his inner console. It was only 2k, so Wayne wasn't tripping, but it did give him a clue to the type of police he was dealing with.

Wayne was smart. He knew this life had no longevity, so the plan was to always get in and out. His little stint in jail made it clear that that's no place he wanted to be and that the time to get out was now. He went straight to his grandma's house to check up on her where he found the house was taped up.

"A Wayne," said Mr. Brown the next door neighbor as he was leaving his house. "I'm sorry to hear about your grandmother. She was a special woman. You have my condolences," he said before getting into his car and driving off.

Wayne's head began to spin. He dropped to his knees and a single tear fell for his grandmother. She was his world. When his mother died giving birth to Kiam, grandma picked up the pieces and kept everything going. Kiam's father couldn't take losing his wife and left Wayne's grandma with a newborn baby and a teenager to raise. Everything Wayne did was for his grandma and Kiam. He put himself in harm's way so they could have a better life. And while he was locked up, half of his world died. Wayne picked himself off of the ground and jumped in the car to go and find the other half.

***

William found Mye resting peacefully rocking a little boy. He could not help but admire her beauty, perfect brown skin, and big curly hair. He preferred her hair bone straight but had to admit she was beautiful either way. He thought for a moment why he even cheats on her and then he remembered why.

"It's me," said Mye through closed eyes.

William said, "I know, I know my wife."

"Oh do you," Mye said

When she opened her eyes, William got an instant hard-on. He loved her green eyes. He never could understand why she would cover up such a unique, attractive feature. Her eyes were low and dreamy opened just enough for him to see them sparkle with each blink. Mye smirked at William's arousal as she put Kiam down on the couch, got up and walked over to him. She gently pulled him into the hall.

"What is he doing here?" asked William.

"I don't know," Mye replied as she looked down at the bulge in his pants. "I haven't seen him in awhile," she smirked.

William adjusted his pants. "I meant the boy."

"Oh," Mye said walking to the kitchen, "He'll be staying here for a while."

"Says who?" asked William.

"Says me," replied Mye.

"That boy-" said William.

"His name is Kiam," replied Mye, "it stands for King I am. Kiam."

"I'm not raising any more kids, and I don't want to live with any kids, what is he like 5?" asked William.

Mye paused and squinted as she walked closer to William and said, "Yes, he is 5. How would you know he is 5?"

"What do you mean," asked William slightly nervous.

"What is your frame of reference for what a 5 year old would look like? Height, weight, size? I see tons of kindergarteners all the time but you, you don't?"

William began to stutter and then said, "I don't want to be around any kids in my house."

Then Mye said, "William, you don't live here though."

"Ouch! That's gotta sting," said Truman walking down the hall.

"Can you please stop walking in my house like you own it?" said William angrily.

Truman replied, "Well, apparently... you don't live here anymore, so, yeah." Truman quickly turned his back to William to face Mye.

"Are you aware that there is a whole kid in your living room right now?" he asked her.

"Yes," she replied.

He leaned in and whispered, "Is it William's?"

"No!" Mye and William said in unison.

"Look, I'm going to go grab some of my things, and I'll send a crew to clean out all of my stuff in the morning," said William as he turned to walk to the master bedroom they once shared.

"All of your belongings were delivered to your condo Saturday morning. I used my key to get in. There was dust everywhere. Even all over the dark hardwood floors, but not a single footprint in sight. Almost like no one's been there for months," said Mye.

William walked slowly toward her nervously. "Well, you know I work a lot. I'm hardly ever there," said William.

"I guess you haven't been there all weekend, that's no longer any of my business though. Please leave William," said Mye.

"This is still my got damn house too!" said William.

"You got the papers?" asked Truman. "We can divide all this up right now or do you want me to write up the papers? I think I might even have a draft in my briefcase," said Truman as he opened his briefcase and shuffled through files.

"I got this Truman," said William with a scowl. "Have it your way Mye. I'll get you those papers," said William as he slammed the front door behind him.

"Now who the hell is that kid in the living room?" asked Truman.

"Long story short. That's Kiam, he's 5 years old, and his grandma passed away today, so he's going to stay with me for a while," said Mye smiling from ear to ear.

Truman said, "Look Mye, I know your son got shot... then tased, and then almost died today and apparently, you adopted a big ass 5 year old, that I low-key think is really 7. But Ima still need those documents for court tomorrow."

Mye could only laugh to keep from slapping Truman. No matter what, Truman was always about his business. He was the most dependable reliable person she knew. Mye and Truman had an inseparable brother and sister bond that real siblings could only dream of. Mye hoped that Tem would get his act together so he and Bhavani could continue to grow there tight-knit relationship to exceed the strength of the bond Mye and Truman had.

"Here you go," said Kiam as he handed Mye her bag and in the process shocked the shit out of Truman. "That's a fast 5 year old! I thought he was asleep," said Truman.

"Hi Uncle T!" said Kiam as he gave Truman the biggest hug.

Truman raised his hands in the air and repeatedly said, "I don't do hugs, I don't do hugs, I don't do hugs," while Kiam just ignored him. Kiam finally lets go, and Truman said, "And its Truman. Not Uncle T."

Kiam replied, "Ok Uncle T! " as he left the kitchen. Truman's phone vibrated. He checked it, grabbed the files and put them in his briefcase.

"Business as usual Mye. So be ready to leave at the same time we always leave and arrange for someone to take that kid to school," said Truman.

"Bye Truman and don't go doing your own private investigation on this Tem cop shooting thing. Let the mayor handle it," replied Mye as she pushed him to the door.

"Ok," said Truman as he walked out of the door.

"I'm serious Truman! Mind your business!" said Mye as Truman closed the door in her face.

Mye walked into the living room and found Kiam asleep on the couch. With all that happened today, she almost forgot to call and check up on Bliss.

"Hi Joyce, my apologies for not calling earlier today. I just wanted to say thank you for keeping Bliss this past weekend."

"Mye get some rest I heard what happened today," said Joyce.

"You did?" asked Mye curious to what Joyce was referring to.

"Yeah, you have Kiam, and I'm sure he has a tough road ahead losing his grandma so suddenly. You have a lot on your plate today. Bliss has practically been living here every other weekend, and I already have a little girl. Your kids are grown, and now you have a 5 year old. That's got to be a lot," said Joyce.

"I'm just glad Kiam is safe. It's like Kiam's a little old man in a kid's body. He seems so familiar like I've known him for years, but he's only 5. He'll settle in just fine. Is Bliss still with you or did she go home today?" asked Mye.

"Oh, Bliss is with me and will be with me for a while. She told me what her mom's boyfriend had been doing to her. I called Ms. Gaines the teacher of our foster care class, and she worked it out so Bliss can stay with me until after they go to court. She could have stayed with her mom but her mom took her boyfriend's side, and she refused to put him out of the house," said Joyce.

"That's sad. I'm glad Bliss now have you and Katie and the weekend overnight offer at the center stands indefinitely. This is a community effort," said Mye, "and that Ms. Gaines is an angel."

***

The next morning, Mye was in the kitchen cutting up fruit and vegetables when Kiam came running down the spiral staircase.

"Amazon Goddess!" yelled Kiam while running down the stairs.

"Slow down!" yelled Mye as she laughed when he fell down the last three steps.

"I'm ok," he said as he picked himself up off the floor.

"What is that?" said Bhavani looking down over the second floor banister pointing to Kiam.

"It's a boy! A real boy!" said Mye trying to keep from laughing. "What are you doing here?" asked Mye walking out of the kitchen to the entryway. "Girl you don't live here. You have a whole penthouse in Georgetown."

Bhavani replied, "I figured you needed me here to comfort you with Tem all shot up in the hospital, but I see you've already traded him in."

"Hi, I'm Bhavani!" said Bhavani to Kiam as she kneeled down to his eye level.

"Hi! I'm Kiam!" he replied. "Look! My tooth is loose. Hopefully, the tooth fairy can find me even though I moved," he said to Bhavani.

"Awwwwww! He is so cute! Can we keep him!" Bhavani said as she hugged Kiam tight.

Mye smiled at Bhavani gawking over Kiam.

"We have to see what Ms. Gaines says, but until then we have to just play it by ear," said Mye.

"I'm going to turn Tem's spare room into Kiam's room. It will be amazing!" yelled Bhavani.

Mye said, "Weren't you just saying how you wanted someone to love? Well, here you go!" laughed Mye.

Bhavani replied, "I guess I should have been more specific. Now don't get me wrong. You are adorable Kiam but Ma I was thinking about someone bigger."

"Ohhhh like a fat kid," said Kiam. They both laughed.

Bhavani replied, "No Kiam. I mean like. A man who is 6'2", 220 lbs, with dark chocolate skin, who adds great value to my life and sees me as an extension of him. A protector who makes my overall safety mentally, physically, and emotionally a top concern of his and he nets 7 figures or more annually. Do you know a man like that Kiam?" asked Bhavani.

"Maybe," replied Kiam. Bhavani laughed.

"Well, if you do Kiam then please introduce him to me," she chuckled.

"Hopefully the universe works just as fast bringing me my man as it did bringing me you," said Bhavani to Kiam. Kiam blushed.

Mye added, "Oh yeah Kiam, whoever this guy for Bhavani is, can you introduce me to his father?"Everyone laughed.

"Gotcha!" said Kiam.

"And mom, I'm loving this look! This big hair don't care; green-eyed diva look. Yassss! Keep it up!" said Bhavani.

"Me too!" said Kiam. "Can you stay like this please?" he added.

"For you Kiam," Mye replied, "do you want a smoothie?" asked Mye.

"What's that?" asked Kiam. Bhavani laughed.

"Ok, what do you want for breakfast Kiam?" asked Mye.

"Ummm pizza!" he said.

"Ummm no. Here drink on this smoothie while I make you some pancakes," said Mye.

CHAPTER SIX

SECRETS IN SECRETS

Emerson woke up feeling tired, and he was alone again in his bed. He didn't sleep a wink last night, and his wife was up and out of the house earlier and coming home later, so he felt like he never saw her. He checked his phone and saw she sent him a text.

"Got home late and didn't want to disturb you, so I slept in the guest bedroom. Had to get an early start so I'll see you later this evening.

This was the third time this week that Delilah had to pull extra hours. Emerson couldn't wait for her department to hire another pharmacist so that his wife didn't have to work so hard. Emerson went to the kitchen to make some coffee when he ran into Jia.

"What are you doing here?" he asked surprised to see her.

"Hello to you too dad," she sassed back, "I'm here to make sure you're alright, after all that happened yesterday," Jia added as she sipped on her smoothie.

"You're amazing, you know that?" he said as he gave her a big hug and kissed her forehead.

"Let me ask you something Jia. Why didn't you call me when Tem got hurt?" asked Emerson.

"Whatcha mean I did. I told you everything," she said.

"Yea but later that day. I first found out by eaves-dropping on some nurses talking," he added.

"Well, that type of news travels fast in the hospital," she said.

"Yeah, but why didn't you call me first?" asked Emerson.

Jia was slightly confused, "You mean like, as soon as the incident happened?" she asked. Jia chuckled slightly as she sipped her smoothie, "Dad that's not how the e-plan goes. You know the first person we call is G-Ma and then she mobilizes everyone. Remember?" Jia shook her head slightly at her dad's forgetfulness.

Emerson observed his daughter as she drank her smoothie and scrolled through her phone. He was convinced that Jia thought that he knew about the emergency plan. When actually he didn't.

"If you had an emergency, who would you call first?" asked Emerson.

"Come on dad, G-Ma, duh!" said Jia.

Jia noticed that her dad looked disappointed.

"Dad come on. Don't do that. She's just good at handling herself in high-stress situations," Jia added.

"I am a brain surgeon," said Emerson in a slightly elevated tone.

"I know dad. You are extremely intelligent and very calculated. All I'm saying is in an emergency you mostly rely on instincts and intuition. G-ma is good with that stuff, so that's why I'll call her. I'm lucky to have her and you because you guys give me the best of both worlds," said Jia as she smiled and hugged her father.

Emerson felt a little better by her response.

"And besides dad, your cell phone is never by you," chuckled Jia.

Emerson couldn't do anything but laugh because she was right and he was happy she had a person like Mye in his daughter's life to fill-in the gaps he couldn't.

***

"Come on Mye," whined Truman as Kiam got in the backseat dragging his booster seat with him. Kiam crawled over to Truman and gave him a big hug while Truman just held his arms above his head trying not to touch him.

"Safety first!" said Kiam as he reached and put Truman's seatbelt on, then he got in his booster seat and strapped himself in.

Mye got in the front seat and turned around to find Kiam looking happy as ever while Truman looked completely annoyed.

"Let's switch," demanded Truman.

Mye laughed, "No Truman. You'll be fine. He doesn't bite."

"I do bite that's how I eat my food," said Kiam.

Mye laughed, "No Kiam, I mean you don't bite people."

Kiam looked at Truman and gave him a sneaky, creepy smile.

"What the hell?" said Truman.

"Language Truman," said Mye.

"Oh, because we have a member of the creep squad here, I have to watch my language," said Truman.

"The driver is a member of the creep squad?" asked Kiam in a loud whisper.

Alex chuckled.

"My apologies Alex," said Mye trying to keep from laughing herself. Kiam sat in his seat swinging his legs and humming.

"Why are you so happy kid? Didn't your Grandma just die?" asked Truman.

"Truman!" yelled Mye.

"My Grandma didn't die, Uncle T. No one can die. I mean your body can die, but you can't die. My Grandma is free! Since she doesn't have her body's liminations."

"Limitations," said Truman.

"That's what I said," said Kiam. "Now she can fly like the birds and go wherever she wants. Besides, she told me I will get another mom and dad, some sisters and brothers, aunts and uncles, and a bunch of cousins! I never had all that stuff before. It was just me, my big brother, and grandma," said Kiam

"So your grandma was creepy too?" asked Truman.

"Truman!" said Mye.

"It's ok. I like Uncle T. He is his true self. He doesn't pretend to be someone else, which is good, because when his body dies... and it will, he will live on with all of the choices he made. Forever," said Kiam smiling at Truman.

Truman responded, "When you say forever. Do you mean like for-ever or like forever ever?

"Are you asking a 5-year-old questions about the afterlife?" asked Mye.

"Look, you got me in the backseat with boy buddha. I'm just trying to make conversation," said Truman.

"Look Kiam, we're at the center," said Mye.

"Yes! Today is pizza day too!" shouted Kiam.

"Bhavani is going to come check up on you just to make sure you're doing alright," said Mye.

"Ok cool! Ummm, can you let her know that I'm going to pretend sad at lunch so I can get another slice of pizza? But I'm not really sad though, just pretend so not to worry," said Kiam.

Mye laughed, "Ok, I'll let her know. Oh and Kiam, I wouldn't tell anyone about what your Grandma told you before her body died. Not everyone will understand."

"Oh, I know. My grandma said I can trust you and your brother because you guys are special like me. Grandma said you are Claira Hearing Uncle T and that you, Amazon Goddess, are many Clairas in one. She said I can tell you guys anything," said Kiam.

"I'm a Claira what? And most importantly, I'm not related to her," said Truman.

Kiam laughed hard and loud, "You so funny Uncle T!"

Mye turned to Truman as Alex opened her door, "His grandma was saying you're clairaudient. Claira Hearing is clairaudient," smiled Mye.

Alex then opened Kiam's door.

"Thanks creep!" said Kiam to Alex.

Alex laughed as he closed the door behind him. Mye grabbed Kiam's hand and walked him into the building.

Truman sat in the car as a million thoughts ran through his head and smiled a genuine sigh of relief.

***

A woman sat in a wingback chair in the corner of her bedroom when her phone rang, "Hello Leah, all is going well I hope."

Leah replied, "Yes, everything is going to plan. He's shopping around for a lawyer now to do his divorce. Then he and I can get married."

"What you do with him after the divorce is your business, Leah. I just want him out of Mye's life," said the woman.

"Well, I've got that well under control. He just walked in the door. Gotta go," said Leah as she quickly hung up the phone.

"Mye will pay for what she did to my family. If it's the last thing I do. I missed the first time but the second time will be dead on. She will pay and feel the pain I feel. Leah better make sure that divorce goes through and I'll handle the rest. Her son won't be so lucky next time," said the woman.

***

William walked into the condo he bought for Leah and instantly became annoyed when he saw she ordered takeout. Again. Leah always ordered takeout. She never cooked. William did his best to regain his composure because he was more upset with his relationship with his son than Leah's lack of cooking. He felt like he had lost all of his son's respect and he didn't know where to start to get it back. William truly loved his son, but he didn't understand where things went wrong or how to fix it. This time around he is going to do this right.

William walked into the master bedroom where he found Leah folding clothes.

"So, how is your son?" Leah asked.

He looked confused, "Why do you ask?"

She stopped folding a shirt midway and had a surprised look on her face.

"What do you mean why do I ask?" she said looking confused.

William moved closer to her slowly with a menacing look in his eyes, "How do you know about my son?" he asked.

Leah dropped the shirt and started trembling as she was backing up, "William you are scaring me," she whispered.

William started to raise his hand, "If you played a part in my son getting hurt-"

"No daddy!" said Tre. "Mommy didn't hurt me. I fell off my bike," the little boy added.

William turned around and hugged his son, William Hart, III really tight, then he tickled him. Leah breathed a sigh of relief.

"Ok Tre, I was just worried that's all," smiled William.

"Look I lost another tooth!" said Tre.

William chuckled. "Be careful on your bike before you lose another one," smiled William.

"I love you daddy," said Tre.

"I love you more," said William as he watched Tre run out of the bedroom. William turned around and saw the look of disgust on Leah's face.

Then she said, "What's going on William? You've never raised your hand at me before." William stumbled over his words.

"I was just asking you about Tre, and you flipped. I know you love your kids but would you really flip out on me like that?" she added.

"I was just angry; I had a rough day, I wasn't going to hit you," he said.

"You need to go William," she said.

"No no... let me make it up to you." He pulled out a silver credit card.

She said, "No, the black one."

He gave it to her reluctantly. "This is a start," she said.

CHAPTER SEVEN

PENITENTIARY BLUES

Mye and Truman went through security at the state prison. Mye ran a therapy group called, D.O.P., Daddies of Princesses. While she held group therapy sessions, Truman did pro bono work for the members. The warden despised the program and thought it was a waste of time because when most people leave prison, they end up right back 6 months later. However, none of the group members who were released from jail have come back. So now every inmate with a daughter was trying to maintain good behavior to get into the therapy group. D.O.P. has a waitlist of 150 inmates who were eligible to be a member. As soon as one member was released, then another inmate was added to the group. Truman has a 100% success rate with the members of this program, and the warden detested it.

"Hello, Kings! It's always a pleasure to see you. I hope you came prepared to experience another great session," said Mye.

Mye scanned the group as everyone filed in, and she noticed someone missing.

"Where's King Tank?" she asked.

"Follow Lil Dicky's hate," said King Brown.

"Thanks, King Brown. I'll follow-up on it after our session," said Mye.

After the session, Mye met up with Truman in one of the private attorney-client rooms. "What happened to Tank? He wasn't in our group session," she said.

"Lil Dicky is hating again. Apparently, Edward Mane from the appeal board is looking to become a prison warden, and Lil Dicky thinks he's coming for his job," said Truman.

Mye replied, "What? Why would Edward want to do that?"

"Prison reform. I think Edward is trying to shake the prison system up from the inside out. Show people there's another way. He's our biggest advocate for this program," said Truman.

"What does this have to do with Tank?" asked Mye.

"Well, Tank is an easy target. He has major anger issues," said Truman.

"But he's getting better," said Mye.

"But he's still angry," said Truman, "I think he is trying to use Tank to prove people can't be rehabilitated and to prove your system doesn't work."

"Where is Tank now?" asked Mye.

"In solitary confinement," said Truman.

"I'm going to see him," she said.

"You can't," said Truman.

"Watch me."

***

Mye walked with grace and poise to Tank's cell. It was only April but it felt like a summer day and the area outside the cell was hot and extremely stuffy. Mye had learned to not breathe through her nose, but even now that wasn't helping. However, you couldn't tell by the smile on her face.

"King Tank! I missed you for our session. What happened today?" she asked.

"My apologies Doc. The guards keep pushing my buttons. They ain't too sweet on the idea of me possibly getting out," he said.

Mye looked around his cell through the little square opening. Prolonged isolation with a lack of natural light and poor ventilation was a punishment on top of punishment. Prisoners are people too, and as much money as these prisons are getting they should be able to give inmates basic human rights. Mye wiped a single tear from her face.

Tank noticed and said, "I'm not going to mess this up for you Doc. Too many inmates are counting on your program to help rehabilitate them. We know no one cares about us, but you do, and we appreciate it. Don't worry about me. I'm not going to let warden Lil Dicky win," said Tank as he smiled through the small square hole.

"Don't forget what we practice King Tank. Remember what to do when you think you feel yourself getting angry," said Mye.

"I know Doc. I close my eyes and imagine feeling the heat of the Sun on my face. Absorbing its energy, strengthening my being. I take four breaths in, hold for two, and release for four. I do this repeatedly until I calm down. Each time breathing in the Sun's energy and breathing out whatever got me mad in the first place. I got this Doc. I promise I won't let you down. Now get out of here before you get caught by a jerk officer," said Tank.

"Oh yeah, your daughter wrote you a book called, "Princess of the Earth and Sky," said Mye. Tank smiled.

"My baby girl is a writer," he said through a big grin.

"I mailed the book to you, so hopefully you'll get it tomorrow. Keep your head up King and stay cool. Bliss needs you."

***

Wayne went to Kiam's school and got nowhere with the front desk. It was like Fort Knox in there. They took privacy and school safety to the highest degree. They won't give Wayne any information. They didn't even tell him if his brother was a student there. Wayne went back to his car seemingly defeated. He just found out his grandmother passed away and now he can't find his little brother. He was devastated.

As Wayne sat in his car trying to figure out what to do next, a sparkling brown Mercedes Benz S 600 sedan pulled in front of him. Out jumped the most unbelievably attractive woman he had ever seen. She had a young fresh face with smooth mahogany skin with long big curly black hair with brown highlights flowing down her back. She walked with confidence and elegance in 4-inch gold strappy heels that showed her perfect toes. She wore a strapless, backless, white pants jumpsuit with a sheer gold cover that dragged behind her as she walked. Her heels made her appear to be about 6 feet tall, with an hourglass shape perfectly sculpted by God himself. Wayne stared at her as she walked into the school. For a moment, he forgot about all of his problems, but once she was out of sight, all of his issues came flooding back.

Wayne sat in his car searching online on his phone to see how he could petition for custody for his brother. He was the only family his little brother had, and he was worried sick about what his brother might be feeling right now. With his head in his phone, Wayne was startled by a knock at his window. He looked up, and it was her. He rolled down the window as fast as he could, but then it got stuck, so he just opened the door.

"They are going to call the cops on you if you don't leave," said the woman.

Wayne was stunned silent by her beauty; she smelled like mangos and pineapples; she was perfect.

"Helloooo…. Did you hear what I said? You gotta go. They are going to call the cops on you," she repeated.

"I can't go. I need to make sure my brother is ok, but they won't even tell me if he's inside," said Wayne.

"So what's your next move playa? Sit here until the cops come and get charged with trespassing?" asked the woman.

Wayne hung his head down in defeat.

"It's been a long week for you huh?" asked the woman.

"And it's only Tuesday," he added.

"Well, If I were you sir, I would fight for my brother. I would go back in there, plead my case, and leave all of my contact information with them. Maybe someone will give you a call later. Then I would wait at the corner off of school property and see if my brother comes out of the building," she said.

Booty, beauty, and brains, he thought to himself.

"Well, I have to go. Good luck with your brother," she said before walking away.

"Hey," he said grabbing her by the wrist. He stood up and watched her size him up then smiled.

"Thanks. Thanks for telling me about them wanting to call the cops and thank you for your suggestion," Wayne said closing his car door behind him. "But how did you know I wasn't a creeper or something?" he asked.

"I could see it in your eyes," said the woman staring deeply at Wayne. "And besides, you're missing your passenger side mirror, your exhaust is hanging on for dear life, and your windows aren't even tinted. Who you kidnapping in that car?"

Wayne couldn't help but laugh. His car was a mess.

"Good luck with your brother," she said as she turned and walked away.

Wayne couldn't help but stare as she walked to her car and opened the door.

"Wayne, the cops. Go in there and talk to them before they call the cops," she said.

"Oh yeah," he said under his breath. Wayne walked to her window and tapped on it.

"Here's my card. Now go," she said before pulling off.

As he walked to the school door, he read the card she gave him.

Bhavani A. Hart, Financial Advisor

***

Truman was sitting in the car with Alex a block from the police station. His inside man came and got in the car.

"So what's the latest?" asked Truman.

"The officer who shot Tem is on administrative leave, but I heard his family is packing up to go to the Dominican Republic," said officer Grey.

"To vacation?" asked Truman confused.

"No to move. Permanently relocate. Word is he has a house, a boat, cars, and all that already down there. He's likely about to resign and just leave," officer Grey added. "He won't stand trial."

"How can he afford that?" asked Truman.

"I don't know. He cleaned out his savings and took out a hardship loan to help pay for some experimental treatments for his wife's cancer. I don't know where he got the extra money from," said officer Grey.

"This was a paid hit," said Truman.

"Now hold on Truman. Let's not go there. That's a big leap," said officer Grey.

"Get me a list of all of the officers with sick close relatives and anyone who was once stressed about money but now isn't talking about it anymore," said Truman. "If this was a paid hit and they missed, then someone will be out to get Tem again. Maybe we can stop them before it's too late."

***

Mye was writing in her journal when her phone rang, "Hello," she said.

"Hi Mye, this is Mrs. Hawkins."

"Hey Mrs. Hawkins, is everything alright with Kiam?" asked Mye slightly concerned.

"Oh yeah, he is great! Well, he was a little sad during lunch time, but it was nothing a second slice of pizza couldn't clear up," said Mrs. Hawkins.

Mye laughed to herself.

"I was calling you because a gentleman came up here claiming to be Kiam's brother looking for him. But as you know per our rules, I couldn't give him any information," said Mrs. Hawkins.

"Of course I understand. If he comes back, you can give him my address and contact info. I'll handle it," said Mye.

"Isn't that a little risky? What if he is a predator or something?" Mrs. Hawkins asked.

"What if he is a young man who feels like he lost his grandmother and little brother the same day? Something inside me is saying to invite him to dinner this evening. So if he comes back, no, when he comes back, please send him my invitation. I'm following my inner guidance system Mrs. Hawkins, and I feel really good about this. Trust me," said Mye.

***

Mye and Kiam went home to find Bhavani playing the piano. Mye went to the kitchen and started preparing

dinner. Kiam went to the living room and started dancing to the music. Wayne pulled up to the house and marveled at its grandness. The landscape was impeccable,
and the house sat high and looked so regal. He parked
his car on the street and walked up the long semi-circle
driveway. When he reached the door, one of the gardeners said, "Go right in. Mye is expecting you."

Wayne didn't know who Mye was but turned the
knob of the huge 8-foot door and walked in slowly. He
closed the door behind him and marveled at how beautiful the house was. The entrance could have been a cover
feature of an interior decorating magazine. The ceilings
were high, and you could see the second-floor walkway
look over into the living room and the entryway. It
looked like someone was building a sliding board around
the spiral staircase. If his brother was here, he felt good
that he was in good hands.

Wayne heard someone playing the piano in the distance and then he heard a child laughing. He walked
quickly towards the living room and said, "Kiam!"

Bhavani grabbed her gun from under the piano and
yanked Kiam to her.

"When I said you should fight for your brother, I
didn't mean this one," said Bhavani while pointing a pink
and chrome beretta at Wayne.

Wayne lifted his hands up and slowly started backing
away.

"Wayne!" said Kiam excitedly while trying to wiggle
out of Bhavani's arms, but she had a tight grip on him

"But he is my brother," said Wayne

"How did you get in here?" asked Bhavani.

"Your gardener let me in. He said you were expecting me," said Wayne.

Mye walked out the kitchen drying a glass on a dishcloth.

"Put that thing away Bhavani. Didn't I ask you to get rid of that and all the others hidden around the house? We have a young guest now," said Mye.

"It's fingerprint activated, so he's safe," she replied.

Mye snatched the gun from her hand, and Bhavani released Kiam in the process.

"Wayne! I've missed you!" said Kiam.

"I told your father we shouldn't have let you take that marksman training," Mye whispered to herself putting the gun on the table.

"That's Wayne, Kiam's brother," said Mye as she dried the glass she was holding.

"I'm sorry I didn't catch your full name," said Mye looking up at Wayne for the first time and she dropped her glass.

Everyone stared at Mye as she stared at Wayne. Memories began to flood Mye's mind from childhood. *This can't be*, she thought to herself. *He looks exactly the same. Just the way I last saw him, but that's impossible. That was nearly 25 years ago.* Mye walked slowly towards Wayne and reached for his face, "Champ?" she whispered underneath her breath as she touched the side of his face.

Wayne shook his head no slowly with her hand still on his face.

"That's not me," he said in a sorrowful tone.

Mye put her free hand on the other side of his face. "Nolan?" she asked.

Wayne shook his head yes. She backed up and put her hand over her heart.

"Nolan Jr.... Nolan Wayne Washitaw, Jr.," he said. Mye was overrun with emotions.

"Nolan Sr., Champ, was my father," he said.

"What do you mean was?" Mye asked.

Wayne looked down and said, "He passed away."

Mye's world crashed. Believing Champ was out there somewhere gave her hope. Whenever she was down, she leaned heavily on the memories of him. He was the one that got away. The thought of him kept her going. She secretly hoped she would run into him again. Seeing Wayne rushed so many emotional memories to her head and then hearing Champ died crushed her. Mye was exhausted from this 10-second emotional roller coaster.

"Did you know him?" asked Wayne looking at Mye.

"Yes," she whispered while trying to hold back tears. "He was my best friend."

"I'm sorry for your loss," Mye and Wayne said in unison.

"Don't cry AG," said Kiam as he hugged her.

"Remember he's free. Probably flying around right now," he smiled.

Mye chuckled to herself, "You're right Kiam. I should be happy he's free," she added.

"Well, thank you for caring for Kiam while I was gone. I can take him off your hands now," said Wayne.

"Unfortunately not," said Mye through sniffles.

"I'm his temporary legal guardian until the courts deem otherwise. Now you can come visit him whenever you want, but until you gain legal custody, I can't let you take him," said Mye. "I hope you understand."

"Wayne, I love it here! They are really good people! They are building me a slide, so I don't have to take the steps. How cool is that!" yelled Kiam.

Wayne was filled with tons of emotions. He lost his grandmother, and he just found his brother. Only to run into a woman who knew his dad and that brought up a ton of old memories. On top of all of that, this woman looked so much like his mom. It was all too much to process at once. He technically didn't have a place to go to since his grandma's house was taped up. What was he going to do? Raise Kiam in a hotel until he figured everything out. That's no life for a kid.

"Ooo, Wayne you can stay here! AG, can Wayne stay here? We can share a room. That way we can be closer," said Kiam.

"He can have his own room Kiam. I mean if you want to stay here," said Mye to Wayne.

"No Ma! Hello I'm standing right here," said Bhavani as her jet black short bob with bangs swung back and forth with each head jerk.

Wayne was slightly confused by Bhavani's appearance. She was equally as beautiful as the first time he saw her, but she looked totally different with short hair. And now she was wearing a black wrap dress with a high split with red stilettos and red lips. Wayne couldn't help but stare at her transformation.

"What!? Why are you staring at me?" she asked Wayne.

"I'm sorry. You just look different from earlier. Just as beautiful, but different," said Wayne.

"Oh, this is the guy you were talking about earlier today," said Mye smiling.

"Ma, seriously," said Bhavani.

"Well, if you're gonna be around here, you have to get used to her switch-ups. She changes up like 2-3 times a day. I hate to see her dry cleaning bill," said Mye to Wayne. "This is my house, and you are free to stay here as long as you want. Bhavani doesn't live here, so if she feels a certain way she can just go home."

"No, I'm good Ms. Mye, but thank you," said Wayne.

"Let me go get a broom to get up this glass. Bhavani I don't really feel like cooking anything right now. Can you and Kiam go pick us up something to eat?" asked Mye.

"Sure mom no problem. Come on Kiam," said Bhavani looking at Wayne.

Kiam added, "Oh hold on. Wayne this is Bhavani. Bhavani this is Wayne," he leaned into Bhavani and whispered loudly, "We talked about him this morning, remember?" said Kiam as he winked obviously.

Bhavani blushed. "Umm, I don't know what you're talking about."

Kiam said, "You remember, this morning you asked me if I knew a man who was chocolate, 62 inches, and 20 pounds."

"I said 6 feet 2 inches and 220 pounds. Get it right boy," said Bhavani.

"That's me," said Wayne quickly. Those are my exact measurements and as you see, I'm chocolate."

Bhavani blushed. "I said a lot more than that Kiam."

"Well I'm only 5 and I can't remember everything. Besides, he's the only man I know," said Kiam.

"Let's go Kiam," Bhavani said as she grabbed Kiam's hand and started to drag him down the hall.

"I'm not feeling the love here. I mean, the Universe can't work no faster," said Kiam. "This is same day delivery."

Mye couldn't help but to laugh.

"Wayne you should join them," she added.

"Ma!" said Bhavani.

"I'd like that," said Wayne as he followed Kiam to the door.

"Alright, fine then, but I'm driving," said Bhavani. "Your car is clearly a safety hazard," she added.

"Safety first!" said Kiam as he grabbed his booster seat by the door.

"Oh heavens no, drop that thing Kiam," said Bhavani. "I got you a new car seat in the trunk. She popped the trunk and asked Wayne, "Can you install the car seat?"

He looked at the car seat and said, "This is a Mercedes Benz car seat."

She replied, "So can you install it or not?"

Wayne installed the car seat without a hitch. "There you go," he said.

"Yay thanks!" said Kiam as he got in the car seat to give it a try.

"I've never seen a Mercedes with this sparkling brown color. What made you get this car?" he asked.

"Who wouldn't want this beauty. Cars are my vice. I have many cars. Besides, what's not to like about something big, reliable, and sparkling brown?" she asked. Wayne was instantly aroused. He couldn't get in the car just yet, so he had to stall her.

"What's her name?" he asked pointing to the car.

"Sheila E.," Bhavani replied.

"And why the Benz car seat? Surely there were other cheaper options," he asked.

"I don't do cheap," she replied. Then Bhavani put on her Gucci oversized embellished square-frame sunglasses and said, "What can I say, I like the glamorous life."

CHAPTER EIGHT

EMOTIONAL ROLLERCOASTER

Mye needed time alone to process her thoughts. She never wanted to think of Champ as being dead. She preferred to think of Champ as missing just like she preferred to think of her mom as missing. At least she knew now that he was gone forever. Mye poured another glass of red wine as she played her Mica Paris album "Whisper a Prayer" on vinyl. She loved the way Mica sang, "Put a Move on my Heart." That was always her go-to song when she was feeling down. It reminded Mye of Champ. She was young, but they were in love. Mye had more questions than answers, but she knew they had to wait until everything settled down.

Tem walked in yelling, "Ma! Where are you?" as he headed to the living room. "What's going on? Who got you over here whispering a prayer?" he asked.

"Why are you here?" Mye asked in between sipping her wine.

"You forgot to pick me up," said Tem.

"Naw you grown. You don't need the black woman anymore," said Mye.

"Ma are you serious? Come on," he said.

"Yes, I'm serious Tem. You need to learn some respect. Your slick little remarks and how you feel about black women are offensive. I don't know where you picked that up from, but it's not cool," she added.

"Ma, this is why. Y'all make everything hard for y'all self. Instead of conforming and taking the easy way. You make things harder for yourself. You used to conform more and keep your hair straight and be dainty, but now look at you. You're getting smart with me and your hair? When are you going to do your hair?" said Tem as he flopped down on the couch beside her. "You're changing Ma, and I'm not sure that I like it," he added.

Mye drank the last sip of her wine and sat the glass down.

"Get out!" she yelled. "Get your ungrateful black ass out of my house! Did you not hear what I told you? I'm through babying you and you have the audacity to come up in my house and tell me how you're displeased with me! Get the hell up out of my house!"

Tem was completely taken off guard. His mother never yelled at him like that before.

"But Ma wait! I might be still a little sick and Jia's on rotation at the hospital," he pleaded.

"Then call a nurse to stay at your house with you," she said.

"I'm going to my room," said Tem heading for the steps.

"Oh, you have no room here Tem. I gave it away," said Mye.

"What?" said Tem.

"Oh yeah, and you might have a little brother and now that I think about it. Possibly a big brother or a future brother in law? I don't know what but I do know is that…" and in her best Jamaican impression from the movie, "Bad Boys 2" she said, "You are not welcome heeeeeah!"

"Alright, Ma. I ain't messing with you today. I'll talk to you in the morning," said Tem as he slammed the front door.

***

Tem sped out his mom's driveway and headed to his place in Georgetown.

"I can't believe Ma is tripping like that," he said as he was weaving in and out of traffic. He pressed a button on his steering wheel and said, "Call Uncle E." The phone started ringing through his car speakers.

"Hello," said Emerson.

"Hey Unc, how are you doing?" he asked.

"I'm good. What about you?" How are you feeling? Are you taking it easy?" Emerson asked.

"I'm trying to but Ma is tripping. She won't let me stay in the house," said Tem.

"Oh, so she was serious," said Emerson.

"Apparently. I was like what if something happens and no one is around to help. Jia is on rotation at the hospital. Ma is gonna say, "Get a nurse Tem," Unc she is wilding out. I don't even know who she is anymore."

"I know a few good nurses. I can send you their numbers," said Emerson.

"Nooooo Unc, you don't understand. I want my old mother back. The "my son can do no wrong" mother back," said Tem.

Emerson laughed, "You are 18 years old. You are a grown man. Maybe it's time you do some things for yourself."

"I did not call you to hear this," Tem said.

Emerson chuckled, "Okay, okay, how can I help?"

"Can you go talk some sense into her? She's acting all different and brand new. Do you know I have to do my own accounting and bookkeeping now or pay Ashley myself? And if I want to ask Truman a legal question, then I have to put down a retainer fee first? Do you know how much his retainer fee is? Ma is tripping," said Tem.

"I'll talk to her Tem, but understand, all those things your Ma is making you do now, she used to do for you. She's not making you do something she doesn't do. I'm going to talk to her to see what's really going on," said Emerson.

"Thank you. In the meantime, I'm going to Bhavani's and Jia's," said Tem.

"But Jia's at work and Bhavani is pissed off at you. She's liable to let you die," chuckled Emerson.

"Ha ha very funny Unc," said Tem sarcastically. "That might be true, but that would greatly reduce her property value, so I know she's not going to let that happen," said Tem.

Emerson bust out laughing, "See, you're getting more creative by the minute. I'll let you know how Mye and our conversation goes."

"Good luck Unc because you're gonna need it," said Tem.

***

Mye was in her downtown office straightening her office after her last client for the day. She called Truman on speaker phone.

"Hey Truman," said Mye.

"You know I hate talking on the phone. Before you start, did you ask yourself if this could be an email?" asked Truman.

"No, shut up and listen. I'm going to tell Emerson today," said Mye.

Truman perked up, "About the divorce or about-"

"Everything. I'm going to tell him about everything," said Mye.

"Ok," said Truman.

"That's it? No slick remarks? No, you lying Mye? Nothing?" asked Mye.

"Nope. I believe you. You are not acting like the Mye I used to know. You are owning your shit. Using your voice. On your 20 year anniversary you told your husband you wanted a divorce, straight yanked the nipple out of Tem's mouth with no notice on the day he almost died and ran around all day Monday with no shoes on. You're a wild woman. I love it!" yelled Truman.

Mye chuckled.

"Just know that when you tell Emerson, he is going to disappoint you. He couldn't handle the old docile

Mye, so he damn sure can't handle this one. However, I think that it's a conversation that needs to be had. It's an "L" that you need to take," Truman said.

"What do you mean?" said Mye.

"I don't know much about L's because I'm a winner, but I've heard that sometimes that W you are looking for is behind that L you are not trying to take. Have this conversation with Emerson, take it on the chin and move on with your life. That way, you can finally close a chapter that has been opened for like 20 something years," said Truman.

"That was good Truman. I think my psychology skills are rubbing off on you. Have you thought about doing some counseling or coaching?" asked Mye.

"Of course not! I don't like people, and FYI, this conversation could have been an email. Goodbye," said Truman as he hung up the phone.

Mye opened her office door and walked over to Kara.

"Hey Kara I'm going to stay late and do some work here, you can go ahead and leave for the day," said Mye.

"It's noon doc. I don't mind staying here with you. I was only about to go home and do some homework. I can stay and do that here. I don't mind," said Kara.

Mye appreciated the offer. She knew Kara was still a little shaken up by the incident earlier that month and didn't want to leave her alone.

"It's okay Kara. Thank you, but I'll be fine," said Mye.

"I don't know," said Kara just as Emerson came running through the doors.

"Is everything okay Emerson?" asked Mye.

"Yeah, I just thought I might have missed you," he said to Mye.

"Hey Kara," said Emerson.

Kara smiled, "Hey Dr. Birch," she said, "I was just leaving, but it was good seeing you."

Kara walked passed Emerson with a big smile, and when she opened the glass door, she winked at Mye and mouthed, "Get yours!" and then went down the steps.

Emerson was wearing Mye's favorite cologne and looked delicious in his tailored suit.

"Just the man I wanted to see," said Mye as she flashed a big smile. "Step into my office."

Emerson followed Mye to her office and couldn't help but watch her hips as they swayed in her emerald green bodycon dress. Her dress matched her eyes perfectly. Her hair was big, bouncy, and curly. He walked in the trail of her natural scent and was instantly aroused. He did his best to position himself before Mye turned around to sit in her chair. He sat on the couch across from her and placed his briefcase on his lap. She smiled at him making him feel like she was reading his mind. This made Emerson blush a little.

"So Em, what brings you here?" asked Mye.

"Oh no, you first. What I have to say can wait," said Emerson.

Mye got up and walked over to her bookcase and grabbed a box. She opened the box and pulled out a picture. She traced the picture with her finger as she walked back to Emerson and sat beside him. She gave him the picture. He took it and noticed that the picture was of the two of them, him 17 and her 14 under the sycamore tree outside of their high school. In the picture he was standing with Mye on his back with her legs wrapped around his waist and her arms wrapped around his neck. Mye's hair was in a big curly ponytail on top of her head, and she had the biggest most beautiful smile he'd ever seen.

Holding that picture took Emerson back to that very day. He remembered everything about that day. Emotions flooded him but he did his best to keep his composure. That's the day he asked Mye to the homecoming dance.

It was Autumn of 1993, and it was Emerson's first day back to school since the bee sting. Everyone was wishing him well and saying they couldn't wait for him to get back on the field. After school, he went to Mye's writing spot by the sycamore tree to wait for her. She would often write and walk which was a dangerous combination. Emerson stood right in front of Mye and let her walk into him. She would say she hated when he did that, and then they would play fight for a minute or two; then she would sit under the tree and write. Emerson would usually study beside her, but that day was different. This day he sat on top of her legs as she sat with her legs crossed and he didn't move. Mye laughed and tried to get him to move, and when he wouldn't, she just wrapped her legs around him and kept writing.

Emerson knew right then and there that he didn't want to be anywhere else but with Mye. She was only a freshman, but they had 6 out of 8 classes together. She was gorgeous, and she saved his life. With his back to Mye, Emerson handed Mye a note over his shoulder.

It read: Will you go to the homecoming dance with me? Yes No Maybe.

Emerson could feel Mye writing on his back and then she handed the note back to him, and he saw she circled, "Yes." Emerson was so excited that he stood up with Mye on his back and he spun her around as she laughed hysterically.

"Emerson, Emerson," said Mye bringing Emerson back to reality. "Do you remember this day?" she asked.

"Who took this picture?" he asked.

"I don't know," shrugged Mye. "I guess someone from the yearbook committee. I found this picture in our high school yearbook," she added. "Do you remember this day," she asked.

"Vaguely," he said lying.

Mye squinted her eyes. She could always tell when he was lying.

"I mean yes. I remember. I remember it fairly well," admitted Emerson. "What's this all about?"

Mye took a deep breath.

"How did you feel that day? The day this picture was taken," said Mye handing him the picture.

Mye grabbed the other end of the picture as Emerson was holding it and a surge of loving energy ran through his body. He let go of the picture quickly.

"Well," she asked.

Emerson stuttered, "I felt... I felt... I felt like I could do anything. I felt like I could conquer the world with you by my side."

Mye grabbed his hands, and they sat down together on the couch. With his hands in hers, she said, "Me too.

And I want that feeling, from that day, every day, with you."

Emerson stood up and walked over to the other side of the office.

"Hold up Mye. What are you saying?" he asked.

"I'm saying I'm ready for whatever," said Mye.

Mye stared at the back of Emerson's head waiting for him to turn around or say something.

She continued, "We've created great lives for ourselves Em, so we know we have the authority and power to create whatever kind of life we want. Let me be true to you and you true to me. We are the real deal. We've loved each other before riches, degrees, kids, -

"Spouses," he added as he turned around.

"Yes. We loved each other before we loved our spouses," she said.

"We've put so much before us. Yes, we have our little lunch dates, but I don't just want a dose of you. I want all of you," said Mye as she walked towards Emerson. Emerson backed away.

"You're married Mye," he said.

"I'm getting a divorce. William hasn't been in the house for months, and all of his belongings were removed from the house last weekend," said Mye.

"Mye what are you saying? What are you doing? You are ruining us! We had a great thing going. I told you things I haven't shared with anyone. Was this your plan? Did you throw me that huge birthday party to butter me up for this?" asked Emerson.

Mye was shocked and taken back, "Wait, what?" she said.

"Who throws someone a huge 41st birthday party? That's an odd number," said Emerson.

"I threw you that party because you are my best friend and it pained me to see how your wife completely ignored your 40th birthday," said Mye.

"My wife. That's right my wife. I have a wife, Mye. What would people say? Huh? I can't just leave my wife and run off with the woman I love. I have responsibilities. We have reputations Mye. Life is more than just you and I. We affect many people around us," he said.

Mye said, "I've been putting everyone else's well being before mine, and that stopped about a week ago. I don't care what anyone thinks about my decisions. I love me, and I'm being honest about what I want."

"Now that you've found yourself, you're caught up in your feelings and putting me in a sticky predicament," said Emerson.

"I'm not caught up in my feelings Emerson. I'm just telling you how I feel. I needed to do this for me. I needed to stop using energy dreaming about what if when I could just ask you for myself," she said.

"Well, now you have your answer at the expense of my feelings. Are you still going to divorce your husband?" he asked.

"Hell yeah! I've embarrassed myself enough. It was easier to pretend in the beginning, but now everyone knows he's stepping out on me. Look, I'm sincerely sorry that I've made you feel anything short of amazing. That was not my intention. However, I needed to express myself, and I'm happy that I did because now I can close a chapter that has been open for over 2 decades," said Mye.

Emerson's heart dropped. He didn't want Mye to close the chapter completely. He wasn't saying that he didn't want to be with Mye. It was just that he couldn't be with Mye under these circumstances. Emerson was a good boy, and he always chose doing the "good thing" over doing what he genuinely wanted to do.

"What was I supposed to do with this information Mye? Go divorce my wife and be with you?" asked Emerson.

"What do you want to do Emerson? Inside your heart, what do you genuinely want to do?" she asked.

Emerson thought to himself for a moment.

"To be frank Emerson, I did think you would divorce your wife, but not for me. You and I are in the same boat, and I honestly thought that this could have been the nudge to get you to give her the walking papers," said Mye as she reached for her make-up pallet in her purse.

"What are you talking about? You're divorcing your husband because he's a serial cheater and sorry to say, but everyone knows it. No one would question you for your decision. That's not the case with me. My wife and I have issues, but cheating isn't one of them," said Emerson.

Mye stopped powdering her nose and looked Emerson in the eye and said, "And to think, all of this time I thought you were pretending not to see like me, but you honestly don't know," said Mye.

"Know what?" said Emerson.

"We are one in the same Emerson. The only difference is my husband cheats down and your wife apparently, cheats up," said Mye as she tossed her makeup back in her bag.

***

Emerson called his wife as he was leaving Mye's office. A million and one thoughts were racing through his head. His wife worked the overnight shift, so Emerson figured she was at home asleep. He rushed home to find his wife up wide awake entertaining a male visitor.

"Oh hi Emerson," said Delilah looking a little flustered as she got up from the dining room table. "You're home early," she said. Delilah noticed Emerson looking at her guest suspiciously. "This is councilman Allen. He's running for mayor," she said proudly.

"I was just in the neighborhood sharing my plan for the city," said the councilman, "well, I should be going. It was nice meeting you Dr. Birch," said the councilman.

"I'll show you the way out," said Delilah. Emerson noticed how Delilah's shirt wasn't buttoned properly and the councilman's pants were unzipped. When Delilah came back around the corner, Emerson just stared at her.

"How was your meeting with Mye?" she asked trying to divert the attention from herself.

"Everyone knows Delilah," said Emerson.

She stood there frozen. This affair had been going on for nearly 6 months, and she had to admit that she was starting to get sloppy. It wasn't that she didn't love Emerson. She did. She just wasn't in love with him. Emerson wasn't a risk taker. In fact, Delilah thought he was downright boring. She wanted someone with some ambition and excitement. She wanted a man going somewhere.

"Everyone knows what Emerson?" asked Delilah trying to play coy. "Everyone knows you turned down the Chief position twice!" she yelled.

She caught Emerson slightly off guard. He wondered how she knew.

"I work in the hospital too Emerson. Word travels around. How could you turn down the position without even talking to me?" she asked. "Why are you so afraid of growing?" she added.

Emerson sat down at the dining room table with his head in his hands.

"Why don't you just be with him?" Emerson asked. "Why cheat? Why not just divorce me and be with him if that's where you truly want to be?

Delilah responded, "Why don't you just be with Mye? Why just settle for a couple of dates a month when you can be with her every day?" asked Delilah.

"Because I'm married to you Delilah!" he snapped. He got up and walked up to her and got eye level. "I'm not with Mye because I married you," he said. Then he headed towards the stairs to go to their master bedroom.

Delilah followed him up the stairs. "Why are you still married to me?" she asked. Emerson took off his jacket and started unbuttoning his shirt.

"I'm married to you because I don't believe in getting a divorce," he said. "I'm a good Jewish boy, and I simply can't file divorce papers, and I also can't cheat on you, which is why I'm still married to you," he added. By now Emerson was standing only in his t-shirt and boxers.

Delilah couldn't pretend not to notice how fine her husband was. His body was impeccable, but she was still upset at his reason for being married to her. Even though she was in the wrong, she still expected him to fight for her. Instead, he did what he always did and retreated. He was never one who was up for a challenge.

"I'm about to take a shower and go grab an early dinner," he said this time standing completely naked. "Don't wait up for me. Do me one better. Don't be here when I get back," he said before closing the bathroom door behind him.

***

Alex opened the door for Mye. She got in the car and avoided eye contact with Truman.

"It was that bad huh?" asked Truman.

"I sent you an email," she replied. "Do you have the files for me to review?" she asked.

"Now that's boss," said Truman as he handed her some files.

CHAPTER NINE

NAME THAT FEELING

Jia and Bhavani went to Mye's house to drop off Kiam. Bhavani was smiling at her phone.

"Who are you smiling at? I'm not texting you," said Jia.

"It's just Wayne," said Bhavani. "What do you think of him," she asked.

"I don't know Bhavani. He seems ok, I guess," said Jia. "I've never seen you like this over a guy before," she added.

Jia's phone vibrated, and she looked at it and smiled.

"Oh no. That's not me texting you. Why are you so happy?" Bhavani mocked her.

Jia laughed. "Whatever. It's Tem," said Jia. Bhavani rolled her eyes.

"A, I didn't roll my eyes at Wayne," said Jia.

"Well yeah because Wayne ain't Tem," said Bhavani. "Tem is so immature. He has so much growing up to do, and you know this."

Jia knew she was telling the truth, but she wanted to believe that he'd change.

"Look Bhavani, after the accident Tem changed. He's different now," said Jia trying to convince herself.

"You don't even believe that," said Bhavani. "Whatever change you think you see is just temporary. He's one of those people with hard heads. He's a slow learner," she added.

"Look Bhavani, you do you and I'll do me, alright," Jia said walking out of the kitchen.

Kiam came running down the hall into Jia.

"I'm sorry Jia," he said. "I like your tutu! Can you do a ballerina dance?" asked Kiam.

Jia just came from teaching dance at the local community center, so she was tired, but it was hard to say no to Kiam, so she said, "I would love to, but I don't have any music."

"No worries Kiam! Bhavani to the rescue!" said Bhavani as she ran to the piano with Kiam hot on her heels. In walked Wayne as Kiam was running down the hall. Jia eyed him up and down as he walked into the house.

"Hi, I'm Wayne," he said extending his hand.

"I know who you are," Jia said unamused, "so do you just walk into everyone's house?" she added.

"No, the mechanic told me I could come in," he replied.

"Damn you, George," she whispered under her breath.

"Come on Jia!" yelled Kiam.

Everyone went to the living room. Bhavani was warming up on the piano.

"We have to stretch first Jia. Safety first!" said Kiam.

Bhavani looked up and saw Wayne.

"Hey Wayne, we are about to put on a little show for Kiam. You can stay and watch if you want," said Bhavani.

Bhavani was giving this Toni Braxton look. The look from her debut album with the short cut dark brown hair, dark red maroon lips, high waist jeans, with a white t-shirt and a leather jacket. Wayne couldn't believe how gorgeous she looked in everything.

"What are you about to play Bhavani?" asked Jia.

"Ummm... let me think. Oh! I'm going to play 'You are my Sunshine,' but I'm going to switch up the lyrics." Bhavani looked at Kiam and asked, "Is that okay with you?"

"Yes!" yelled Kiam.

"Good. Do it slowly because I'm already tired," said Jia as she got in position and Kiam pulled up his chair.

"Ready when you are," Jia said.

Bhavani began to play the piano while Jia started to dance.

Tem walked in while all of this was happening and was instantly entranced by Jia's dancing, while Wayne hung on to every word Bhavani sang.

What is this feeling?

This funny feeling,

That makes me happy,

On rainy days,

You can't imagine,

How much I need it

Please don't take this feeling away.

Then Jia put her hands over her head onto the piano and did a back walkover onto it. Kiam was clapping hysterically, and Tem was trying to contain his excitement, but he couldn't stop cheesing.

Wayne shook his head yes as if responding to Bhavani's proclamation and Tem was mesmerized by Jia's dancing. The fellas were doing their best to control themselves, but the energy in the room was electrifying.

In walked Mye, "Are you dancing on my Shadd 9'3" concert grand piano Jia?" she asked.

"Not at all G-ma," she replied sliding off of the piano.

Kiam was standing on his chair screaming, "Yay! Good job everybody! AG you missed it!"

"Chairs are for butts not feet," said Mye. Kiam laughed as he got down from the chair.

"AG said butts," he whispered loudly to Wayne while trying to control his amusement.

"What are you doing here Tem?" asked Mye.

"Ok Ma," said Tem in defeat, "you got it. I'm out," he added as he started walking to the front door.

"Wait up," said Jia as she followed him out.

"Dr. Hart-" said Wayne.

"Mye. It's Mye," said Mye.

"Ok, Dr. Mye," said Wayne. Bhavani chuckled.

"Do you mind if I take Kiam around back to shoot some hoops?" Wayne asked.

Mye looked confused, "Well, of course, you could, but we don't have a basketball court back there."

"Um yes we do," said Bhavani enthusiastically. "It's a half court but to scale," she added.

Kiam tugged at his brother's shirt and whispered loudly, "Just call her Ma. See," pointing to Mye. "Doesn't she look just like her. She looks just like the pictures! Don't we look alike?" smiled Kiam to his big brother.

It was hard for Wayne to be around Mye. It made him a little emotional. She reminded him so much of his mother physically, but Mye's energy was way stronger. More intense than his mother's ever was. His mother was more timid but sweet. Mye was direct yet gentle and had this way of commanding attention and respect with few words. Memories of his mother had been flooding back since he met Mye, and it was like an emotional rollercoaster for him.

Fighting back a tear Wayne said, "Yeah, you guys do look alike," kneeling down to his little brother's eye level. "She does look like mom," he said looking up at Mye. Wayne stood up and chuckled, "Yeah, dad clearly had a type."

Kiam added, "Yeah… beautiful," he smiled.

"Let's go outside Kiam," said Wayne as he grabbed his brother's hand.

"Can Bhavani come?" ask Kiam.

Wayne looked Bhavani in the eye and said, "If I had my way, I would never leave her side. Of course, she is welcomed to join us."

Mye sipped her tea as she watched a beautiful love affair began to unfold.

Bhavani replied, "No, it's ok Kiam. You guys need guy time. Guy time is important. I'll be here when you're finished."

"You promise?" said Wayne and Kiam in unison.

Bhavani laughed, "Yes, I promise."

Bhavani walked the guys to the kitchen door. After the boys left out, Bhavani leaned on the door and smiled to herself as she walked to the stove to make some tea.

"Bhavani," said Mye in between sips.

"I know what you're gonna say Ma, and no it's not like that between Wayne and I. We are just friends," said Bhavani as she dipped the tea infuser in the hot water.

Mye said, "What I was gonna say was you don't live here child. Stop adding stuff to my house. First a spiral slide around the staircase and now a basketball court. Remember, you don't live here woman," chuckled Mye as she left the kitchen and went to her bedroom.

Bhavani stayed in the kitchen daydreaming about Wayne. She went to the kitchen window to take a peek and see what Wayne and Kiam were doing, making eye contact with Wayne by mistake. She couldn't look away quickly because she wasn't a punk. She was determined to make him look away first. He never did. He just played basketball with Kiam while looking at her, almost seemingly putting on a show for her. He looked at her as if she was all that mattered in the world. She giggled as she looked away, "What's going on with me?" she said as she walked out of the kitchen.

"Hey Ma," said Bhavani as she walked into her mother's bedroom. Mye had oversized gold headphones on while typing on her laptop. Bhavani walked over to her mother's California king bed and flopped down. Mye looked up and lifted her finger while saying "One-second sweetie." Bhavani picked up her mom's phone and noticed she was listening to her "Champ" playlist. Mye

stopped typing, closed her laptop and pulled her headphones around her neck.

"What's up little lady?" smiled Mye, "how can I be of
service?" said Mye as she moved her laptop aside and
placed her headphones on top of them.

"You've been listening to this Champ playlist more
than usual. Walking around humming and smiling," said
Bhavani.

Mye shrugged her shoulders, "You know, it makes me
feel good. It takes me to a good place," said Mye as she
motioned for Bhavani to hand her the phone. Mye took
her phone and put it on her laptop. "When you feel
good, you can make better decisions. You can see things
clearer, and from different perspectives," added Mye.

"Yeah, but why now? Why are you listening to it so
much now? All this time I thought Champ was some
sort of allegory or metaphor or something. I peeped
how you pulled out this playlist when dad made you
mad. Almost pretending some knight and shining armor
would come save you from him," said Bhavani.

Mye was shocked by how observant her daughter
was. She threw a pillow at her and Bhavani ducked only
to catch a second pillow to the face. They both laughed.

"It's not my business Ma, but for whatever it's worth,
you deserve better. Don't put up with any kind of abuse
on my account, and Tem's an idiot, so he doesn't count,"
said Bhavani.

Mye wasn't sure how much her daughter knew and
surprisingly her words lifted a weight Mye didn't even
know she was carrying.

"Thank you," said Mye.

"Now back to this Champ guy. Do Kiam and Wayne remind you of him? Champ? Is that why you keep playing this Champ playlist?" asked Bhavani.

Mye's heart began to race at the mention of Champ's name. However, externally she kept her composure. Mye had a killer poker face.

"I know you didn't come in here to ask me about my choice in music. So what's up?" asked Mye.

"No, you're right. Ummm, I came by to ask you about Wayne," said Bhavani. Mye perked up and motioned for Bhavani to come closer tapping the bed beside her.

"Ok, tell me more," said Mye.

"Well, maybe it's not about Wayne but men in general," said Bhavani. Mye smiled with her hands clasped resting her chin on them.

"Why are you acting like that? All excited and extra interested?" asked Bhavani.

"You're 17, and you've never asked me about a guy before," said Mye.

"What? Did you think I was gay?" asked Bhavani.

"Nope, but if you were, I wouldn't care. I'm just happy that you are feeling something for someone. You had a hemispherectomy done when you were 3-"

"Ma that was nearly 15 years ago, I'm about to be 18 in a few months," interrupted Bhavani.

"I know your birthday, I was there. Sweetie after your surgery, you had a severe loss of emotional attachment. You were like a kid robot who wasn't programed for empathy or compassion. Very logical in your understanding and approach to life. I low-key thought I was raising a sociopath," said Mye.

"Ha, ha, ha," laughed Bhavani, "you are being so extra right now Ma," said Bhavani.

"I'm serious. I was concerned that you would have difficulty empathizing with people which makes it difficult to love people. And baby, what is a life without love? So I figured if I could somehow teach you to love yourself. If you could understand self-love and the unconditionalness of it, then you would be able to love others at least the way you love yourself. You would be your point of reference of what love is and what it feels like. Over time you started to build your emotional connections back with Tara, Tem and Jia, then John, which pissed your dad off, then your dad, then me," said Mye.

"Why did it take so long to connect with you? I remember you doing everything for me," said Bhavani.

"I don't know. I think you thought I was your servant or something. I don't know," said Mye.

"Ma you are making this stuff up!" laughed Bhavani, "you should have checked me."

"No, I'm not making this up. You were always very direct and intentional with your words. Something I never was. I never wanted you to lose that, so I allowed you to boss me around a little. Jia was my little bodyguard though. She would check you for me," said Mye.

"Yeah, that sounds like Jia, and she's still checking me," said Bhavani.

"That's good. We need friends to help keep us aligned. But babes that's why I'm so excited about this talk about Wayne," Mye said clapping her hands. "Loving friends and family that's supported you for years is a little different than loving a person who was a complete stranger only a couple of weeks ago."

"Hold up Ma; no one said anything about love. I don't know if I love him. I mean I only love like a couple of people. And I trust even less, but that's what I wanted to talk to you about. I feel like I can trust Wayne like I trust you, but that's stupid because I barely know him. So I've stopped talking to him as much, and I'm keeping my distance because I'm feeling all stupid inside."

"So if you've made up your mind, then why are you here?" asked Mye.

"Cause of Jia! She said I was being stupid for thinking I was being stupid. She doesn't really care for Wayne, but she does believe I should trust myself and I should never stop trusting myself," said Bhavani.

Mye laughed.

Bhavani added, "Jia told me that if I was falling in love with him then that's a beautiful thing if he meets the 3 requirements all potential life partners need. And then I asked her, what are the 3 requirements and then she was like, ask your mother. Soooo, that's why I'm here. I need to know what are the 3 requirements all potential life partners need and why do I feel so stupid."

Mye replied, "That stupid feeling you feel is less stupidity and more illogical reasoning. Logic and observation plays a huge part in how you in particular love. You love and care in a logical manner. What you've observed from myself, John's, and Jia's actions is how you come to the conclusion that we love you and you love us. The way we are taught to love is in a very conditional manner in general which doesn't help. But to love a significant other is different. How you've come to feel how you feel about Wayne is a combination of observation and feeling. This feeling is energy, a vibration. When you are on the same energetic frequency as another, it can make a complete stranger feel like someone you've known for years," said Mye.

"So if I feel this way then this means I love him and we are supposed to be together?" asked Bhavani.

"No, of course not, don't be silly. It's a feeling, which is good. It's an indicator that you two could possibly be more. Now it's time to use your logical side and further evaluate this person and your feelings, which brings us to the 3 requirements of a potential life partner," said Mye.

Bhavani sat up straight and attentive as her mother spoke.

"A potential life partner should be appreciative, want to be kept, and want to grow into their best self. First, they should be an appreciative person. Appreciation is closely related to gratitude. An appreciative person does a better job at seeing the brighter side of things than an unappreciative person. Second, they have to want to be kept. The person has to want to be involved in a relationship with you. All parties must be on the same page regarding relationship terms, being it's monogamous, polygamous or what have you. If you want an exclusive relationship, then you should be with a person who also wants an exclusive relationship with you. And last but not least, they should want to grow into their optimum self. Everything alive is either growing or dying. Your partner should want to not only grow but grow towards a better version of themselves and not just want to acquire more things," said Mye.

Bhavani said, "Well, if Wayne is all of those things, then he is a good potential life partner?"

"Yes. Now you have to check yourself to see if you're maturing into a woman who is vibrationally aligned with that type of man," responded Mye.

"Whenever your love finds you, remember you still reserve the right to move at your own pace. There's no right or wrong way to do this thing called life. However, you either walk according to your inner guidance system, or you're just existing. Always stay true and honest to yourself lady," smiled Mye.

CHAPTER TEN

GOOD MAN

One of the guards gave the warden the latest numbers on the D.O.P. therapy program.

"Damn it! She is killing me with this program!" yelled the warden. Prisoners are doing whatever it takes to meet her requirements for the program. Fights are down. This is terrible. We are not going to get the extension added if things keep going as good as they are."

"Cut off the funding," said a guard.

"The program is free. Her and that lawyer do everything pro bono, and I've been trying to get you idiots to break Tank, and you continue to fail me! He has the worst temper. He was our problem boy. Now he's changing. If this program fixes him, then I'll have a hell of a time getting her out of here," said the warden.

A guard said, "He's doing whatever it takes to get his daughter back."

The warden perked up, "Oh really. Tell me more about his daughter. How long is her wrap sheet? Which juvy is she in?"

The guard replied, "She's 5. She attends Dr. Hart's school. Her mother's boyfriend was recently arrested for molesting her. The mother gave up custody of her daughter, so now she's a ward of the state."

The warden looked perplexed, "Well, how did the mother lose custody? Was she selling her daughter or something?" he asked.

The guard replied, "No sir. The mother took the side of her boyfriend and accused her daughter of lying. She voluntarily relinquished custody."

"That's cold. Good for business nonetheless. There is no bigger funnel to the prison system than foster care. As long as families ignore each other and neighbors turn a blind eye, we will always have a job," laughed the warden.

"They say it takes a village," added the guard.

"And it's true… and the more dysfunctional the village, the more lucrative this industry becomes. Forget Bitcoin. Longevity is in prison stocks. Mark my words. All you have to do is take the dad away; families begin falling apart, then communities start falling apart and so on. Keep the disaster quarantined with real estate prices and use property taxes to fund the neighborhood schools. That's how you can legally segregate education. The system is genius I tell you! With our lobbyist and now a proven successful businessman as president, we will see huge gains in this industry. I'm telling you. Buy your stocks now," said the warden.

Another guard entered the room. "Sir, Edward Mane called and left another message. He wants to see the latest report for the D.O.P. program. Do you want me to send it over?" asked the guard.

"No! Not yet," the warden yelled. "He wants my job so bad. He is Mye's biggest advocate. He wants to reform the prison system and how we run it. Rehabilitation, trade skills, business class, etc. Why would we do that?! This is a business! We are in the business of housing prisoners, not making valuable citizens."

The guard interjected, "Excuse me sir, but Edward Mane wanted me to tell you that if you don't send him the report, then he will be forced to come get it."

"Screw him!" yelled the warden as he knocked all of the papers off the desk. He hung his head in frustration then lifted it slowly with a devilish grin.

"Find out what prison that kid's molester is in and do whatever you got to do to get him transferred here. I'll get Tank to snap one way or another and be done with Mye and Edward for good. Talk about killing two birds with one stone," laughed the warden.

***

"Mom! Dad!" yelled Emerson as he walked into his parent's house. He placed his keys and briefcase on the front table and hung his coat in the closet. He preceded to jog upstairs to his parent's room.

"Wait!" yelled his mom, "here we come," she added.

He went back down the stairs to grab something to drink from the kitchen. His mother came downstairs in a silk cobalt blue long robe with matching slippers with fur on them. She had the smoothest dark chocolate skin with curly thick grey shoulder-length hair. Petite standing only at 5'2" yet she always managed to command the attention of a room with her presence. Her laugh was infectious, and smile was perfect. She was a perfect balance of poise and bluntness. A woman who could speak her mind without being offensive and now he needed her blunt honesty more than ever.

"Hey baby," she said as she kissed him on the cheek. "What brings you over without a call or text? It must be serious," she said as she put some water in the kettle.

"That key is for emergencies son. So this better be an emergency," said his dad as he walked into the kitchen. Emerson's dad was husky about 6'2" with a full neatly groomed salt and pepper beard. He always wore his yamaka. He was hairy, but it couldn't hide his pale skin. You could see his pot belly pushing against his two-piece pajama set that perfectly matched his mother's robe. Emerson's dad walked behind his mom and slid his hand in her robe.

"Stop it," she said playfully, "I think Emerson has something serious to discuss."

Emerson admired the love his parents had for each other. He couldn't think of a time when his father didn't adore his mother. Emerson had grown accustomed to his parent's display of affections and wish he had someone in his life that made him feel like his ma made his dad feel.

"Two minutes Emerson. Then you gotta go," said his dad as he slapped his mom on the butt.

"Senior, stop it," said his mom playfully. "Go ahead, baby. Talk to us," said his mom as she handed a cup of tea to her husband.

"Be quick son. You got about 20 minutes before this pill kicks in," said his dad.

Emerson shook his head in disgust as he tried to find the right words. He had been going back and forth in his mind trying to figure out what his next move would be. He has a great relationship with his parents, and he knew they wouldn't steer him wrong, but he just didn't know where to begin.

"Well, spit it out boy," said his mom as she sat down on his father's lap.

"19 minutes," his dad said.

Emerson took a deep breath and said, "Mye came on to me. I mean really hard. Talking about us being together, us leaving our spouses and just living life for us and-"

"Yesssss!" screamed his mom as she jumped up and down holding her robe closed. "You're finally leaving the one I hate for the one I love! Yes! This is great news. I'm so happy for you guys. Mye dropped off my prescription yesterday and made no mention of it," said his mom slightly confused. "Well, it doesn't matter. I'm just happy for you. Mye is going through her divorce now, so the sooner you get yours started, the better. Actually, a legal separation would work in the meantime," she added.

Emerson was frozen in shock. His father stood up and put his cup in the sink.

"That was some good tea. Congratulations son. Mye has a special place in both your mother and our hearts. She's been there for you and us for years. Consider yourself lucky son. She was almost the one who got away. I think it's about that time baby," said his dad as he walked up behind his mom.

"Well, son. It's been a pleasure talking to you and congratulations on your new love affair. Your father and I have some affairs of our own to take care of upstairs," said his mom as she walked out of the kitchen with her husband right behind her.

Emerson watched his parents leave the kitchen confused by what he just heard.

He yelled, "No!" as his parents were going up the stairs.

"No what?" asked his mom.

"I said no to Mye. I can't just divorce my wife and get with Mye," he added. "I mean I couldn't then, but maybe I can now?" he said confused while rubbing the back of his neck.

"Now I'm confused," said his father, "why can't you divorce your wife and marry Mye?"

"Dad what do you mean? It's not right! You can't do that. Marriage is til death. I mean look at you two. 40 plus years and you still excite each other," said Emerson.

Emerson's father replied, "Because we like each other Emerson. We have more common interest than most couples. So many people marry people they don't even know that they don't even like. They grow to love and care for the person genuinely, but they don't like them. You should pick your spouse like you would pick a business partner with a common mission, vision, and goal. Making sure that you like them because that's what keeps you growing together."

Emerson said, "Everyone can't take a 3-week trip to Egypt and find the love of his life dad. You got lucky."

His dad walked down the stairs to get eye level with him. "Emerson, I was married when I met your mom in Egypt."

"And I was engaged when I met your dad," said his mom.

Emerson was shocked. He never knew that.

His dad said, "Neither of our significant others wanted to go to Egypt and it was by coincidence that we both went alone and were staying in the same hotel. It was the best 3 weeks of my life," he added grabbing his wife by the waist pulling her close. "When we got back to the states, I filed for a divorce and she called off her engagement."

Emerson walked to the living room and sat on the couch trying to process all of this information.

"Son listen to me. You've made me so proud. You've never given your mom and I any trouble, but don't you think it's finally time to start living according to how you feel in here?" said his father pointing to Emerson's heart. "It's true that sometimes when you are true to yourself, you will break a few rules, but I promise you it's worth it," said his father.

"Your dad and I aren't a conventional looking couple. I mean seriously, he wears a yamaka and I wear a cross, I'm black he's white, and we have a son darker than me. You should have heard the whispers. Our families didn't speak to us for a few years, but I didn't care. Being in your father's arms is like having heaven right here on earth," said his mom.

"And I wouldn't have changed anything for the world," his father said as he kissed his wife's forehead. "Everyone eventually got with the program and moved to gossiping about someone else," he added.

"And don't worry about Jia baby," said his mom. "She's nearly grown, doesn't even live at home and she's understanding. Besides, she loves Mye probably more than us all."

"Son, your mother and I stand behind you in whatever decision you make," said his father.

Emerson's mom asked him, "If you weren't married, would you ask Mye to marry you?"

Emerson paused and thought about his mom's question. Him and Mye both got married early and while he loved her he never really thought about them getting married because he knew it wasn't possible.

"Leave her alone then, Emerson," said his mom as she crossed her arms. "Mye is a wonderful woman and I'm glad you turned her down. You aren't even sure if you love her or just the idea of being with her," she added.

Emerson was quiet. His mother was right. Mye could be intense sometimes and that scared him. Mye was very ambitious and pushed him to do more. She didn't speak to him for a week after he turned the Chief Physician job down for the second time. She was disappointed not because he turned the job down but because of his reasoning. Mye had a way of pulling the best out of people and sometimes Emerson just wanted to be the best amongst average people.

Emerson's dad said, "Look, son, sometimes it can seem that you like to be the big fish in a small pond. However, if you go and pursue Mye, she will constantly urge you to go explore deeper waters. She will help take you to new heights. If you are not ready or don't desire that type of growth, then I don't think you should pursue Mye."

His mother said, "This conversation is practically null and void. The chances you'll even get the girl is slim. The poor woman poured her soul out to you and you shut her down; because of your cheating wife who is screwing a councilman by the way."

Emerson looked surprised and embarrassed.

"When you get to this social status, your circles get smaller, and everyone knows everything. The crazy part about it is that the councilman is screwing every desperate housewife in town. Anyways, you shut Mye down because you're scared baby. Scared to fail, scared to grow, just scared to walk into a new life where you don't have all of the answers. It's my fault though. I praised you so much for being good that I raised a man who doesn't know how to be genuine," said his mom in defeat.

His father grabbed his wife tight, "Oh no baby. It's not your fault our son has small balls," he said.

"Senior," laughed his mom.

His dad added, "Look son. When I was young, I too had small balls, but then I met your mother. She was the greatest thing that happened to me. She pushed me and helped me to grow myself and my business. I was afraid at first but as long as I had her by my side, I knew I could do anything," his father said as he kissed his mother.

"Look son, go get your girl and work overtime, triple time, to win her back. Do whatever to get in her good graces. You can do it only if you are willing to put in the work," his father added.

Emerson felt the wind get knocked out of him with some hard truths. He sat for a while not saying anything. He knew he had to do something but didn't know exactly what.

"Thanks mom and dad. I guess I have some things to consider. Carry on with your day. Sorry for coming over unannounced," said Emerson as he hugged his parents and left the house.

Emerson's dad followed his wife up the stairs and asked, "Sweetie, what do you think Emerson is about to do next?" She turned around and replied, "Nothing. Absolutely nothing."

***

Mye and Truman were on their way to Truman's Law office when his phone rang. He answered it and said, "Speak quickly."

"Something is about to go down today. The warden put in a request to have Tank's daughter's molester transferred here. He's trying to do whatever it takes to keep Tank here and to shut you guys down," the lady said.

"Thank you. I'll take care of it from here," he said as he hung up the phone. "Alex change of plans. We need to get to the jail as soon as possible," Truman said.

"What's going on?" asked Mye.

"It's about Tank," he said.

"We got the appeal?" Mye asked excitedly.

Truman gave her the side eye with a confused look. "Of course he got the appeal. I'm his lawyer. I get what I want," he said.

Mye chuckled at Truman's arrogance, but she couldn't argue with him. He was that good.

"I need you to talk to Tank because he's about to confront his biggest challenge yet," said Truman.

"What's that?" asked Mye.

Truman replied, "His daughter's molester."

***

"Edward, Paul, what a pleasant surprise," said the warden.

"I told you I was coming today," said Edward.

"And you asked me to come," said Paul from the Appeal Board, slightly confused. "What's going on?" he added.

"More importantly, where are the stats on the D.O.P. program?" asked Edward.

The warden said, "Look down there gentleman at the yard. You see those men. They are unfit to live in society, and so they live here. We take care of them to protect the rest of you from their criminal behavior. Take Wilbert for example right there in the corner doing push-ups. Many people affectionately call him Tank because of how he's built. Strong, solid, like an ox. He has arguably one of the worst tempers out of anyone here. He has been a problem."

"Are you that desperate warden James?" asked Mye as she interjected in his monologue. "Good day, Edward, Paul," said Mye as she shook their hands.

"What's going on?" asked Edward staring in utter confusion at the warden. "Stop stalling and give me the report!" he demanded.

From her peripheral vision, Mye saw a guard walk over to Tank and say something to him. No one could hear what the guard said since they were inside but it was clear that whatever he said made Tank furious. The warden smiled as he watched Tank start to walk slowly across the yard.

"Soon you will see why all of you are here," said the warden.

"You better call this off," demanded Mye.

"No!" the warden yelled. "Now everyone will see that your little program is nothing more than a distraction and false hope. These criminals cannot be rehabilitated. The best place for them is here. It's the best place for society!" he added.

"You called to specially request for his 5 year old daughter's molester to be sent here so that you could try to make me look bad? Are you so afraid of prison reform that you would stoop to this level?" asked Mye.

Mye's eyes darted from the warden to Tank back and forth over and over as Tank walked across the yard.

"I promise you warden, if Tank lays one finger on that man who molested his daughter, I will have you charged with psychological abuse and emotional harm, and I will win warden William James and it will open the floodgates for prison reform and propel it further than any program I could have created," said Mye

"Is that a threat Dr. Mye Hart?" snarled the warden.

"No Lil Dickey," she replied.

The warden was instantly pissed off. He hated the nick name the prisoners gave him. But no one ever had the courage to call him that to his face. Until now.

Mye added, "Think of it as a formal promise, a guarantee." Then she walked over to the glass and leaned on it. While looking out through the window whispering, "You got this Tank."

Everyone stood in silence as Tank finally approached his daughter's molester. Tension filled the room. Tank stood behind the molester as he sat not knowing what was coming. Tank was approximately 70 lbs larger than him and had so much rage and hatred in his eyes. No one warned the accuser of what was about to come. Molesters are amongst the lowest in the prison hierarchy. The yard was frozen still, and it seemed everyone was watching anticipating what was to come. It seemed as if everyone knew that the future of this prison and how it operated lied on the actions of this one man. Tank stood behind the man breathing hard. You could see his chest moving up and down, and his body was tensed, and both fists were clenched tight.

Mye whispered to herself, "Look to the sun, feel the heat on your skin, take a deep breath, in four counts, hold for two, absorb the sun's energy. Breathe out four counts, release the anger, release the guilt, release the shame. You got this Tank."

Tank closed his eyes, looked to the sun, and fell to his knees. This startled the guy he was standing behind causing him to jump up from his seat. Everyone was stunned. Tank cried loudly and released every built up emotion he was holding on to. He sobbed at the thought of his daughter being abused, the thought of him not being there to protect her, and the thought of not being able to comfort his daughter Bliss.

"Let it all out and leave it in the yard. Bliss needs you to be emotionally available to help her heal," said a soft woman's voice in Tank's right ear. Soft but ever so clear. Tank turned to see where the voice was coming from and looked up to the window and saw Mye smiling with her arms across her chest making an 'X.' He wiped his face with his arm and responded back with the same gesture.

"I've seen enough," said Edward with a clenched fist as he banged his hand on the wall beside him. "You've sunk to a new low Lil Dickey! I mean warden James," he said as he walked toward the warden. "You put an inmate in direct harm by having him moved to the prison of his victim's father. What if this Tank fellow beat him to death? Then what? You called us all here to witness a potential homicide! I've never been in a fist fight a day in my life, however, today you have pushed my limits! Prepare to start looking for a new job warden James because your days here are numbered! Mye I would like for you to present this program to the board. There is hope for these men and Tank's self-control in such a difficult environment confirms it. I'll be in touch," said Edward as he stormed out. Paul shook his head in disapproval at the warden as he exited behind Edward and gave Mye a wink and a smile.

CHAPTER ELEVEN

THE SINS OF THE FATHER

"Junior!" yelled William's mom as she opened the door and hugged him. "You look beautiful as always mom," he said.

She replied, "Oh that's thanks to my grand baby. Bhavani keeps me looking so nice. This is hand stitched, you know?" she added while she made different poses for her son. William chuckled to himself. His mother Dorothy Gene Hart was breathtaking, people close to her called her DD short for Dorothy Dandridge because she looked just like the actress. She's petite, fair skin, with dark brown big loose curly hair. Her smile was big, but her big brown eyes showed a hint of sadness no matter how much she tried to cover it up. She was only 58 years old but didn't look a day over 45. She married William's father on her 18th birthday, and he was 15 years her senior. Then she gave birth a week later. The only love she has ever known was William Senior.

"Mom, is dad here?" asked William as he handed his mother his coat.

"Yes, he is in his cigar room," she replied while hanging up his coat. William walked to the cigar room and knocked on the door.

"Come in," answered his dad in a husky voice. William Senior was 73 years old, and an avid smoker. You could tell by his voice that it had taken a toll on his body. He was about 6 feet, average build with a small pot belly. He had brown skin and was completely bald. William Senior sat in his chair and smoked his cigar never looking up at William as he entered the room. William hated smoking just like his mom, but neither of them ever said anything to his dad about it. No one ever questioned William Senior.

"Dad I'm divorcing Mye," said William. Senior looked at his son suspiciously.

"Are you divorcing her or is she divorcing you?" Senior asked. William was immediately irritated, but he kept his cool.

"I'm divorcing her," he replied.

"Good. I initially liked her. I thought. Finally, you did something right. She met the criteria for a good wife, but then you let her go to school," Senior said.

"She was already in school when I met her. You know that," said William.

"Not to become a doctor!" spat Senior. I was sitting at the dumb graduation thinking she was about to get a certificate or something. What does a woman need a doctorate's degree for? What is she planning on doing? Delivering her own baby or something? I knew she was going to be trouble then," he added.

"I didn't know she was getting her doctorates. She was only 18, how was I supposed to guess that?" William rebutted.

There was a knock on the door. "Come in," said Senior.

In walked Dorothy with two plates of food. "She sat them down on the table in front of Senior then she walked out without speaking or making eye contact.

"See son; you got to get them young and dumb. Then you can make a good woman out of them," said Senior as he grabbed one of the plates and started eating his food.

"You should have divorced her as soon as you found out she had ambitions outside the home," said Senior in between bites.

"She got pregnant with Tem as soon as we married. Just like you suggested. Trap em' young you said," he replied.

"Look, you ruined your life not me. She didn't even name your son after you. You never had control over her, and that's why you've suffered throughout the years," said Senior as he ate his food.

William didn't come over to hear this. He already knew how his dad felt about his wife. He just wanted to tell him about the divorce and make his dad think that it was his idea.

"I'm glad you've finally got some sense and are trading up to a new model," said Senior with a big grin. William smiled as he thought about Leah, but he didn't say anything. Senior leaned over and fist-bumped his son then said, "My man." Then he coughed a nasty cough. "I was about your age when I traded up. It comes a time in a man's life when he needs a younger woman. See son, as women get older, they get set in their ways and can be harder to control. That's why it's imperative to upgrade when you are around 42 - 43 years old. You're young enough to attract them still and seasoned enough to teach them their role quickly. This is a smart move," said Senior.

William was pleased to have his dad's approval. That's all he pretty much ever wanted from him.

"How old is she?" asked Senior.

"28," replied William.

"Whew, that's a little old, isn't it? I mean that's almost 30," said Senior.

"I got her at 21 so, yeah, she's with the program," said William.

"My man!" said Senior as he ate his food. "Whatever you do son, don't get her pregnant, and if you slip up, get that baby tested. Women who know they are side pieces and have played that role for that long always have their own side pieces too. Believe that."

William thought about his father's words and how there might be some truth to it.

As Senior was finishing his food he added, "When you marry again, make sure you have a son and name him after us. We have a legacy us Hart men. I had 4 girls with my first wife and was pissed that she couldn't give me a boy. That was part of the reason why I left. But then I met your mother, and she gave me twin boys. Hotdog! I knew that woman was special when I met her. Damn, I miss Charles."

William didn't know how to respond. Charles was his dad's favorite. Charles was everyone's favorite. But William's.

Senior continued, "If Charles were here, he would already be Mayor by now. That boy was going places!" chuckled Senior. "You were lucky to have a brother like him to learn from and follow."

William stood up and began to button his coat, "I am Deputy Commissioner dad. I rank higher than you ever did. A little respect would be appreciated," he said.

Senior smirked at William's temper tantrum. He knew his brother was a sore subject, but Senior didn't care.

"Respect. Please Junior. You have lost complete control of your life. If you were smart, you would stay married to your wife then run for Mayor. Everyone knows she has connects. After you win, then you divorce your wife, and then trade up."

William gave what his father was saying some thought.

"See son, all you have to do is break her down. All the way down. Mye's not a bad woman; she just doesn't know her place. Be a man, break her down and show her her place. Show her who's in control. You're the man, right?!" asked Senior.

"Of course! I'm the man," said William.

"Well, then act like it!" yelled Senior. "Teach Mye her place, become mayor, then trade up to the new model. Mye has been embarrassing you for far too long. She doesn't know how to treat you how you deserve. She owes you, William. The least she can do is get you to the Mayor's office. All you have to do is figure out how to break her all the way down and then show her her place. It would make me so proud to say my Junior is Mayor. All I ever wanted was to be proud of you like I was of Charles. Can you make me proud son?" ask Senior.

William smiled sinisterly, "Of course I can dad, and I know the perfect way to do it."

***

On the ride home from the jail, Truman watched Mye as she reviewed some files. He was impressed by how relaxed she seemed after such an intense situation. He's never seen her act like that before. This new Mye was causing big waves and had the courage to check people and put them in their place. He's known Mye for years, however, it seemed that she was evolving into a new version of herself. Still her, but better. Truman beamed with pride quietly taken the credit for her growth as he chuckled to himself.

Of course she's growing into a beast. How can you hang out with me and not be one, he thought to himself. While he was genuinely happy for his friend, he was also secretly a little scared that she would outgrow him. He quickly shook the thought out of his head and handed her some more files.

***

Mye and Truman got to her house to find Tem and Emerson sitting in the living room.

"What are you doing here Tem?" asked Mye. "You're really starting to annoy me. I don't know how many times I have to have the same conversation with you about the same thing," she added as she leaned on her grand piano.

"See Unc," said Tem, "I told you she was tripping. Can you please talk to her?" he asked.

Mye looked at Emerson in anticipation waiting for him to say something. Emerson stood there in silence for a moment. As soon as he began to speak, someone barged in the front door loudly.

"Mye!" yelled a man's voice. Everyone went to the hallway to find William standing in the doorway.

"What are you doing here William?" asked Mye. You don't live here anymore," she added.

"This is my got damn house too!" he yelled.

"Not anymore!" yelled Mye. "Now leave and take your son with you!"

Emerson grabbed Tem by the arm and said, "Let's go. Right now isn't a good time."

As Emerson dragged Tem to the front door, an older gentleman came inside. Mye began to tremble.

"What's the matter? Not so big and bad now," said William to Mye.

"Granddad?" said Tem as he looked at his grandfather in confusion. "What are you doing here?" he asked.

The question was rhetorical. Tem knows his grandfather has severe dementia and some type of delusional disorder that prevented him from being able to take care of himself properly. Mye put her dad in a really nice home with great care. Bhavani and Tem visited him from time to time, but he never recognizes them, and he never acknowledged them as his grandchildren.

"Elroy?" whispered Emerson in shock while pulling Tem behind him. William stared at Mye as she stared at her dad. He smiled as he watched his plan unfold.

"Well, aren't you going to say hi to your dear old dad? Word is you haven't seen your dad in years, but his expenses are paid in full, so I guess you're doing your part. I guess that makes you a good person. Aye guys, did you know that Elroy here has never been to this house. We've lived here nearly 20 years, and he's never been to a family dinner, birthday party, nothing. Why is that?" said William looking at Mye. "Why do you treat your dad like shit Mye?! Are you no longer his Mi Amor?!" yelled William.

"Mi Amor?" whispered Elroy as he slowly walked towards Mye. Elroy was 60 years old and in impeccable physical health. His smooth chocolate skin was wrinkle free and glowing. He was wearing khaki pants, a white tailored button up shirt, with a navy and grey sweater vest. Mye was happy to see he looked so strong and healthy, but she knew mentally he wasn't all the way there. Mentally he was not her father, but her mother's lover. The last time she saw him was over 5 years ago, and his episode was so bad that the doctors forbid her from seeing him again. At least not until he makes more progress in his therapy sessions. Mye backed up slowly as he approached her.

"Is that you, baby? Is it really you?" asked Elroy as he walked closer to Mye.

Mye trembled uncontrollably as she backed into her grand piano.

"Mi Amor," Elroy cried as he walked closer to Mye.

Mye stood frozen as her father gently grabbed her face. "I've missed you so much," he said as he slid his hands down her arms. He stepped back and said, "You look exactly the same! Like no time passed at all," he smiled.

Mye stood frozen, trembling.

"Oh Mi Amor," Elroy said excitedly as he grabbed Mye with both hands, one behind her head and the other on her butt while trying to kiss her passionately. Mye pushed him as hard as she could before anyone could say anything causing him to fall to the floor. The room was dead silent. Everyone looked a combination of disgusted and confused.

"Mi Amor!" yelled Elroy. "Why?!" he added. "You've been gone for over 30 years, and then you just treat me like this!" he cried. Mye ran around to the other side of the piano.

With a shaky voice, Mye said, "Daddy it's Mye. Remember, your little girl? Remember I'm Mye. Mommy is not here. She's gone. She's been gone for many years."

"No, you are Mi! You are Mi Amor Almonte! I'm not crazy!" he yelled as he got up from the floor and started walking around the piano.

"No you are not crazy daddy," said Mye as she walked around the piano away from her dad. "And yes, I am Mi Amor Almonte, and I'm named after my mom. Remember, you had a little girl March 23, 1979, remember? You named me after my mom. Remember?" said Mye.

Elroy stopped following her for a moment.

Mye said, "Remember mom was kidnapped in 1985? Remember you decided to change your daughter's name to Mye? This would help you not to confuse mom and I. Remember dad? Dad please try to remember," pleaded Mye as she fought back the tears.

Elroy sat on the floor in the corner and rocked. "You are my daughter Mye. You are my daughter Mye," he repeated over and over.

Elroy slowly started to get overwhelmed with emotions. He rocked harder and faster.

Mye stormed at her husband, "Is that what you want!?" she yelled, "you want me to go crazy? Why would you bring him here? And in front of our son? Why are you trying to break me? Don't you see what you've done? When my dad sees me, he gets confused, and then he has these emotionally painful episodes," she said as she looked at her dad in pity.

William replied, "So you have been ruining the men in your life since you were a kid?"

The words were painful to hear. Mye looked to Emerson for comfort, but he just stood frozen, still with nothing to say. Tem punched his father in the face so hard he went flying across foyer.

"No one talks to my mother like that! No one!" yelled Tem.

"Yesssss!" yelled Truman. "My man!" he said as he dapped Tem up and hugged him. "No retainer fee needed. I got you!" said Truman extra hyped.

Tem ran to his grandfather trying to stop him from hitting his head against the wall. "You gotta help me Ma! You gotta help him!" yelled Tem.

Mye stood frozen in her foyer as everything seemingly went quiet. Painful memories flooded through her head. Her mom being snatched by two men and pushed into a car. Leaving a 6-year-old Mye hiding behind a dumpster in the cold rain until the trash men discovered her the next morning only for her to go home and have to console her father. She changed her name from Mi to Mye to help her father not confuse her for her mother even though she loved her name. And then there was that God awful night after the school dance. Now she has to deal with and process the incident that happened today. Mye had experienced so much trauma throughout her life and yet was always required to care for others despite how she felt or what she was going through. The weight of her past traumas began suffocating and breaking her down. Right before she broke and gave into the heaviness of it all, she heard a small still voice say, "Stop operating at a deficit. You owe no-one anything."

She was knocked from her trance by confusion. She was a great businesswoman and all of her businesses operated in a surplus. She owed no-one anything. She stayed in the black.

"But your life," whispered the voice again. "It's time to live your life in the black. Your power is in the black. Use your black power."

Then it hit Mye. Since her mom was taken, she had been living her life from a state of lack. This childhood trauma of not being able to save her mother manifested into a woman who felt she needed to try to save everyone she could. A woman who operated from a perspective of not having enough. A woman with a self-obligated debt to pay for her inability for not being able to save who she loved the most. At this moment, Mye realized that she has been taking vital resources and energy from herself, giving it to others not just to help them, but to somehow make living with this guilt of not being "enough" more manageable. Tearing herself apart trying to prove to others that she is capable of providing services that are not even her responsibility. Continuing the bleeding out of her 6-year-old self so that she could help heal grown people who have chosen to suffer; a right that is theirs to choose. She realized that she was forcing healing on others that she has yet to accept for herself.

Truman walked to Mye and gave her a tight hug. She cried loudly into his shoulder as Tem was on the ground holding his grandfather trying to keep him from hitting his head. Emerson stood motionless as William smiled from Mye's pain. Mye slowly pulled herself together as Truman handed her his handkerchief to wipe her tears. Truman looked Mye in the eye and then whispered in her ear, "Now tell them how you really feel."

She gave him his handkerchief back then Truman stepped away and pulled out a chair from the kitchen island to sit on. Mye took a deep breath, closed her eyes, turned around, and faced the music.

In a low whisper she said, "Be quiet please." Everyone kept talking likely not able to hear her. Tem pleaded for her to help his granddad. William was filled with rage and Emerson remained frozen with shock.

"Quiet!" she yelled with authority. Everyone fell silent. Even her father.

She spoke with insistence and said, "The treatment I've allowed years past, yesterday, and 5 mins ago, is now inadmissible thereby being irrelevant. This moment forward, everything will be different. Different for me, inadvertently becoming different for you. My father is ill.

When I was 12, he was so ill that I had to move out. I, at 12 years old, moved out of my father's house. I'm hurt, and I'm finally acknowledging this hurt. I've also decided to work on my healing. You see, these lives you guys have built for yourself was built on my back. I was bleeding out while helping you and caring for you. The sad part is that my story is not unique to just me. Millions of black women had whole families, corporations, nations built on their backs. Queens snatched from their families and sexually exploited and trafficked for the sole purpose of expanding a legal free labor force. Made to nurse her captor's children. Forced to the labor force when their husbands were forced to the frontlines of wars for a country that envied them. Mandated to relinquish the love of her mate and forced to exile him in order to receive any type of government assistance. Only to become the highest educated group of people in America while receiving the lowest pay. You and the rest of the world actually expect us to continue, indefinitely, in the nurturing and care of our abuser. We have been fueling so many at the expense of ourselves, and I say all that ends today. At least, it ends today for me. I will no longer set my desires and dreams ablaze just to keep you ungrateful migrants warm. Now I have some self-healing work to do so I am going to ask you all to leave."

Tem got up and said, "But mom, what about granddad?"

Mye looked her son in the eye and said, "Listen to yourself son. Even in the midst of my own trauma, you want me to take care of my abuser. How inconsiderate is that?"

Tem looked down in embarrassment. He knew his mother was right and when she put it that way, his request sounded downright disrespectful. It was just that he was used to his mother solving all of his problems. Asking her for help was a natural impulse.

Mye added, "Now gentleman, please leave."

"Let's go Tem," said Emerson as he pulled Tem by the shoulder and walked towards the door.

"Tem," said Mye, "you're forgetting someone," she said as she pointed to her father. Tem helped his grandfather off of the floor and out of the door.

"This isn't the end Mye," said William as he stormed outside and slammed the door behind him.

"I couldn't agree with you more," she smiled.

Truman walked over to Mye and stood beside her looking at the front door.

"So right now wouldn't be a good time to ask you for the Miller file?" asked Truman.

"Out now," said Mye through a smirk trying not to laugh.

"I know, I know. I was just checking," said Truman as he grabbed his briefcase and left the house.

"Some things will never change," she said to herself as she closed the door behind him. "But these locks ain't one of them," she chuckled.

CHAPTER TWELVE

SAME SCRIPT DIFFERENT CAST

Jia rushed to her parents' house but her key didn't work. Her mother opened the door and closed it quickly behind her.

Jia said, "I came as fast as I could. What's going on Ma? And why doesn't my key work?"

"I'm leaving your father," said Delilah as she rushed up the stairs. "I had a courier send the papers to him today at work," she added. Before Jia could process the information, the doorbell rang.

"That's him," said Delilah. "I changed the locks and turned off the garage opener so he couldn't come in."

Jia stood stunned with her palms up as her mother rushed down the stairs to the table to grab something. She ran to Jia and said, "Here's the new keys. You're my witness. In case he hits me or something," said Delilah.

"Why would dad hit you Ma?" asked Jia confused.

"And prepare for a huge argument," said Delilah. "You need to understand Jia that men have a hard time losing the one they love most. They can treat you like crap, but the minute you say you're leaving, they can get emotional and sometimes combative. Men are very territorial," she added.

Jia rolled her eyes and rushed to the door and opened it.

"Are you Delilah Birch?" the gentleman asked.

"That's me," said Delilah as she opened the door wider.

"This package is for you. Can you sign here?" he asked.

Delilah signed for the package and shut the door.

Jia quickly opened the door and said, "Thank you sir!" to the delivery guy and closed the door.

Delilah threw the package on the table without even opening it.

"He refused the package," said Delilah as she walked upstairs to finish packing.

Jia grabbed the big envelope and opened it, "No. Dad accepted the package, signed it, and agreed to all of your terms."

Delilah ran down the stairs, snatched the papers from her daughter and flipped through them quickly.

Jia said, "Maybe he's not as territorial as most men." As she headed up the stairs towards her childhood bedroom, she stopped at the top of the stairs and looked down at her mom and said, "Or maybe you're simply not the woman he loves most." Then she went into her room and closed her door.

Delilah ran up the stairs and bust into Jia's room.

"Your father is a weak man! An indecisive over thinker. You may think the world of him and think he's so amazing, but I'm here to tell you, sweetie, that he is not. He is weak and masks around with this artificial ambition, but the real true ambitious people know that he's a coward. He would have never married me if I didn't make it painstakingly easy for him. He didn't have the courage to go after a woman like me."

Jia snapped back, "So I get it. Daddy likes things easy," she said as she looked her mother up and down, "but who does he love?" asked Jia with a smirk.

Delilah threw a lamp in rage. "Argh! Shut up! You don't know what you are talking about! You can never understand what it's like to be me. I've been through some shit little girl; some stuff that would make your little head spin. I deserve to be loved how I want to be loved. I deserve passion and desire," said Delilah as she adjusted her skirt, "and now I've found it. A man not afraid to pursue me and satisfy my dreams. A man with ambition that's going places," gleamed Delilah.

Jia shook her head in utter disappointment in her mother. "Mom, you are correct. You do deserve to be loved how you want to be loved. However, just because a man doesn't speak your love language doesn't mean you cheat on him. You talk to him; you seek counseling, you figure out how to effectively communicate your desires to him. You simply don't cheat!" she yelled.

"For what!" yelled Delilah. "Why? I know he's simply what I don't want. He can't give me what I need."

"No mom! What you need is to face those old traumas and heal!" said Jia.

Delilah sat down on her daughter's bed.

"I don't know what happened to you in the past, but you're projecting all of your hurt and pain on to everyone else. Including me! You want dad to fill a void only you can fill. Divorce dad fine! I don't care! But work on yourself mom. I get it. Things are changing. I've grown up and moved out of the house. All the distractions you've once had to keep your past traumas at bay are gone. Now you have to face it. Face the hurt, face the guilt, face the shame," said Jia. She went and sat down beside her mom and said, "This new man isn't the answer. He's just a numbing agent, and you deserve more than that," said Jia as she hugged her mother.

Delilah sat there for a moment and shed a single tear. Then she broke free from her daughter's arms and snapped, "You ain't shit just like your father! I'm tired of pretending like I like you. Every time I see you I see him. Every time I try to make you more like me, you act more like him. You both think you know everything and I can't take it! I finally found a man who loves me for me! And no one's getting in the way of it! Not you, not your father, not no one. Now give me my keys and get out!" yelled Delilah.

Jia silently cried as she reached into her lab coat and handed her mother the keys. "I always felt that you never really wanted me, but to hear for myself that you don't like me cuts deeper than I could have imagined. Thank you for continuing the cycle of trauma. However, unlike you, I am going to handle mine so the cycle will end with me. I pray God has mercy on you and that you get some help."

Jia went to walk out of her bedroom when she turned around and said, "Oh and FYI, my friend Christine's parents divorced because of Councilman David Allen. Well, back then he was just getting into politics. Apparently, he promised to marry her mom within 6 months of her divorce being finalized. Christine's mom used her influence to get him his current seat," sniffled Jia. "Word around town is he is up to his old tactics and has a couple of married women caught in his web. I just thought you should know," said Jia as she left the room, ran down the steps and out of the door, never looking back.

***

Truman's cell phone rang while he was preparing for a case.

"Make it quick," he answered. The call was from the private investigator.

"The officer who shot Tem secured a large house in the Dominican Republic right before he shot Tem. There's no proof of purchase though. Apparently, it was a gift. I'm tracing the gift back to the gifter, but it's gonna take me a while. The gifter doesn't want to be identified. They did a good job covering their tracks but no one's perfect. I'll figure out who it is soon enough," said the private investigator.

Truman asked, "Well, are there any other cops you could find who received any recent huge gifts?"

The P.I. replied, "Yeah, there is this one guy."

***

Jia bumped into her dad at the end of his shift.

"What's up baby girl?" he said as he put the back of his hand on her head, then neck. "Is everything ok?" he asked concerned. "You've been distant the last few days."

"I'm fine dad," said Jia unconvincingly, "mom told me what she did. She told me what you guys decided," she sniffled.

Emerson felt horrible. He didn't think Jia would take it this hard. He hugged his daughter and said, "I'm sorry you have to deal with this sweetie. No child should have to deal with their parents divorcing."

Jia lifted her head and said, "Oh no dad. It's not that. I'm glad you're getting a divorce. You deserve better. Now you can stop being Mr. Good Guy and go after what you want or who you truly want."

Emerson smiled, pleased to have his daughter's approval.

"Then why are you crying?" he asked.

"It's something else that mom said," said Jia as she wiped her face. "But we can talk more about that later. Go tell G-Ma how you really feel and stop playing these little games," smiled Jia as she gave her dad a push.

***

Emerson rushed to Mye's office with three dozen long stem roses. Kara's eyes lit up as she saw Emerson walking in. Breathing heavily he asked, "Is Mye in?"

Kara smiled eyeing the roses and replied, "No, Dr. Birch. She's not in at the moment. Can I take a message for her?" she asked.

"Please, Kara. I need to know where she is. I've been hiding my true feelings for her for years, and I simply can't hold it in anymore. I love Mye and today is the day I'm going to tell her," he said with pride.

Kara cried softly at the professing of his love.

"Is she home? No worries Kara, I'll just go check there," he said as he turned around to leave.

"No wait," she said, "she's at Tara's."

"Thank you Kara and have a nice day!" he said as he jolted out of the office.

"Get your girl Doc!" yelled Kara.

***

"Tell me again how Tem punched William's lights out," said Penelope as she played in Mye's curls. Tara and Mye bust out laughing.

"I think 3 times is enough Nelly," said Mye.

Penelope was Truman's younger sister. She was the same age as Mye, 38, three years younger than Truman. She was about 5'9", fair skin, with freckles and long straight red hair with bangs. She had an athletic build at about 190 pounds with big brown eyes and a perfect smile. She owned and operated a multi-million dollar publishing and licensing company, and she commissioned paintings on the side. She shared her time between her home in California and her home in London, England. Mye met Penelope first, and then Penelope introduced her to Truman. They have all been friends for nearly 20 years.

As Mye laid her head on Penelope's shoulder, all of her pain momentarily subsided. Penelope had a very soothing effect on Mye since they first met in college.

When Mye was around her, she always felt that everything would be okay. Mye was now eating her third blueberry cheesecake cupcake from 'The Sweet Lobby.'

"These cupcakes are my favorite," she said in total bliss.

"Well if we can listen to Mary J Blige's 'What's the 411' on repeat, while watching you eat a dozen cupcakes, then you can tell the punching story one more time," said Nelly. Everyone laughed.

Tara flopped down on the oversized cream sectional with another bottle of 2007 Duppy Conqueror "Port"-style Dessert Wine from Brown Nappy Valley.

"More wine please," chuckled Mye.

"Thanks for the Chanel sweat suits," said Nelly.

"Don't thank me. That was Bhavani. She said I couldn't have a girl's day in without proper attire," said Tara. The ladies laughed.

"Thank you for flying into town Nelly," said Mye sitting up to get eye level with her, "you really didn't have to, but I truly appreciate it."

Nelly stared at her for a moment. Mye pushed her hair out of her face. "I know it's been a long time since you've seen me like this, but I kinda like it," said Mye as she ran her hands through her curls. "I think I'm slowly falling back in love with them," she added.

"I never fell out of love with them," Nelly replied. Mye blushed as she shook her index finger. Nelly raised her hands in surrender.

Tara's phone rang breaking the tension.

"Hello. Of course, send him up. Thank you!" said Tara, "that was the front desk. Emerson is on his way up."

Nelly smiled a devilish grin, "The infamous Emerson," she said.

Tara laughed.

"Behave Nelly and don't encourage her Tara," said Mye.

"Let's see how he fucks up today," said Nelly through a big smile.

"He won't. Not this time," said Tara.

"Bet money," said Nelly, "1 thousand," she added.

"10," said Tara effortlessly with a smirk.

The elevator dinged.

"Bet," said Nelly.

"Stop it," whispered Mye as the elevator doors opened.

Emerson walked out of the elevator with three dozen long stem roses. Tara stuck her tongue out at Nelly. Emerson walked into the penthouse looking delicious in his lab coat but also a bit nervous.

Mye spoke first, "Hi Emerson. Did you come straight here from the hospital?" she asked.

"Well, kinda," he replied, "first, I went to your office then I came here."

Everyone waited for Emerson to say something else but he didn't. He just stood there holding the flowers.

Nelly said, "Hey Emerson, it's been a minute. Anything new going on?" she asked as she placed her arm on the couch behind Mye.

Emerson didn't know what to make of the gesture. He began to stutter, "Um no, it's the same ole same ole," he replied.

"Do you want to have a seat?" asked Tara.

"Oh no no," he replied. "I just want to drop off these flowers," he said.

Mye's eyes lit up as he walked to her but then she was confused when he only gave her one bouquet. Then he proceeded to give Nelly and Tara the other two bouquets.

The elevator dinged and in walked Truman.

"What's with the flowers?" he asked.

Emerson turned and said, "I brought the ladies flowers just because," he said proudly.

"You knew Nelly was here?" asked Truman.

"No," said Emerson.

"Well, how did you know to bring 3 bouquets?" asked Truman. Before Emerson could respond, Truman added, "Tara prefers her flowers planted, Nelly is allergic to roses, and Mye thinks they smell like shit. Mye's favorite flower is lavender. Everyone knows that," said Truman as Nelly and Tara shook their heads in agreement.

"Is there something I can help you with Truman," said Mye through clenched teeth.

"Um yes, the Miller file," he replied.

Mye reached under the table and handed Truman the file.

"Thank you. It has been a pleasure, but I gotta go," said Truman sarcastically as he walked to the elevator and pushed the down button.

"Um, I have to go too. I need to head back to the hospital, so I'll see you guys later," said Emerson as he jogged to the elevator just as the doors opened.

Truman sucked his teeth when Emerson got in the elevator with him and the ladies laughed.

"Truman hates sharing an elevator," chuckled Mye.

"Run me my money," said Nelly to Tara.

Mye laughed.

Tara replied, "How about this? Fly with John and I to London. We leave in 2 days.

"In the Lear?" asked Nelly.

"No the Challenger. We leave in 2 days, so you'll have to keep yourself busy until then," said Tara.

"Oh, I'm sure I can think of something to do until then. You gotta deal," said Nelly. Then she looked at Mye, "24 plus years and he doesn't even know your favorite flower," said Nelly as she got up from the couch. "I remembered your favorite flower. I remember everything about you," Nelly said walking away.

***

"Hey baby," said Councilman David Allen in a low whisper on his cellphone. "I'm finishing up a meeting, and then I'll be right over. Wear that little red teddy I like... or nothing at all," he chuckled into the phone. "I gotta go babes, see you in a few."

David hung up the phone right when Delilah was entering the room.

"Your shower is amazing. I have to get me one of those," she said as she dried herself off. She stood naked as she grabbed her body butter.

"Do you need help with that," asked David walking up behind her.

"No babes," she said. "You have a meeting in less than 45 minutes, and DC traffic can be bad. You have to keep your commitments and be a man of your word. You can't be late," she said as she put her bra and panties on. "As future mayor, you have to be a man of your word," she smiled.

He loved how committed she was to him succeeding. David was glad to have her on his team along with all his other women.

"What would I do without you?" he said as he kissed her forehead.

She said, "Play your cards right, and you won't ever have to find out," she smiled. "Can you zip my dress please?"

David did as she requested while also feeling her up and down. Delilah turned around and kissed him passionately.

"When are we going to finally get married?" she asked.

Without missing a beat, David grabbed her tight, kissed her forehead and said, "As soon as your divorce is finalized we can get married within 6 months after that. Let's focus on the election for now and worry about all that other stuff later." Then he walked to his dresser and grabbed his keys and wallet.

Delilah forced a fake smile as her daughter's words ran through her mind. She shook the thought away and told herself that what she and David have is special and no one could tell her otherwise.

***

"I don't know about this anymore," said the man in a dark grey hoodie with an oversized baseball cap. He fidgeted with his wedding ring and couldn't stop biting his nails.

"Relax," said the woman. "Everything will be fine. There's a 6 bedroom house, car, and boat waiting for you in the Dominican Republic right now. Consider this an early retirement with blue waters and no financial worries," she said easing his nerves.

"What if I get caught?" asked the man.

"What? How?" replied the woman, "this kid has already had a run-in with the law before, and we all know that blue law is above all. The department will have your back fully, and Internal Affairs is going to waste very little looking into the shooting of a kid like him. I mean, let's be serious. He's black."

The man didn't seem convinced, and this irritated the woman although she did a good job concealing her frustration.

"Look, your wife is all prepped and ready for surgery. As soon as you complete the job, I'll give the orders for the doctors to perform the transplant," said the woman.

The man perked up.

"Your wife is an alcoholic and has been kicked off the list because she couldn't stop drinking. She won't be getting a liver, and we all know you need your liver. So do the job, save your wife, and live the rest of your days however you want," smiled the woman.

"I'll do it," he said.

"Perfect," she replied.

CHAPTER THIRTEEN

MAMA KNOWS BEST

Mye was glad Ms. Leena Dean her house executive and friend, was able to come over the house to watch Kiam. The mayor sent Tem an invitation to her charity event, and Tem asked his mom to be his plus one. Mye had her own invitation but appreciated Tem wanting her to tag along with him.

Tem sent Mye a text, "Hey Ma, I'm 5 minutes away. Be ready. I gave Alex the night off so I'll be driving us to the event."

Mye put her phone face down on Kiam's dresser with an attitude as she tucked him into bed.

"AG, what are you trying to do? Make me into a burrito? I can't move my arms," said Kiam.

Mye chuckled, "My apologies baby. I just found out that Tem will be driving us to the Mayor's charity event and I hate that little coupe he drives. I get claustrophobic," she said.

Kiam replied, "Well, why don't you drive?"

"I don't like driving. Especially not when I'm all dressed up. I mean, I'm too cute to drive. My dress could wrinkle," said Mye.

Kiam rolled his eyes and face palmed his head.

"And Tem is not likely going to drive one of my cars because he doesn't like driving other people's cars. He's so particular and spoiled," Mye added.

"I don't know AG. You sound a little particular and spoiled yourself," said Kiam. Ms. Dean laughed.

"I'll take it over from here," said Ms. Dean. "Tem is waiting for you downstairs."

Mye walked down the spiral staircase in a soft pink, long fitted gown, with a sweetheart neckline, and an 18-inch train. Her hair was pulled back into a low ponytail with long full bouncy curls. Her gold earrings perfectly matched her bangles and hair tie. She walked down the stairs with grace and poise. Tem stood proudly in his tux as he admired how youthful and beautiful his mother was. He was ashamed of his behavior over the years, especially after finding out about some of his mother's past. She didn't look like a woman who had been through all that hurt and pain. She looked radiant. Tem decided from that moment forward that he would make a better effort at dealing with his own traumas while also being a better son, brother, and friend.

"You look amazing Ma," said Tem as he kissed his mom's hand. "That's your new Maybach outside?!" asked Tem excited.

"No," said Mye confused. That's just a new Mercedes. That's Truman's and I new car. Alex will be here in the morning to get it. George had to inspect it first. That's why it's still here," she said.

"Ma! That's a Maybach! You gotta let me drive it. Please?" said Tem. Mye was happy she didn't have to ride in that small coupe of his.

She said with a smile, "Of course we can take the May-Back."

"Ma it's Maybach. That thing has to be at least 20 feet long," said Tem as he opened the door for his mother. "After you," he said.

"See AG! You don't have to ride in his small car, and you don't have to drive. Look at God!" Kiam yelled from the top of the stairs.

"Go to bed Kiam!" yelled Mye as she tried to keep herself from laughing. "We're gone Ms. Dean!" Mye added.

***

Traffic was light, and the moon shined bright as Tem drove to the Mayor's charity event.

"Ma I just want to say-"

"It's ok baby," said Mye cutting him off as she looked out through the window into her side mirror.

Tem said, "No Ma I just want to-"

"I said it's ok baby," smiled Mye as she tapped her son's knee and went back to looking at her side mirror.

"Ma just let me say this," said Tem in an authoritative tone.

Mye gave him her undivided attention. Her green eyes sparkled in the moonlight, and the intensity of her focus was slightly intimidating.

Tem stuttered, "Ma, I'm I'm... I'm sorry for, you know, all the stupid stuff I've done and said. It's going to be a long process, but I'm going to make being a better man a priority."

Mye smiled and said, "Apology accepted," as she rubbed her son's head and went back to looking out her side mirror.

Tem noticed his mom constantly looking at her side mirror. "Mom what are you looking at?" asked Tem.

"Look Tem. I need you to do exactly what I say. No need to think, just simply do what I say. Do you understand?" said Mye.

Tem looked confused.

"Do you understand?" Mye said sternly.

"Yes, I understand," said Tem.

"Now remain calm, put both hands on the steering wheel, maintain your speed and keep looking straight," said Mye calmly. Tem obliged. "Someone is tailing us," said Mye. Tem turned to look behind him and caused the car to swerve. Immediately they heard sirens.

"I'm sorry Ma," said Tem.

"It's ok sweetie. You know the drill. Pullover slowly, keep your hands on top of the steering wheel and turn on your inside lights. Keep your answers short and be very polite," said Mye. Tem was shaking a little.

"I'm usually not this nervous but considering what's happen," said Tem.

Mye laid her hands flat on the dashboard and said, "I understand. The officer can see our hands, and we will remain calm no matter what. This is why we keep our registration and license in the sun visor so the officer

can always see our hands. I know it's a pain to keep taking your license in and out your wallet, but we do this to
make sure the officer feels comfortable and safe. We
have to be smart incase we come across an officer who
isn't trained." said Mye.

"It's humiliating Ma," said Tem.

"What did I tell you happens to a black person's civil
liberties when in encounter by the police?" asked Mye.

"We have none," said Tem softly.

"That's right Tem. We have none. Our civil liberties
go out of the window when encountered by the police.
So we must be smart. You must be willing to accept humiliation and disrespect, in order to even make it to the
court room. You only have two options, to do what the
officer says and let the courts take care of the officer
later or to be prepared to take the officer out and deal
with the courts later. We do not have equal protection
under the law and discretion is often confused by dis-
crimination in law enforcement. Now get it together, "
said Mye.

***

The police officer pulled out his burner phone and
called the one number saved in it.

"I got him pulled over," said the officer.

"Great! Now do your thing and be an ass. Pull the
power card and make him feel beneath you. Agitate him.
Once he takes the bait, then ask him for his license and
registration, that's when you take him out; as he's reaching for his wallet or glove compartment. Whichever
gives you a better shot," said the woman.

The officer was scared and didn't want to do it, but his wife really needed that liver, so he felt his options were limited.

"Consider it done," said the officer. The officer walked to the car as Tem was rolling down the window, "Do you know why I pulled you over?"

"No sir," said Tem looking forward. The officer noticed Mye and got spooked. He didn't know someone else was in the car.

"Who's car is this?" asked the officer nervously.

"My mother's sir," said Tem still looking forward. Mye made eye contact with the officer for the first time and noticed how nervous he was as he had his hand on his gun.

"License and registration boy," said the officer.

This infuriated Tem, but he remained calm, lifted both hands to the air and flipped the sun visor down. He didn't notice that the officer unlatched his gun from his holster and was holding it at his side, but Mye did.

The officer didn't know what to do. He couldn't justify the shooting if the items he requested were in the sun visor. The officer took the documents and went back to his car and called the woman back.

"Deals off," he said. "There's a woman in the car. His mom. His freaking mom is in the car with him," he said.

The woman got excited and said, "Do them both. The boy then her. I wanted her to suffer, but this works too."

"No, I can't do it. Not a mother and son," he said.

"Listen, your wife is waiting prepared for surgery right now. Are you going to let her down? I'll even sweeten the pot for you. I'll double everything and throw in another liver for your wife for after she drinks this new one away," smiled the woman.

"Ok," said the officer reluctantly. "You have a deal."

***

Tem sat nervously in the car when it started pouring down raining.

"Something's not right," said Mye, "Tem start the car."

"Oh hell no Ma. You're trying to get us killed. I already been shot and I ain't trying to give him a reason to get gully," said Tem.

"I'm serious Tem start the car and drive off now!" she yelled.

"No Ma!" he yelled back.

The officer ran to the car and knocked on Tem's window surprising him.

"Don't roll down the window Tem!" yelled Mye. "Stop rolling down the fucking window!"

"Chill out Ma!" yelled Tem looking at his mother as he rolled his window down.

"Get out the car!" screamed the officer with his gun drawn. Mye was shocked into silence.

Tem put his hands in the air and nervously asked, "What what's the problem sir?"

"Open the door and get out the car! Stop resisting," yelled the officer.

Tem opened the door and got out of the car. Tem stood in his tux as it poured down raining on him and the officer. The officer's hands were shaking terribly.

"Get on the ground! Stop resisting and get on the ground!" yelled the officer.

Tem got on his knees with his hands still in the air. He said a silent prayer and thought about all of the things that went unsaid and how he never did properly thank Jia. *At least I got to apologize to my mom*, he thought.

Click! "Don't fucking move," said Mye as she held a Smith and Wesson 500 Magnum. It was matte black so you could barely see it in the dark but each time lightning struck the sky it was clear she was holding a powerful weapon. She held both hands on the gun inches from the officers left temple. The officer was about 2 feet from Tem with his gun still pointed at the middle of Tem's forehead. Rain poured down on Mye causing her dress to cling tight to her body and her curls to disappear. She was confident and calm. Fully prepared to do whatever it takes and to deal with whatever the consequences to protect her son.

"Put your gun down," said Mye. "I don't want to shoot you. If I did want to shoot you, then I would have done it already." The officer shook uncontrollably.

"I want to know who sent you and why," she said in an authoritative tone.

"I don't know," said the officer still pointing his gun at Tem.

"I don't know what?!" yelled Mye.

"I don't know why," said the officer fighting back tears.

The thunder roared forcing Mye to scream, "Then who! Who sent you! Who sent you after my son!" she yelled as she pushed the revolver into the side of the police officer's head. Police sirens can be heard coming down the street. The officer dropped his weapon and put his hands in the air.

Mye kicked his knee forcing him to drop to the ground.

"I'm going to give you to the count of 3 to tell me who sent you," said Mye as 3 police cars came to a screeching halt one beside the other blocking the two-lane road and the shoulder. "1... 2...-"

"No Mye!" yelled Truman as he ran from one of the police cars to her. She looked to the right slightly confused as to why Truman was there but focused her attention back on the cop.

"Who sent you!" she yelled at the cop as the rain masked her tears.

"It's ok Mye. Put the gun down," said Truman as he pushed the revolver to the ground. "We got him," whispered Truman to Mye. "This was a paid hit," said Truman.

"By who?" asked Mye.

"I don't know yet, but I will find out," said Truman.

The officer on his knees dropped his hands with a sigh of relief. He called to the other officers that were running towards him and said, "Arrest this crazy bitch!" Mye hit him in the head with the butt of the revolver knocking him to the ground. The officer winced in pain.

Mye dropped to the ground and hugged her son tight. She didn't know how much time she would get in jail for her actions or if she would be arrested at all. So she just hugged her son as long as she could. There's no love like a genuine mother's love for her child. 6 police officers ran to the scene and grabbed the officer on the ground and began to read him his rights, "You have the right to remain silent anything you say can and will be used against you in the court of law-"

"What! She pulled a gun out on me and assaulted me! What the hell is going on here?!" he interrupted.

"Everything will be explained at the precinct," said officer Grey in disgust. "It's officers like you who make the rest of us look bad. But now I'm done protecting you. We tell kids that the streets "no snitch policy" is bad but we have the same policy in our own police departments. Well, not me. Moving forward, I'm calling bad cops like you out! Put him in the car!"

Tem saw the officer being taken away in handcuffs. He tapped his mom's back and pointed to all the commotion.

Mye grabbed Tem by the chin and said, "When I give orders listen to me. Trust me. I know you're a grown man now, but sometimes mother knows best," she smiled as she rubbed his chin. The rain slowly stopped and the clouds dispersed allowing the moon to shine brightly.

"Yeah, I could have driven off but then what if he had started shooting at us? Did you think about that?" said Tem to his mother.

Mye grabbed the officer's 9mm that was on the ground and fired two shots right by Tem's head. One into the door and the other into the window. She leaned up against the car and took deep breaths to center and calm herself. While cuffing his ears trying to stop them from ringing. Tem looked at the car in shock. Even at point-blank range, the bullets didn't go through.

***

Early the next morning, Mye woke up to Kiam's foot in her face, Bhavani behind him, and Tem laying across the bottom of the bed. She smiled as she admired her family sleeping. She did her daily routine, drank 2 cups of lemon, ginger, and mint water, meditated, did yoga, then she took a shower. She was journaling on the kitchen island drinking hot tea when Truman came in.

"You're here earlier than usual," said Mye as she took a sip of her tea. "Hold up. I changed the locks. How did you get in?"

Truman replied, "With my key, but that's not important. Listen, the cop rolled on everybody. He's probably still at the station singing like a canary." Mye paused hanging on to Truman's every word.

Truman added, "Someone named Lo-Ruhamah was the mastermind behind it all."

Mye perked up, "I know her," she said. "She came to my office about two months ago, on the day of my 20th wedding anniversary. She had a mental breakdown. Kara had to call the police to escort her out."

"Who would name their child 'no mercy'?" said Truman.

Mye walked over to Truman and said, "How do you know Lo-Ruhamah means 'no mercy'?" asked Mye.

Truman replied, "Look, I am Jewish, Christian, Muslim, Hindu, I'm whatever religion my client needs me to be." Mye laughed to herself as she shook her head in disbelief. Truman added, "So Hosea married Gomer and had 3 kids, Jezreel, Lo-Ruhamah, and Lo-" Truman froze and stared at Mye with sadness in his eyes.

"What?" asked Mye sipping her tea. "Hosea's third child was Lo who?"

Truman replied, "Ammi."

FLASHBACK - THE NIGHT OF THE SCHOOL DANCE 1993

Emerson pulled up to Mye's house 5 minutes before her curfew. She lived in a large 4 bedroom house in Potomac, Maryland on a quaint street lined with mature trees.

"Thank you for tonight. I had a blast," she smiled. Mye wore an emerald green sequin mid length dress, with off the shoulder sleeves, and a bateau neckline. Her natural curls reigned free as she used her hand to comb them over to one side of her hair to keep from obstructing her view. She fidgeted with her hands as Emerson admired the worry she tried to hide behind her smile.

"What's wrong Mye?" he asked as he pushed a loose curl behind her ear. Mye took a deep breath inhaling his cologne in the process.

"You smell amazing Em," said Mye. Emerson blushed and looked away. His high top fade was flawless, and his suit was black and tailored made. His green bowtie was the perfect accent to Mye's dress.

"Seriously what's going on Mye?" he asked.

Mye closed her eyes and said, "It's Ammi."

"Your stepbrother?" asked Emerson, "what about him? I mean he's a little weird but what's up?"

"He's been freaking me out. He's always freaked me out, but it's way worse now. He's too big to like hover over me, and he stares at me all the time. It's scary. I don't trust him, and I feel like he's gonna snap or do something," said Mye.

Emerson was smiling while looking down at his lap reading a text. He sent a quick text and looked up to find Mye scowling.

He laughed it off and said, "Look Mye. He ain't gonna do anything. Especially not tonight. He's probably out celebrating with the team or with some shortie."

Mye looked down and fidgeted with her fingers, "Can I just go with you? I mean back to your parents, not out with you with your friends or nothing," she said.

Emerson thought about it for a minute. He knew if he took her back to his house, his parents would make him stay there with her. He was heading to see big booty Judy, and he couldn't mess that up.

Mye could sense his hesitation, so she said, "Or you can just come inside. At least until my dad or his wife gets home. I just don't want to be alone with him. Please,"

Emerson's phone vibrated again. It was another text from Judy telling him all the things she couldn't wait to do to him.

"Look Mye you'll be fine. Ammi is weird but not violent. Stop overreacting. His name means 'God's people' for heaven's sake. Who can be violent with a name like that? You're an over thinker Mye. Now stop worrying about nothing and get some rest," smiled Emerson as he started his 93' Camaro.

Mye smiled a fake smile as she got out of the car and closed the door. She walked to her front door and waved bye when she got inside. Emerson loved Mye, but she was young, and he had needs now that Judy could fulfill that Mye couldn't. So he chose Judy that night over Mye, and it changed his life forever.

PRESENT - 2017

Bhavani came running in the kitchen with Kiam hot on her heels.

"Are you okay Ma?" said Bhavani helping her mother pick up pieces of her shattered mug.

"I'm sorry guys," said Mye, "oh don't touch that Kiam. Thank you, but I got it," she said as she wet a paper towel to get up the small pieces of glass while still visibly shaken.

"Bhavani can you get Kiam dressed please while I finish up with Truman?" asked Mye.

"Of course," said Bhavani as she picked up Kiam.

"Hey Truman," said Bhavani.

"Hey Uncle T," said Kiam grabbing Truman unexpectedly by the neck as Bhavani carried him.

"What the hell," said Truman as he pushed Kiam off of him. Kiam laughed as Bhavani carried him up the stairs. "It's bad enough I had to sit in a nasty police car. Now this," said Truman as he straightened his suit jacket.

Mye was looking out of the kitchen window trying to keep it together.

Truman said, "She's in custody now, and we have everything we need to send her away forever. I can push for the death penalty if you want.

"No," said Mye quickly, "I want to speak to her." Mye turned around with tearful eyes and asked, "Can you make that happen?"

CHAPTER FOURTEEN

O TASTE AND SEE

Mye sat patiently in a hard chair in a cold room. Truman stood in the corner of the room behind her. Two guards walked in Lo-Ruhamah. She was wearing an orange jumpsuit with her hands and feet chained. Lo-Ruhamah glared at Mye, filled with hate and anger, grinding her teeth mustering the strength to keep from jumping across the table. Lo-Ruhamah's left eye began to twitch as the two sat there staring at each other.

Then Mye broke the silence and asked ever so softly, "Why?"

Lo-Ruhamah spat, "I just wanted my mother back! She went crazy after you had my brother locked up!" she screamed. Then she started to cry, "I thought I could make it up to her by taking your son from you. You know, an eye for an eye," she cried. "I tried to give you a chance to make things right, but you blew me off! You ruined our lives! Now my mom is in a mental institution, and my brother is in jail!" sniffled Lo-Ruhamah in between screaming. "You seduced my brother and had sex with him, then when you got caught you said he raped you! You, you, you little whore!" yelled Lo-Ruhamah.

FLASHBACK - IN THE HOSPITAL AFTER THE DANCE 1993

Mye woke up to a beautiful caramel complected Indian nurse named Bhavani. The nurse informed Mye that she had been unconscious for three days and that she had been raped, but all of the tests came back negative. As Mye was processing this information, a social worker barged in.

"Mi Amor Almonte?" she said looking down at her files.

"Yes," she replied, "but everyone calls me Mye."

The social worker continued, "I'm here to inform you that you are officially a ward of the state of Maryland. You've been placed in an Independent Living Program. Here is the address for your new home and you have a mandatory court hearing tomorrow at 9 am," the woman said in a matter of fact tone.

"But where is my dad? Is he coming to get me?" asked Mye.

The social worker was annoyed as she looked through her files, "Look I really don't have time for this, I have other cases," she said. "Wait, here it is," she said pulling out a piece of paper, "your father had been placed on psychiatric watch involuntarily. So, no. He won't be picking you up. Make it to court tomorrow, or you will lose your housing placement," said the woman as she walked out of Mye's hospital room.

Nurse Bhavani made a note of the social worker's unprofessional stark treatment as she listened from outside the room. Mye laid in the hospital bed with bruises all over her body, in pain inside and out. She could feel what felt like her heartbeat pounding, in her face, in her vagina, but mostly in her back. Mye cried in pain at the thought of losing everything at once. Nurse Bhavani came in to the room and comforted her.

"Shh shh…. There, there," nurse Bhavani said as she wiped Mye's hair out of her face.

"But it hurts so bad," Mye cried trying to reach for her back.

"No, no," said the nurse as she handed Mye a cup of water and some pills. "Take this medicine. It will help you feel better."

Mye obliged.

"My child, you are strong. You gave your attacker a good fight. He pushed you into your bedroom window, and you got cut up really bad, but you still kept fighting. You have 35 staples in your back right now, and you must try not to touch them."

Mye stared off into nothingness as she thought about how she lost her home, dad, and virginity all in the same night. She felt like nothing. She just wanted to give up.

"Stop it Mye! Stop it!" yelled the nurse. "You can't give up," said nurse Bhavani seemingly reading her mind. "You have too much to accomplish. Your life will positively affect hundreds of thousands, possibly millions. You are gifted many gifts my child. You are not what happens to you in life but how you respond to life. Choose to keep living and watch how Ganesha gets you through everything," said the nurse as she handed Mye a small statue of Ganesha.

PRESENT - 2017

"I was raped!" yelled Mye as she slammed her hands on the metal table.

Mye had never said that out loud. She made it a priority to bury the details of that night.

"Your brother raped me," said Mye. "I was only 14. He was 18 years old, 6'3", 265 lbs," said Mye.

Lo-Ruhamah replied, "You broke 3 of his ribs!"

"I was scared!" yelled Mye. "I thought he was going to kill me. He pushed me into my bedroom window, and glass and blood were everywhere. I thought I was going to die! Every day I see this scar on my back, and I am reminded of that night," said Mye.

"You hit him so hard with one of your awards that he got amnesia," said Lo-Ruhamah. "He doesn't even remember that night. It's all foggy. He's on constant suicide watch because everyone told him what he did and he can't believe it. And if he did do it, which he didn't, he is not that person anymore! He's serving life for a night he doesn't remember. Hasn't he been punished enough?" asked Lo-Ruhamah.

Mye calmly said, "Look, I want you to know that I do not get any pleasure from your pain or your brother's pain. However, I also do not feel pity for you or your mom or your brother."

Lo-Ruhamah replied, "You had it easy compared to me. I had a whole life of hardship and pain Mye. Life wasn't roses. I had no father to love me like you. I think maybe he thought I wanted it, maybe it was my fault," cried Lo-Ruhamah.

Mye didn't understand what she was saying. She watched her cry and try to console herself while handcuffed.

Then Lo-Ruhamah said, "My mom had 2 kids with my father. Me and my brother. My father was already married, and his wife couldn't have kids. When my dad's wife found out he had kids outside of their marriage, she left him. My dad was furious with my mom. He never loved my mom and never wanted us. That's why he named us Lo-Ruhamah and Lo-Ammi. We moved into my dad's house 6 months after his wife moved out. Then on my 6th birthday, my brother and mother moved out. After that, I would see my mom once a month, when she came by to get some money and then when I turned 14, she stopped coming."

Lo-Ruhamah put her head in her hands and sobbed loudly. Mye could hear the pain in her voice. Then she said, "I did everything my father told me. I tried to be the best daughter and listen and did well in school, but, but, he wouldn't stop touching me. Every time he would get really mad at me afterward. He would blame me, then beat me for making him do it. It was all my fault. I made my dad do those terrible things, and I drove my mother and brother away," said Lo-Ruhamah looking at Mye. She continued, "My father died unexpectedly from an aneurysm when I was 18. He left everything to me. 5 rental properties in the Dominican Republic, 2 apartment buildings in Maryland, and a 2.5 million dollar insurance policy. I went to find my mother and brother to share the wealth, and that's when I found my mother in a mental institution," sniffled Lo-Ruhamah. "It's like she didn't even recognize me. Then I found out about you, and what you did to my family and I thought if I could just avenge my mother then, maybe, just maybe she would want me back," whispered Lo-Ruhamah.

Mye wept silently as she tried to wrap her head around a crazy concept. She thought to herself, *Did Lo-Ruhamah's mother really leave her daughter in the hands of a pedophile for money? Did her mother sell her 6-year-old daughter to her father? Did her father do to her what my father did to me?* Mye's thoughts raced a mile a minute as she felt undeniable empathy for the woman who sat across from her. A woman physically, but still very much a traumatized and abused 6-year-old little girl inside. Mye reached across the table, grabbed Lo-Ruhamah's hands, and asked, "Can I meet you where you are?"

Lo-Ruhamah shook her head and said, "Yes."

SIX-YEAR-OLD MYE MEETS SIX-YEAR-OLD LO-RUHAMAH

In an all-black room, 6-year-old Mye was wearing an emerald green dress with puffy gold tulle underneath. Her hair was in two ponytails with curls so big it almost covered the center part in her head. She has gold shoes on that tapped when she walked, and 2 gold bangles on each wrist. She walked to the far side of the dark room to find 6-year-old Lo-Ruhamah crying in the corner. Mye sat beside her and hugged her. My used her dress to wipe her tears. 6-year-old Lo-Ruhamah was wearing a dirty brown dress with rips and holes, with no shoes, and her hair was all over the place. Mye held Lo-Ruhamah tight and rocked her back and forth.

"What's the matter?" asked 6-year-old Mye.

Never looking up, 6-year-old Lo-Ruhamah said, "Nobody wants me. I'm a good girl I promise I am, but still nobody wants me," she cried.

"Why do you think that?" asked Mye still hugging Lo-Ruhamah.

"Because, because, my mom left me, but took my brother," cried Lo-Ruhamah into Mye's little shoulder. "And my dad doesn't want me because I make him touch me."

"How do you make him touch you?" asked Mye.

"Because I was born," cried Lo-Ruhamah. "I should have never been born," she cried.

6-year-old Lo-Ruhamah asked Mye, "What are you doing here?"

"I'm here for you. I love you silly," giggled Mye as she squeezed Lo-Ruhamah's cheeks together. "I know what it feels like to not be wanted. I used to think about all the people who didn't want me," said Mye as she hugged Lo-Ruhamah, "I used to be sad like you, but that's old news now," smiled Mye.

"How did you change their minds?" asked Lo-Ruhamah.

"Change whose mind?" asked Mye confused.

"The people," said Lo-Ruhamah. "How did you make the people who didn't want you, want you?" she asked while wiping her tears with her dirty, ripped dress.

Mye got up and played imaginary hopscotch. "I didn't," she said picking up a pretend rock then throwing it. "How can anyone do that? How can you make some-one want you who doesn't?" asked Mye looking at Lo-Ruhamah.

Lo-Ruhamah stood up confused. "But you're so hap-py," she said watching Mye pretend to be an airplane. Mye zoomed around Lo-Ruhamah in circles before she fell to the ground from being dizzy.

"So do the people want you?" asked Lo-Ruhamah leaning over Mye as she laid on the ground.

"I don't know," shrugged Mye. "But why does that matter?" asked Mye as she sat up to get eye level with Lo-Ruhamah.

Lo-Ruhamah sat down confused, "But how can you be so happy if you don't even know if anyone wants you?"

Mye leaned her forehead against Lo-Ruhamah's and whispered, "Because I want me and me wanting me is all that matters." Mye jumped up and put her hands on her little hips. " I want me to grow up big and tall, so I can ride a sparkling unicorn," said Mye as she galloped around Lo-Ruhamah causing her to giggle. "You can only grow up big enough to ride a unicorn if you love yourself. You can't grow without love. You can get old and wrinkled, but you can't grow. And since ponies were soooo last year, I have to grow big and tall to ride a uni-corn," Mye said stretching her hand high in the air on her tippy toes. "Don't you want to grow big enough to ride a unicorn?" asked Mye with big bright eyes.

Lo-Ruhamah smiled and said, "Yeah, because ponies were soooo last year." The girls laughed together. "How can I grow big enough to ride a unicorn?" asked Lo-Ruhamah.

"You gotta choose you," said Mye. "You gotta want you and love you. No matter what anyone says or does. You can't ever stop loving you," said Mye.

Lo-Ruhamah said, "What if you were-"

Mye cut her off and said," Still love you."

Lo-Ruhamah said, "What if I did-"

Mye said, "Still love you."

"Look, you're not letting me finish," said Lo-Ruhamah.

"Because it doesn't matter what you say. There is nothing you can do or can be done to you that can make you unlovable," said Mye with both hands on Lo-Ruhamah's shoulders.

"I want to want me. I want to love me, but I don't know how," said Lo-Ruhamah with her head hung low.

"You had me fooled," said Mye. "You're looking better already," smiled Mye.

The room lightened up and all of a sudden the girls were outside in a green meadow with beautiful flowers by a crystal clear pond.

"Open your eyes and look at yourself," said Mye.

Lo-Ruhamah opened her eyes and immediately saw her reflection in the pond and started to cry tears of joy.

"That's me?" she asked Mye.

Mye nodded, "Yep!"

Lo-Ruhamah was wearing the same dress as Mye, but it's purple with puffy silver tulle underneath. Her hair was in a single ponytail with a long braid that went down her back with curls at the end. She was wearing platinum shoes with platinum bangles. Two on each wrist.

"The first step to loving yourself is to first want to love yourself," said Mye. She put her hand out and said to Lo-Ruhamah, "Thank you for allowing me into your beautiful heart. Now let's go love ourselves together!"

Lo-Ruhamah grabbed her hand and said, "Thank you for meeting me here and showing me the way!"

"Look a unicorn!" yelled Mye. "Let's go see how much more bigger we have to get before we can ride it!"

"Yeah! Let's go!" said 6-year-old Lo-Ruhamah.

PRESENT - 2017

Lo-Ruhamah cried as Mye held her hands. Mye got up and dragged her chair beside her, "Can I hug you?" whispered Mye. Lo-Ruhamah shook her head yes. Lo-Ruhamah cried into Mye's shoulder.

"I'm not a horrible person," said Lo-Ruhamah in between tears. It's just, it's just.... Has your father ever touched you in your private places?" she cried.

"Yes," said Mye seemingly sucking the air out of the room. Lo-Ruhamah gasped.

"My mom was kidnaped in front of me at 6, and as I grew older, I began to look more like her. Big curly hair, green eyes, brown skin, same face, build, everything. My father often confused me for her. For the last 20 plus years, I've worn my hair bone straight or pulled into a bun, wore brown contacts to cover my green eyes, and maintained a very strict diet just to be smaller than my natural build. All in an attempt to stop feeling guilty. For so many years, I felt guilty for tricking my dad into thinking I was his lover, my mom. For years, I felt on a subconscious level that I tricked my dad into touching me," said Mye.

Lo-Ruhamah sobbed, "So you understand? You know the guilt."

Mye shook her head yes as her eyes watered. "All too well," said Mye.

"So how did you stop feeling guilty for what someone has done to you?" asked Lo-Ruhamah.

Mye replied, "You start loving yourself. You don't have to start loving your whole self at once. Just start loving yourself. One layer at a time. We were children. Two little girls who lost their mom and had troubled dads. None of this is our fault. The trauma is not our fault. But the healing Lo-Ruhamah. The healing is totally our responsibility," said Mye.

Lo-Ruhamah asked, "Do you think there is hope for me? I mean, Jesus was raised from the dead but not from the pyre. There's no coming back from some things."

Mye replied, "Yes! Yes, yes, yes!" Lo-Ruhamah smiled. "I believe self-love is the ultimate healer. It can release you from anything that you feel has you trapped, and anyone can love themselves to freedom."

"I'm sorry," said Lo-Ruhamah in a whisper. "What I did was wrong. You didn't deserve that."

"You didn't deserve what happened to you," said Mye, "you don't belong here Lo-Ruhamah. You deserve to get help that was denied to you all those years ago. I'll see what I can do," smiled Mye.

"Times up," said one of the guards. "We have to take her back to her cell," said the guard to Mye sympathetically. The guard lifted Lo-Ruhamah by one of her arms, "Wait a second," Lo-Ruhamah said, "I know I have no right but can I ask if you can do another thing for me?"

"Sure," said Mye.

"Can you have my name changed? Clearly, God has shown mercy on me today," smiled Lo-Ruhamah. "My name is so sad and bitter."

"So you need a sweet name," said Mye.

"Yeah," said Lo-Ruhamah lighting up. "Like... 'Caramel,'" smiled Lo-Ruhamah. "I think I like that. How does that sound?"

"It sounds perfect," smiled Mye. "So what about your middle name?" asked Mye.

"I don't have a middle name now. Um, you pick a name," said Caramel.

"Ummm, how about Phoenix? Since you are rising from the ashes renewed, stronger and better," smiled Mye.

"I love it! Not even Jesus did that," said Caramel.

Mye laughed.

"Okay let's go," said the guard.

"If I had a sister like you growing up, things would have been different," said Caramel as the guards were taking her out of the door.

"Well, you have a sister now," smiled Mye. "Bye Caramel Phoenix!" yelled Mye as they took her sister back to her cell.

***

Truman and Mye were in her home office with boxes of files. Mye was going through a stack of papers, highlighting and taking notes.

"You're better than me," said Truman not looking up from the file he was reading. Mye dropped her papers in shock.

"What," she asked mouth wide open. "There's actually someone better than Warren Truman," she gasped.

Truman looked up and said, "Tell anyone I said that and I will deny it." Mye laughed as she went back to reviewing the files.

"How did you do it Mye?" asked Truman genuinely. "How did you forgive a woman who tried to kill your son, not once, but twice, and who knows how many other ways she's tried to sabotage your life? How did we go from prosecuting her and talks of the death penalty to defending her and trying to get her into a mental institution? How can you look at her and not hate her?" he asked.

Mye closed the folder she was holding and stared off into the distance. "I did hate her, at first. It wasn't until I stopped looking at her at face value, that my perspective changed. It wasn't until I stopped looking at what people told me to look at, that I was able to see. She came with a narrative, but I chose to see her for myself. And what I saw was a 6-year-old little girl who had felt unwanted and was sexually abused for most of her childhood. I didn't relate to her as an adult. I related to 6 year old her. The root of all of the pain and all of the trauma," said Mye.

"But so were you Mye," said Truman throwing a folder across the table. "How come you didn't turn out like her? This is about personal responsibility. Yes, messed up things happen to children, but as adults, you have to figure things out," he added.

"I agree Truman. As an adult, you are responsible for your healing. However, I acknowledge my privilege, and I had opportunities that were denied to her. We are all created equal but presented with very different opportunities. I know love. I was the center of my Mom's parents, and my parent's world. I went through hell from 6 to 12, but I had Champ and his Aunt Gayle from 12 to 14. Champ saved my life, Truman. He showed me love and taught me how I should be treated. I am forever indebted to him. And yes, I was raped," said Mye cringing, "but then I met my nurse Bhavani, Penelope, Tara, you!" she said.

"You could have skipped the others and just mentioned me," said Truman.

"It would make me a monster if I did not acknowledge my privilege. I mean, who does that?" asked Mye in a tone just above a whisper.

Truman looked her in the eye and whispered, "Everyone, Mye. Nearly everyone." Truman couldn't understand how that woman had the capacity to love the way she did.

"I submitted your new sister's name change, and I would like to let you know that I think the name Caramel Phoenix sounds like a stripper," said Truman.

Mye burst out laughing, "Shut up! No it doesn't. I think it sounds sweet and magical," said Mye.

"It sounds like she's about to make that ass clap," said Truman.

Mye replied, "This is coming from a man with two first names and two last names at the same damn time." Truman gave a fake laugh causing Mye to laugh even harder.

William interrupted Mye and Truman's meeting and brought in a beautiful woman with him. William threw a stack of papers down on the table and said, "Give me my divorce."

Mye never looked up. Truman browsed through the papers and asked the woman, "Is this divorce to the letter of the prenup as we've discussed?"

William was confused, "You two know each other?"

Truman responded, "Mrs. Hagler is the go-to divorce lawyer in the tri-state area. Of course, we know each other." Truman read through the papers methodically, then said, "Mye and I saw her years prior to ensure when you approach her, because we knew you would, that she would adhere to the prenup as is."

"You are working with them?" asked William looking at his attorney.

"No, I'm working for you. You want to ensure you receive everything you are entitled to per the prenup. Correct?"

A confused William said, "That's correct."

"Mr. Truman just wanted to emphasize that when the time comes, his client doesn't want to fight. She just wants a clean break," said attorney Hagler.

"Great. Now break me off 1/2 of everything that is mine per the prenup!" yelled William.

Mye signed the divorce papers without even looking up from the document she was reading.

"Anything else Truman?" asked Mye.

"No. That's it. You are a free man William," said Truman as he handed the papers to his attorney.

"Now can you two please see yourself out? We are in the middle of something very important," Mye asked politely.

"Of course Mrs. Hart-"

"It's Miss Almonte," said Mye. "It's Mi Amor Almonte, but you can call me Mye."

The attorney smiled, "That's a beautiful name. Good day, Miss Almonte."

Attorney Hagler began to turn to leave. William stopped her and yelled, "We are not going anywhere, this is half my house, and you are still Ms. Hart until you officially change your name."

Truman laid some papers on the table. "Her name was officially changed yesterday," said Truman. "And if I may William, this is not half of your house."

William looked shocked and wide-eyed with his mouth open. "What?" winced William.

Attorney Hagler said, "Per your prenup, you keep everything you brought into the marriage and Mi Amor Almonte keeps everything she brought into the marriage. This house is in Miss Almonte's maiden name and her name alone. All of her businesses were started the day before you two married. You insisted that we stick to the prenuptial agreement. Adamant about that and would not listen to me. You used me for my position and representation, however, you did not value my advice. You have nothing William; this is not your house, that is not your car outside. This all belongs to Mi Amor

Almonte. You wrote a prenup to protect your assets, however, it also happened to protect hers."

William realized he has nothing. Mye added fuel to the fire and said, "You do have a couple of things in your name William, like 4 maxed out credit cards. Don't try to use the black card because it has been deactivated. Oh yeah, here's your ring back," said Mye as she opened a small box on the table, took out her wedding ring and slid it to William.

"Not so fast," said Truman. "You paid for that, I checked with Ashley. She has receipts," said Truman as he grabbed the ring back. Tem and Bhavani walked into the office to see what all the commotion was about.

"You fucking bitch!" yelled William.

"A dad, Ma ain't going to be too many more bitches. You played the game and lost. You always told me to own my losses just as much as I own my wins," said Tem.

William looked at Bhavani for support, "I don't know what to say, dad. I don't know what to tell you," said Bhavani, "but please leave."

"So now you've turned my kids against me?" proclaimed William.

"Bhavani, Tem, this has nothing to do with you. This is between your dad and I," said Mye.

Bhavani said, "You did this to yourself dad. You think we don't know you cheat on Ma? Tem and I have known for years. Everyone knows. You're sloppy. It's disrespectful dad. Is this how you would want a man to treat me? Is this how you want Tem to treat women?" asked Bhavani with tears in her eyes.

William held his head low in defeat.

"Baby girl," sighed William. "Life's more complicated than nails, shoes, and hair. You live a glamorous life baby girl. One day you will have to work and make money versus spending my money all day. Life's more complicated. It's too much to worry your little self. You're a kept woman, and if you marry well you won't have to worry about anything. Life is far more complicated than what you can imagine."

"I grossed 16.8 million dollars last year dad, and I'm on schedule to double that this year. I made my first million at 13. Yes, I do love hair nails and shoes, but I'm also smart. I graduated high school and also received my first bachelors at the same time. I have a masters in Finance and will have another one in Economics by this summer. I have many jobs but being a financial advisor is where I make the bulk of my money. I'm smart dad!" said Bhavani.

"Why didn't you tell me?" asked William.

"I've allowed you to think I'm dumb to make you happy. I didn't want you to be intimidated by me like you are by Ma. I know you don't like a strong woman and I just wanted you to like me. I've watched Ma shrink herself for too long to make you feel important. No more shrinking Ma! No more! I'm glad you two are getting a divorce. Now Ma can finally live. It's your time now Ma. I love you dad I do... but I'm tired of pretending. Women should not have to lessen themselves to make men feel better. You step up to the plate and be better or just check your ego at the door," said Bhavani.

"Ma taught us to be our best. You taught us to be better. Better is in comparison to-" said Tem.

"Being your best is a stand alone goal," added Bhavani.

William started to leave, "I get it. So the whole house is against me. That's fine. I have someone who appreciates what y'all didn't."

William stormed out of the office.

"Wait," yelled Mye as she followed him down the hall. William turned around with a look of anger and defeat.

"What Mye?!" he spat.

She knew there was nothing she could say to brighten this dark moment in his life, however, she knew this needed to be said.

"William, I love you. But, over time, I started to realize that for me to love you how you wanted to be love, it meant I couldn't love myself how I needed to be loved. Even though I came to this realization, I still loved you how you wanted me to love you. Until it became apparent that the way you wanted me to love you, was by me not loving myself at all. It forced me to an impasse. It was either you or me. I was either going to love you or love me, and I chose me," said Mye as she shed a single tear. "I want to say thank you, William," she added.

William was confused, "Thank me? For what?" he asked.

Mye replied, "Thank you so much for pressing me. Pressing me so hard. Forcing me to choose. It's because of you that I'm on this journey of authenticity. If you had let up just a little, if you had gotten your shit straight and apologized and begged for my forgiveness, I wouldn't be here, standing in my truths. Now I'm fully committed to loving myself and taking care of myself wholeheartedly. I'm committed to healing myself and building healthier relationships with people and things. There are things I want but thought I couldn't have that I'm now considering going after. I feel liberated William, and I would be amiss to not thank you for the role you played in my liberation. You helped me to discover my authentic voice, allowing me to merge the path I was originally on with the path to my optimum self. The love provided from my higher self to myself freed me. I literally loved myself to freedom. And for your role in the sweet death of old pain and trauma, I like to say, thank you."

CHAPTER FIFTEEN

FORGIVE THEM

It was the end of Summer and Bhavani earned her masters in Economics. It was a few days until September and has been three months since Mye or Tem spoke to William, but Bhavani speaks to him weekly. Mye allowed William to keep his three luxury cars and paid off his four maxed out credit cards that were more than 374,000 in total. A little more than two years of his salary. William wasn't certain of his ex-wife's net worth, but he knew she was worth 8 figures at least, and her generosity was peanuts to her. Still, the prenup was ironclad thanks to his dad, so William was entitled to nothing.

A few days have passed, and Mye was preparing for her first session with Caramel. Truman managed to get her in an amazing in patient facility, and Mye got to meet with her weekly. Mye suggested Caramel journals daily to help her start the process of peeling back the layers and learning to love herself little by little. Mye knew all too well how painful it could be to face fears and painful truths, but she felt journaling was a therapy in itself.

Helping to ease the burden of confronting the past by first writing it down, then speaking it. It helps to decrease anxiety and focus more on your goals. Mye couldn't wait to see Caramel to see how she was doing. Caramel had a long road ahead, but Mye was willing to stick it out until the end.

Emerson was calling Mye's cell phone. He had been calling daily for the last couple of months. She had been ignoring his calls, and whenever she saw him in person, she just kept it very short. She couldn't deal with her role of having to always comfort him while he just turns around and disappoints her. She just watched her phone as it rang. Then it stopped. Now he was calling again. She hadn't spoken to him in private since that day in her office when she confessed her love to him. Mye cringed from embarrassment at the thought. She didn't know what he had to say or if she wanted to hear anything he had to say at all. However, her curiosity got the best of her, and she answered.

"Hello Emerson," she said.

"Mye they just brought William into the hospital," he rushed. Mye jumped up from her chair. "It's bad Mye. It was a bad accident. I don't know if he is going to make it. I'll keep you updated, but I gotta go. They need me in the OR," he said before hanging up the phone.

***

Tem and Bhavani got to the hospital at the same time to find Mye praying over William. Even though they parted ways, Mye never wanted him to end up like this. Her children needed their father. Bhavani came into the room and cried at her father's side. Tem did his best to keep his composure, but the site was too much to bear, so he sobbed silently in the corner with his shirt pulled up covering his face. Tubes were everywhere. The top of his head was wrapped in bandages, he wore a neck brace, and his eyes were purple and completely swollen shut. There were bruises and scrape marks everywhere, both legs were in a cast, and he had bandages from the top of his left shoulder down to his left hand. Dr. Johnson walked in and hugged Mye. She got herself together and motioned for the doctor to break the news to her.

Dr. Johnson asked, "Can we talk in private?"

"No," said Tem as he walked over to his mom and put his arm around her. "We can talk right here," he sniffled.

Mye nodded to the doctor to continue. "William has sustained life-threatening injuries. He had a collapsed lung, there was heavy internal bleeding, multiple breaks, and fractures in both legs, and a significant amount of skin was removed from his left arm. These things I believe are things he can come back from."

Mye and her children let out a sigh of relief. Then the doctor said, "If he wakes up."

Mye let a single tear fall. The doctor added, "He sustained a major head injury when he was ejected from his car. We currently have him on life support, but we need your permission to keep him on life support or to take him off. His emergency surgery was a success, however, it's touch and go from here. How do you want to proceed?"

"Keep him on life support and do whatever you have to do to get him back," she said looking at William. "He's strong-willed. He will pull through," smiled Mye.

"I disagree," said Leah as she walked into the room with a tall brown skin man in a tailored black suit.

"Hello doctor," said Leah as she shook his hand. I'm William's wife, and I do believe I have the final say," said Leah staring at Mye. "This is my attorney Mr. Royds, and he has proof that I'm Williams wife. The hospital's counsel should be calling you shortly to confirm this," she added.

William's room phone rang, and Dr. Johnson answered. "I understand," he said before hanging up. He looked at Mye with pitiful eyes then turned and began to tell Leah about her husband's medical condition.

"Pull the plug," Leah said cutting him off.

"Well, don't you want to hear about his chances of survival? If he pulls through this, he can have a good quality of life with some therapy of course," said the doctor.

"Pull the plug!" she yelled. Dr. Johnson called the nurses in to take him off of life support. As the nurse came in Bhavani screamed and tried to stop them. Tem held her back and covered her face. She cried loudly in her brother's shoulder. Mye hugged her children as their father slipped away. Leah stood beside Mr. Royds seemingly pleased with herself.

Truman walked in with Officer Grey and handed Mye some documents.

Truman said, "Officer Grey checked the scene of the accident and noticed that there were no skid marks anywhere. The mechanic at the impound said the car had faulty brakes. The car was just serviced 1 month ago by George, and you know how serious he takes brake maintenance. I say William was murdered and who would stand to gain the most from his death? His new wife," said Truman looking at Leah.

Leah looked scared, "Why would I kill him? I loved him," she said looking around nervously. "I didn't want to do this, but William committed suicide. I know because he left me this note," she said reaching into her purse.

In walked attorney Hagler, William's divorce attorney. "Let me guess, does the note you have start like this? Dear Leah, Thank you for doing me the honor of making me your husband but-"

"Not even your love could save me from me," said Officer Grey as he read the note Leah pulled from her purse. He compared the two notes, and the wording was nearly identical.

Mrs. Hagler said through tears, "You stole my son from me just to get his money! You black widow! You killed my boy! I tried to warn William. When I found out about you, I tried to warn him. But he wouldn't listen. Then I figure he was safe. After all, he had no money or access to money once the divorce was settled, but I was wrong. He wasn't safe," she said through tears.

Officer Grey arrested Leah, "This is lies! All lies! What about my children! William and I have children you know?! And they are entitled to his money!"

"What money?! What money Leah? William doesn't have any money. He didn't tell you did he?" asked Mye.

Leah stopped fighting officer Grey and froze in shock. "No…. What, what do you mean William doesn't have any money?" Leah asked looking for someone to respond. "I don't have any money!" she yelled. "Well, well, what about his insurance money? Surely the kids will get that," she said.

Truman replied, "You obviously didn't read the prenup he made you sign. In the event of his death, his biological children receives if any and all inheritance. Not his wife."

Mye added, "And besides, they are not his biological children. William got a vasectomy after I got pregnant with Bhavani. Tem and Bhavani had multiple complications as young children because of the genetic disorder he hid from me."

Leah couldn't believe it. After all these years and all this planning, she is left with nothing. Her children are left with nothing.

"Our cards are maxed out! What do I do now! No, no, I don't believe you! Lies! You're lying," said Leah as officer Grey pulled her out of the room. "Their grandparents will provide for them!" she yelled.

"She obviously hasn't met Grandpop Senior then," said Tem. Mye grabbed her son and daughter and hugged them tightly.

***

On the way from the hospital, Tem, Bhavani, and Mye rode in silence. So many thoughts ran through Mye's mind. She had to be strong for her children and help them to process their father's death and comfort them through their grieving process. Leah was charged with 2 counts of 1st-degree murder, and she implicated her attorney who turned out to be the father of her two children, William Hart III age 5 and Gene Leah Hart age 9 months. The children are now wards of the state and are in foster care.

The family arrived home to find Truman standing outside the front door. Tem and Bhavani went inside, but Truman stopped Mye.

"I hate to have to do this to you today. She had an aneurysm last night, but she left you a letter," he said in all sincerity as he handed her a manila envelope. "Call me if you need me," said Truman as he got in the car for Alex to take him home.

Dear Mye:

I just want to say, thank you. I've been hurting since I was a little girl and needed help for a long time. But I didn't know I needed help because this has always been my life. I never knew what it felt like to matter and this was my normal. It's difficult to know what's missing if it never was there. I've done a lot of horrible things to you, and I wish I could take them all back. I'm sorry for not seeing how I was projecting my hurt and pain on to you. You've been better to me than anyone ever has. You've been better to me than I've been to myself.

You melted the ice around my heart with sunshine that I'm now seeing for the very first time. Just to know a woman who's been through all you've been through but still is as loving as you is amazing. Just knowing "you" are possible is all I ever needed to know. I assumed there was no hope for me, but you've shown me otherwise. You give me strength to be better and to go further. The world may never be able to forgive and love me, but now I know that my true power is in forgiving and loving myself. There is nothing I can say to make what I've done to you less horrible, and I can't brighten past dark days. But I can tell you thank you and how much I appreciate you. You are what my soul needed. Meeting you was what my ego needed to experience. Thank you for being an example of self-love freeing a person. You have loved yourself to freedom, now promise me Mye, that you will dream yourself to love. You deserved to be loved, protected, and cherished. Imagine up the stallion of your dreams and make sure he is a champion. Be fruitful and multiply.

With Love,

Caramel Phoenix

Mye fell to the ground, sobbing uncontrollably. All these emotions were bubbling up from deep within, pouring out at once. She was deeply saddened by Caramel's sudden transition, but also extremely relieved that Caramel didn't have to carry that pain any longer. Mye grieved William's death and understood the void that it left in their children. A hole that Tem and Bhavani would have to learn to fill themselves. A hole that only self-love could heal. She wept for the thought of all the unhealthy fillers that could dwell there until her children learned how to fill it properly. She was angry at the lack of internal satisfaction she received from Leah being arrested. She had compassion for Leah's 2 children having to learn how to fill two voids due to their mother and the only father they knew being taken away. Mye cried and cried as she purged her heart and cleansed her soul the best way she knew how - through her tears.

Then she thought of him. She cried as she mentally prepared to release all of the love and desire to be with Emerson from her heart. She ached from the thought. She cried for all the kisses they would never share. She didn't realize how difficult letting go of a dream could be. However, she knew it was necessary for her to move forward. She began to hyperventilate. She couldn't do it. She loved him too much. She was still too heavily attached to the hope of what could be to let him go. Mye shook her head "no," holding her hands over her mouth trying not to speak, trying not to say what she truly feels.

Then she just blurted out, "I wish he was here! I wish Emerson was here," she cried. A sense of relief fell over her. She closed her eyes and took deep long breaths trying to calm herself and regain control of her breathing. After she composed herself, she got up, but her heel was stuck in the cobblestone causing her to fall backward. She braced herself for the fall.

"I'm here Mye," said Emerson with the sincerest look she'd ever seen. "I'm here for you, and if you have me, I want to be right here by your side forever. I love you so much Mye, and I'm ready," he said shaking his head 'yes.' "I'm ready for whatever, whenever you are ready. No rush. No pressure. In the meantime, I just ask if you allow me to share the load with you. Can I be right here with you now and always?"

Mye wept silently as she shook her head yes. Emerson wiped her tears and hugged her tightly as she cried in his arms. His phone rang, but he ignored it.

"You should get that, it could be the hospital," she said wiping her face.

"Doesn't matter. I took off today, and Dr. Johnson is on call for me. I'm here for you Mye," he said. She smiled at the thought of him taking off to be with her. "In fact, I took off for the rest of the week. I'm not messing up my chances with you. Not this time. You are my top priority. We're going to get through everything together and build something amazing. If that's alright with you," he smiled.

Mye got up from the ground with Emerson's assistance. She smiled as she straightened her skirt and brushed the dirt off.

"I like the sound of that," she said. She took a step, and her knees buckled. Emerson caught her again. She blushed, "Must have a loose heel." She bent over to take off her shoe when Emerson scooped her up in his arms.

"I got you," he said as he carried her to the house. Caramel's words rang in her ear, "*You've loved yourself to freedom, now dream yourself to love.*" Mye laid her head on his shoulder and imagined a beautiful new life... with Em.

The Beginning

EPILOGUE

Self-love is the most underutilized resource of mankind. If we could only manage to love ourselves. Allow the ego to experience love to itself from it's higher self. Lifting the dense fog that blinds us and short sights our vision of ourselves. We're overworking the ego demanding an understanding of the "how" when it was only made to feel. The ego was only designed to experience. As a coping mechanism, the ego is often frozen into fear and inaction due to its inability to comprehend the how and slowly it seems to make peace with mediocrity; finding tranquility in the comfortability of settling. This is where Mye once lived.

Building a sad quaint home in the feeling of being stuck and stunted. Free from the effort and energy required for inspired action. Only attempting tasks, she can see completely through with huge margins for error. Carefully she lived being sure not to overshadow her husband or upset her children. She's perfected this life and from the outside things couldn't be better.

However, when you release your ego from the duty of having to understand and comprehend the how, then a mighty surge of energy is redirected into experiencing the experiences bringing on a rush for the need to grow. This inspired growth comes with various catalyst often called growing pains. You must continue to think positive and understand that a heating, a burning, of the old energy must first happen. See this pain as a pivotal step into the new. This type of pain is inevitable, necessary, and absolutely unavoidable if growth is to occur. Embrace this pain and find solace in this process. The sexual alchemy of chaos and creation is needed to transform old traumas into new relief. Energy never dissipates. Energy only transforms, and everything is energy. Love; the source, can transform nothing into multiple universes and dimensions and this love is in you. The source is in you. Everything that breathes or had breath has a piece of this love inside it. The higher your conscious abilities, the stronger your ability is to will this love and use it to transform one energy to another. So raise your consciousness my Queens and Kings, and use this love on you and transform all of your hurt, guilt, and shame, to peace, relief, and tranquility. Free yourself from a life less than what you are worthy of experiencing. Merge into your authentic self and live the life you want. Love yourself to freedom.

Get Book Two

The Merge II: Dream Yourself to Love

www.TheMergeBook.com

Pre-orders get a bookmark, a special exclusive short story, and a signed paperback copy in the mail.

PRE-ORDER *THE MERGE II: DREAM YOURSELF* TO LOVE **NOW**!

www.TheMergeBook.com

We kindly ask that you leave a book review on Amazon.

It's a great way for authors with small publishers to gain exposure and help sales.

ABOUT THE AUTHOR

Morgan B. Holland lives in Baltimore, MD and is an author and the business owner of www.GoalCare.com. There she goes by the pen name, "Madam Goal Slayer." She helps women build a fulfilled life they love through coaching and goal-specific strategies. While also teaching women how to identify, strengthen, and use their authentic voice. She is now at work on, *The Merge II: Dream Yourself to Love*, the sequel to THE MERGE: LOVE YOURSELF TO FREEDOM. Visit Morgan at www.-MorganBHolland.com.

Author photography by Jeffrey Perkins

THE MERGE

Dream Yourself to Love

CHAPTER ONE

LET'S GET MARRIED

The historic Baltimore Basilica Cathedral was filled with love and tears of joy with standing room only. Mye stared in adoration at Emerson as the priest officiated the wedding ceremony. She wore a Cushnie Et Ochs white lily beaded silk gown that perfectly framed her neckline with a beautiful beaded collar. The silk dress cascaded down her body giving a sultry yet elegant look. Her hair was pinned up with curls naturally perfectly twined, adorned with strategically placed white flowers. Her mahogany skin glistened with a natural glow as she held tightly to each word the priest spoke. She flashed her infectious smile causing Emerson to blush. Her cosmo red lipstick made her bright smile appear even whiter than ever. She'd dreamed of the life she and Emerson would have moving forward, fighting back tears as she thought about all they'd been through together. Then the priest said the magical phrase all came to here, "We now pronounce you husband and wife. You may kiss the bride." Mye and Emerson clapped enthusiastically as Kara and Martin kissed passionately as if no one was watching.

"I's married now!" said Kara loudly while waving her hand for all to see. Everyone broke out in laughter as the couple kissed again then walked down the aisle out of the church.

***

The reception had been in full swing for about an hour, and Mye still hadn't gotten a chance to grab a dance with Emerson. She spotted him across the room, sashayed over to him, and grabbed him from behind. He jumped startling her.

"What are you doing?" he whispered looking around to see if anyone saw what just transpired.

"What's wrong Em?" Mye questioned slightly confused by his reaction. "Stop acting weird. Let's dance," she said as she grabbed both of his hands.

He quickly pulled his hands back, "I don't think that's a good idea. I'm actually a little tired, it's been a long day. I'm going to go home a little early."

"Okay, let me grab my coat," she replied.

"No," Emerson said quickly, then he slowed down his speech. "Enjoy yourself and say your proper goodbyes and such. Then come over my house later," he smiled.

Mye agreed reluctantly. She leaned in to give him a kiss on the lips and he turned his head so she could kiss he cheek instead. She gave a him a weak smile and then disappeared into the crowd. Emerson left, and Mye enjoyed herself the rest of the afternoon at the reception.

Mye and Emerson had been spending more and more time together since the death of her ex-husband and the start of Emerson's divorce proceedings. Emerson agreed to Delilah's terms and gave her everything she wanted: the house, the cars, and half of the savings account he solely put into. She still was not happy. There seemed to be no pleasing this woman. Emerson did his best moving on with his life as he braced for another outrageous request from Delilah's attorney. Emerson leased a house that Bhavani and Jia flipped in the Burleith Neighborhood, 3900 block Georgetown Court. It was 5 minutes from the University hospital and fully decorated and furnished to his specific style. It was smaller than his martial home but way more peaceful.

Emerson's phone vibrated, "Hey Em I'll be there in less than 5 minutes." He smiled as he finished his last set of bench pressing. He lived for these moments with Mye. He didn't know where things were going, but he knew he wanted to be with her and only her. There lied his problem.